Will You Be There?

Will You Be There?

Guillaume Musso

Translated by George Holoch

HODDER &
STOUGHTON

Originally published in 2006 as SERAS-TU LÀ? by XO Editions, Paris, France
This English translation first published in Great Britain in 2008
by Hodder & Stoughton
A division of Hodder Headline

A Hodder & Stoughton Book

3

A CIP catalogue record for this title is available from the British Library

ISBN 978 0340 93371 8

Typeset in Sabon by Hewer Text UK Ltd, Edinburgh
Printed and bound by Clays Ltd, St Ives plc

Hodder Headline's policy is to use papers that are natural, renewable
and recyclable products and made from wood grown in sustainable
forests. The logging and manufacturing processes are expected to
conform to the environmental regulations of the country of origin.

Hodder & Stoughton Ltd
A division of Hodder Headline
338 Euston Road
London NW1 3BH

Will You Be There?

We have all considered this question at least once: if you had the chance to go back in time, which parts of your life would you change?

If you could do it all again, which mistakes would you try to put right? Whch moments of pain, of remorse or regret, would you choose to erase?

Would your really dare to try and bring a whole new meaning to your existence?

But what would you become?

Where would you go?

And with whom?

Prologue

The Red Cross helicopter landed bang on schedule.

Perched on a high jungle plateau, the village consisted of a hundred primitive wooden huts. It was a place that time had forgotten, far from the tourist meccas of Angkor and Phnom Penh. Everything was steeped in mud, the humidity intense.

The pilot didn't bother to cut the engine. His mission was to return a humanitarian medical team to the city – not too complicated in normal weather conditions. Unfortunately, this was September, and the torrential rain made it hard to maneuver the aircraft. Fuel reserves were low, but there was enough to bring everyone back safely, as long as they didn't dawdle.

Two surgeons, an anesthetist, and two nurses came running out of the makeshift clinic where they had been working since the previous day. Over the last few weeks, they had traveled around the villages in the area, doing their best to treat the ravages of malaria, tuberculosis, and AIDS, and providing artificial limbs for the amputees. This was a region still riddled with anti-personnel mines.

At a signal from the pilot, four out of the five of them rushed into the helicopter. The last one, a man of about sixty, held back, his gaze fixed on the group of Cambodians surrounding the aircraft. He seemed unable to bring himself to leave.

'We have to go, doctor!' the pilot shouted. 'If we don't take off now, you'll miss your plane.'

The doctor nodded and was about to climb into the helicopter when his eyes met those of a child held out to him in the arms of an old man. How old was he? Two, three at most. His small face was horribly disfigured by a cavity splitting his upper lip in two, a congenital deformity that would doom him to eating nothing but soup and porridge for the rest of his life and make it impossible for him to speak a single word.

'Hurry!' one of the nurses begged.

'We have to operate on this boy,' the doctor shouted, trying to be heard over the noise of the turning rotors.

'We don't have time! The roads are flooded, and the helicopter won't be able to come back for us for several days.'

But the doctor didn't budge, unable to tear his eyes away from the little boy. He knew that it was not unusual for babies born with a harelip in that part of the world to be abandoned by their parents, and their deformity ruined any chance they might have of being adopted from an orphanage.

The nurse tried again: 'You're expected in San Francisco the day after tomorrow, doctor. You have a very heavy schedule of operations, you've got meetings, and . . .'

'Leave without me,' he said, bringing the discussion to an end and walking away.

'In that case, I'm staying with you,' the nurse decided, and jumped to the ground.

It was Emily, a young American who worked in the hospital with him.

The pilot shook his head and sighed. The helicopter lifted off, hovered for a brief moment, then headed west.

The doctor took the boy in his arms: he was deathly pale and shrank away from the touch. Followed by the nurse, the doctor carried him into the clinic and took his time, talking to him and soothing his anxiety before giving him anesthesia. When the child was asleep, he delicately detached the vela, and spread them to cover the split palate. Then he went on to rebuild the lips and give the little boy a real smile.

When the operation was complete, the doctor came out and sat for a minute on the veranda, precariously roofed with corrugated iron and dried leaves. It had taken a long time. He had hardly slept for two days, and suddenly he felt completely exhausted. He lit a cigarette and looked around. The rain had subsided, and through a break in the clouds came a brilliant shaft of purple and orange light.

He was not sorry that he'd stayed. Every year he spent several weeks in Africa or Asia working for the Red Cross. These humanitarian missions never ceased to affect him but they had become like a fix to him too, a way of escaping from his orderly life as chief of surgery in a California hospital.

As he put out his cigarette, he felt a presence behind him. Turning around, he recognized the old man who had held the boy out to him as the helicopter was leaving. He looked to be one of the village elders, dressed in traditional costume, his back bent and his face furrowed with wrinkles. He lifted his joined hands to his chin in greeting, holding his head erect, and looked directly into the doctor's eyes. Then he beckoned the doctor to follow him to his house, where he offered him a glass of rice wine before speaking his first words: 'His name is Lu-Nan.'

The doctor nodded.

'Thank you for giving him a face.'

The surgeon humbly accepted the thanks and then, almost embarrassed, turned away. The windows had no glass. He could see the dense green jungle pressing close to the village. He found it odd to think that only a few miles away, just a little higher up in the mountains of Ratanakiri, there were still tigers, snakes, and elephants living wild.

Lost in his reverie, he had trouble making sense of his host's words when the old man asked him: 'If you could be granted one wish, what would it be?'

'What's that?'

'What do you wish for most in the world, doctor?'

At first the doctor tried to think of a witty answer, but overcome by exhaustion and in the grip of unexpected emotion, he said quietly, 'I would like to see a woman again.'

'A woman?'

'Yes, the only . . . the only one who ever mattered.'

And in that remote place, far from Western eyes, something solemn passed between the two men.

'You don't know where this woman is?' asked the old Cambodian, surprised by the simplicity of the request.

'She died thirty years ago.'

The old man raised his eyebrows and sank deep into

thought. After a moment's silence, he rose to his feet and went toward the back of the room where his possessions were piled on precarious-looking shelves: dried sea horses, ginseng roots, poisonous snakes preserved in formaldehyde . . .

He rummaged through these odds and ends for a minute before laying his hands on what he was looking for.

When he came back to the doctor, he was holding out a tiny blown-glass bottle. It contained ten small golden pills . . .

ONE

First Meeting

One fine day the future turns into the past.
It is then that you turn around and see your youth.

Louis Aragon

Miami Airport
September 1976
Elliott is 30

It was a sunny Sunday afternoon in Florida. A young woman was driving a Thunderbird convertible to the airport. With her hair streaming in the wind, she accelerated past several cars before stopping briefly in front of the departure terminal, just long enough to drop off her passenger. He retrieved his bag from the trunk and leaned into the car to give his driver a kiss. A moment later he was inside the steel-and-glass building.

Elliott Cooper, a good-looking, rangy man, was a doctor in San Francisco, but his leather jacket and unruly hair made him look more like an adolescent.

He automatically headed for the check-in counter to pick up his boarding pass for the Miami–San Francisco flight.

'Missing me already?'

Surprised by the familiar voice, Elliott turned around.

The woman gazed at him. The look in her emerald eyes conveyed both defiance and vulnerability. She was wearing low-slung jeans, a belted jacket with a 'peace and love' button on it, and a T-shirt in the colors of Brazil, her native country.

'When was the last time I kissed you?' he asked, stroking her neck.

'At least one long minute ago.'

'An eternity.'

He embraced her and held her close.

This was Ilena, the only one for him. He had known her for ten years and she brought out everything that was best in him: his professional skill as a doctor, his openness to others, and certain standards in the way he conducted his life.

He was surprised that she'd come into the airport, because they had always agreed to avoid long goodbyes, well aware that those few extra minutes would end up feeling more painful than comforting.

Their story was complicated: she lived in Florida, he in San Francisco. Their love affair was experienced through a haze of jet lag, at the mercy of the four time zones and three thousand miles between the East and West coasts.

After all those years, they could, of course, have decided to live together. But they hadn't, at first because they were wary of routine: while being together every day would have made their life easier, it would have deprived them of the rush of emotions they felt every time they met again – it was their oxygen.

And besides, each had built a separate professional life on a different coast. After seemingly endless medical studies, Elliott had just gotten a position as a surgeon in a San Francisco hospital while Ilena was the veterinarian in charge of dolphins and killer whales in Ocean World in Orlando, the largest marine park in the world. For the last few months she had also been giving a lot of time to Greenpeace. Founded four years earlier by a group of militant pacifists and ecologists, the league of 'rainbow warriors' had become known through its campaign against nuclear testing, but Ilena had joined up mainly to participate in their campaign against the massacre of whales and seals.

Each of them led a full life, with no real opportunity to grow bored; yet every new separation was more unbearable than the last.

'Immediate boarding for all passengers on flight 711 to San Francisco, gate number 18.'

'Is that your flight?' she asked, loosening their embrace.

He nodded and, knowing her so well, said, 'You wanted to tell me something before I left?'

'Yes. I'll go with you to the gate,' she said, taking his hand.

Walking alongside him, she launched into a speech with that hint of a South American accent that he always found irresistible.

'I know the world is heading for disaster, Elliott: the Cold War, the Communist menace, the nuclear arms race . . .'

Every time they parted, he looked at Ilena as if seeing her for the last time. She glowed with beauty.

'. . . the depletion of natural resources, not to mention pollution, the destruction of tropical rainforests, or—'

9

'Ilena?'

'Yes?'

'What are you getting at?'

'I would like us to have a child, Elliott . . .'

'Here, right now, in the airport? In front of everyone?'

It was the only answer he could come up with; a clever crack to mask his surprise. But Ilena was in no mood for jokes.

'I'm not kidding, Elliott. I want you to think about it. Seriously,' she said, letting go of his hand, and heading for the exit.

'Wait!' he shouted, trying to call her back.

This is the last call for Mr Elliott Cooper, passenger on flight 711 for . . .

'Oh, shit!' he said, stepping onto the escalator for the departure gate.

Almost at the top, he turned around to wave farewell.

The departure lounge was bathed in September sunlight.

Elliott waved, but Ilena had already disappeared.

Night had fallen when the plane landed in San Francisco. The flight had lasted six hours and it was after nine in California.

Elliott was about to leave the terminal and take a taxi when he changed his mind. He was dying of hunger. Upset by what Ilena had said, he hadn't touched the meal served on the plane, and he knew that his refrigerator was empty. He spotted a bar on the second floor, the Golden Gate Café. He'd been there before with his best friend, Matt, who sometimes went with him to the East coast. He sat down at the bar and ordered a salad, two bagels, and a glass of Chardonnay. Worn out from his trip, he rubbed his eyes before asking for change for the telephone at the other end of the room. He dialed Ilena's number, but there was no answer. Because of the time difference, it was already after midnight in Florida. Ilena was certainly home, but she was obviously not eager to talk to him.

I might have known . . .

And yet, Elliott was not sorry for the way he'd reacted to Ilena's proposal. The truth was that he didn't want to have a child, and that was that.

It was not a question of feelings: he adored Ilena and had love to spare. But love was not enough. Now, in the mid-seventies, humanity seemed to be bent on self-destruction and, quite honestly, he didn't want to take on the responsibility of bringing a child into the world. Which was something Ilena wouldn't want to hear.

Back at the bar, he finished his meal and ordered a coffee. He was nervous and cracked his knuckles almost without noticing. In his jacket pocket, he felt the pack of cigarettes tempting him and gave in to the impulse to light up.

He knew that he should stop smoking. There was more and more talk around him about the harmfulness of tobacco. For the last fifteen years, epidemiological studies had demonstrated the dependency created by nicotine, and as a surgeon, Elliott was fully aware that the risk of lung cancer was higher for smokers, as was the risk of a heart attack. But like many doctors, he was more concerned for the health of others than his own. Besides, it was normal to smoke; and cigarettes were glamorous and seemed to symbolize social and cultural freedom.

I'll stop soon, he thought, exhaling a stream of smoke, *but not tonight* . . . He felt too depressed to make the effort right then.

Idly, he let his eyes wander, and as he gazed through the glass wall, saw him for the first time: a man dressed oddly in sky blue pajamas who seemed to be observing him through the glass. Elliott squinted to get a better view. The man was about sixty, still in quite good shape, with a slightly graying beard that made him look like an aging Sean Connery. Elliott frowned. What was this guy doing, barefoot and in pajamas, at this late hour in the middle of the airport?

It was none of his business, but a mysterious compulsion made him get up and leave the bar. The man seemed disoriented, as though he'd just been dropped here. The closer Elliott got to him, the more he was overcome by a feeling of unease that he didn't quite acknowledge to himself. Who was this man? Maybe he was a patient who'd run away from a hospital or an asylum. In that case, as a doctor, didn't Elliott have a duty to help?

When he was less than three yards away, he finally understood what had disturbed him so much: the man somehow reminded him of his father, who had died five years earlier from pancreatic cancer.

Disconcerted, Elliott went still nearer. Close up, the resemblance really was striking: the same shaped face, the same dimple in his cheek that he himself had inherited . . .

Suppose it's him . . .

No, he had to get a grip on himself! His father was dead, completely dead. Elliott had witnessed him being put in his coffin and cremated.

'Can I help you, sir?'

The man took a few steps back. He seemed as disturbed as Elliott.

'Can I help you?' he repeated.

The man merely murmured: 'Elliott . . .'

How did he know his name? And that voice . . .

To say that he and his father had never been close would be an understatement. But now that he was dead, Elliott sometimes regretted not having tried harder to understand him.

Dazed yet fully aware of the absurdity of his question, Elliott couldn't help asking, his voice choked with emotion: 'Dad?'

'No, Elliott, I'm not your father.'

Oddly, this sensible answer didn't reassure him in the slightest. It was as though he had a premonition that a greater surprise was in store.

'Then who are you?'

The man put his hand on Elliott's shoulder. There was a familiar glint in his eyes, and he hesitated for a few seconds before answering, 'I'm *you*, Elliott . . .'

The doctor took a step back and froze as though paralyzed while the man finished his sentence: '. . . I'm you in thirty years.'

Me, in thirty years?

Elliott raised his arms in bewilderment. 'What do you mean?'

The man opened his mouth, but had no time to give any further explanation; a flow of blood suddenly gushed from his nose and fell on his pajama top in large drops.

'Keep your head back!' Elliott ordered, taking out of his pocket a paper napkin he had unconsciously picked up in the bar and clamping it on the nose of the man he now considered his patient.

'You'll be all right,' he said in a reassuring tone.

For a moment, he regretted not having his medical bag with him, but the bleeding quickly subsided.

'Come with me, we have to put a little water on your face.'

The man followed close behind him without any fuss. But when they got near the rest room, he suddenly started shaking, as though he were about to have an epileptic seizure.

Elliott tried to help, but the man pushed him away forcefully.

'Leave me be!' he demanded, pushing open the door to the rest room.

His good intentions curbed, Elliott decided to wait outside. He felt responsible for the man and was not happy with his condition.

It was very odd. First there was the physical resemblance, and then the bizarre statement – *I'm you in thirty years* – and now the nosebleed and this trembling.

Jesus, what a day!

But it was far from over. After a minute, thinking that he'd waited long enough, he decided to go into the rest room.

'Sir?'

It was a long narrow room. First of all Elliott inspected the row of sinks. No one. The place had no windows and no emergency exit. The man must be in one of the stalls.

'Are you there, sir?'

No answer. Fearing that the man had fainted, the doctor rushed to open the first door: no one.

Second door: no one.

Third, fourth . . . tenth door: empty.

14

In desperation, he looked up at the ceiling: none of the panels seemed to have been disturbed.

It was impossible and yet he had to accept the evidence of his own eyes: the man had disappeared.

TWO

I'm interested in the future: that's where
I intend to spend the next few years.
                                    Woody Allen

San Francisco
September 2006
Elliott is 60

Elliott opened his eyes with a start. He was lying sideways on the bed. His heart was beating furiously and he was drenched in sweat.

What a rotten dream!

Usually he never remembered his dreams, but he'd just had a really strange one: he'd been wandering around San Francisco airport when he'd come upon . . . his double. But this double was younger and appeared as surprised as Elliott was to see him. Everything had seemed so disconcertingly genuine, as if he *really* had traveled thirty years back into the past.

Elliott pressed the switch that opened the shutters then cast a worried glance at the bottle on his night table holding the little golden pills. He opened it and saw that there were nine left. The night before, when he'd gone to bed, he'd swallowed one out of curiosity. Was that the source of his mysterious dream? The old Cambodian who had given him the pills had been evasive about the medicine's effects, although he had solemnly warned him '*never* to use it for anything but its intended purpose.'

Elliott stood up with difficulty and moved toward the bay window that looked out on the marina. From here he had an unrestricted view of the ocean, Alcatraz, and the Golden Gate Bridge. The rising sun bathed the city in a deep red light that changed hue from moment to moment. In the distance, ferries and sailboats criss-crossed to the warning hoot of foghorns, and despite the early hour a few joggers were already running along Marina Green, the wide stretch of grass at the edge of the water.

Seeing these familiar sights calmed him a little. His troubled night would soon be forgotten, that was for sure. Just when he'd convinced himself of this, he saw a disturbing image reflected in the window: a dark circle on his pajama top. He lowered his eyes to examine the spot more carefully. *Blood?*

His heartbeat speeded up, but not for long. He must have had a nosebleed during the night and he'd incorporated the incident into his dream. It was a common response, nothing to get upset about.

Partly reassured, he went into the bathroom to shower before going to work. He adjusted the temperature and stood motionless for a moment, lost in thought, while the room filled with steam. Something was still bothering him. What was it? He began to undress when a sudden instinct made him reach into his pajama pocket. In it was a bloodstained paper

17

napkin. Underneath the traces of blood it was possible to make out a sketch of the most famous bridge in the city, headed with the inscription *Golden Gate Café – San Francisco Airport*.

Once again his heart began to race and this time he found it harder to calm down.

Was it his illness that was making him lose his grip?

A few months earlier a scan had revealed that he had lung cancer. It hadn't come as much of a surprise; he was paying the price for smoking a pack a day for forty years. He'd always known the dangers and accepted them. That was just the way of it; one of the risks you take in life. He'd never tried to lead a sanitized life or to protect himself at any price from its knocks. You could say he believed in fate: things happened when they were supposed to happen, and you owed it to yourself to endure them.

Viewed objectively, it was a vicious cancer: a variety that spread very rapidly and was extremely hard to treat. Over the last few years, medicine had made progress in the field and new drugs made it possible to prolong the lives of patients. But it was too late for him: the tumor had not been detected early enough and tests had shown the presence of metastases in other organs.

It had been suggested that he follow the classic treatment – a cocktail of chemotherapy and radiation – but he had refused. At this stage, there wasn't much left to try. The outcome of the battle was already known: he'd be dead in a few months.

He'd managed to conceal his illness until now, but he knew that he couldn't go on indefinitely. His cough was becoming persistent, the pains in his ribs and shoulders were more acute, and he had sudden bouts of fatigue despite his reputation for being tireless.

It wasn't the pain that frightened him. What he dreaded more than anything were the reactions of other people, particularly Angie, his twenty-year-old daughter, who was a student in New York, and Matt, his best friend, with whom he'd always shared everything.

He got out of the shower, dried himself quickly, and opened the closet. He chose his clothing with even more care than usual: a short-sleeved shirt of Egyptian cotton and an Italian suit. As he got dressed, the shadow of sickness was dispelled, giving way to a man still in the prime of life, full of masculine strength. Until recently, his undeniable charm had enabled him to date pretty young women sometimes half his age. But these relationships never lasted. Anyone who was close to Elliott Cooper knew that only two women counted in his life. The first was his daughter, Angie. The second was Ilena, and she had been dead for thirty years.

He went outside where he was greeted by sun, waves, and wind. He took a minute to appreciate the dawning day before opening the door to the little garage under the house. He slid into an ancient orange VW Bug, the last vestige of his hippy days. With the top down, he cautiously edged into the road and drove up Fillmore Street toward the Victorian houses of Pacific Heights. The steep streets of the city acted like roller-coasters, but Elliott was past the age of getting his car to lift off the ground at intersections. He turned left on California Street and passed a cable car that was taking the first of the day's tourists to Chinatown. Just before he reached the edge of Chinatown, he drove into an underground garage two blocks behind Grace Cathedral. Close by was Lenox Medical Center, where he had been working for more than thirty years.

As head of the department of pediatric surgery, he was considered one of the leading lights of the hospital. But the promotion was recent and had come late in life. Throughout his career, he had devoted himself primarily to his patients, making every effort – which was rare for a surgeon – not to stick merely to technicalities, but to take their feelings into account too. Honors did not impress him, and he had never tried to build a network of connections with golf games and weekends at Lake Tahoe. And yet, when his colleagues' children needed surgery, he was the one they turned to; an unmistakable vote of confidence in his profession.

'Can you analyze this for me?'

Elliott handed Samuel Bellow, the chief lab technician, a little plastic envelope in which he had placed some residue he'd found at the bottom of the pill bottle.

'What is it?'

'That's what I want you to tell me.'

Then he swept through the cafeteria for his first dose of caffeine and went up to the operating room to change and meet with his team, made up of an anesthetist, a nurse, and an Indian female intern whose work he was supervising. The patient was a frail seven-month-old baby named Jack, suffering from cyanogenetic cardiopathy. This malformation of the heart, which interfered with the flow of oxygen to his blood, made him look cyanotic: it made his fingers rigid, and turned his lips blue.

As he was about to make an incision in the infant's thorax, Elliott couldn't help feeling a kind of stage fright. For him, there was still something miraculous about open-heart operations. How many had he done? Hundreds, probably thousands. Five years earlier, a television station had even aired a report on him, praising his 'golden fingers' that were able to repair blood vessels as slender as a needle with the help of thread invisible to the naked eye. But every time he operated he felt the same tension, the same fear of failure.

The operation lasted more than four hours, during which heart and lung functions were taken over by a machine. Like a plumber of the heart, Elliott sealed the hole between the two ventricles and opened a pulmonary channel to avoid the flow of venous blood to the aorta. It was meticulous work, requiring a high degree of skill and concentration. His hands did not shake, but a part of his mind was somewhere else, thinking about his own disease, which he could no longer forget about, and his strange dream of the night before. Suddenly becoming aware that his thoughts had wandered, he rebuked himself and focused again on the task at hand.

When the operation was over, Elliott explained to the baby's parents that it was too soon to determine the outcome. The child would be kept under observation for a few days in the intensive care unit, where his breathing would be mechanically assisted until his heart and lungs gradually resumed their full function.

Still in his surgeon's scrubs, he went out to the hospital parking lot. The sun, already high in the sky, blinded him, and for a fraction of a second he felt dizzy. He was exhausted, out of steam, his head full of questions: was it really reasonable to ignore his own condition as he had been doing? Was it wise to continue operating, at the risk of putting his patients' lives in danger? What would have happened this morning if he'd felt faint in the middle of the operation?

He lit a cigarette to clear his head and inhaled the first puff with relish. That was the only comforting thing about this cancer: now he could smoke as much as he liked and it would have no effect on the progress of the disease.

A slight breeze made him shiver. Since he had known that he was soon going to die, he'd become more sensitive to everything around him. He felt the rhythms of the city almost physically, as though it were a living organism. The hospital overlooked the small elevation of Nob Hill. From here, one could sense the vibrations rising from the port and the docks. He took a last puff and put out his cigarette. His mind was made up: he would stop operating at the end of the month, and he would tell Matt and his daughter about his disease.

So, it was over. No going back. Never again would he accomplish the only thing which made him feel useful: taking care of others.

He contemplated this sudden decision a minute longer, feeling old and miserable.

'Doctor Cooper?'

Elliott turned around and saw Sharika, his Indian intern, standing in front of him. She had changed out of her surgical gown into faded jeans and pretty tank top with thin straps. Almost timidly, she offered him a cup of coffee. Everything about her exuded beauty, youth, and vitality.

Elliott accepted the coffee and thanked her with a smile.

'I've come to say goodbye, doctor.'

'Goodbye?'

'My US internship ends today.'

'That's right,' he remembered, 'you're going back to Bombay.'

'Thank you for making me feel welcome, and for your kindness. I've learned a lot from you.'

'Thank you for your help, Sharika – you'll be a good doctor.'

'But you are a *great* doctor.'

Elliott shook his head, embarrassed by the compliment.

The young woman moved a step closer. 'I was thinking . . . I was thinking we might go out to dinner tonight.'

In less than a second, her beautiful copper skin had turned scarlet. She was shy, and it had cost her a lot to make this suggestion.

'I'm sorry, but that's not possible,' he answered, completely surprised by the direction this conversation was going in.

'Oh, I see,' she said.

She let a few seconds go by, then went on, 'My internship ends officially at six o'clock. Tonight you'll no longer be my superior and I will no longer be under your supervision. If that's what's holding you back . . .'

Elliot looked at her more closely. How old was she? Twenty-four? Twenty-five at most. He had never flirted with her, and now he felt uncomfortable.

'That's not it.'

'It's funny,' she said, 'I always thought that you might be interested in me . . .'

How should he respond? Should he say that part of him was already dead, and the other part was about to follow? That people claim age doesn't matter in love, but it's a load of bull . . .

'I don't know what to say to you.'

'Then don't say anything,' she murmured and turned on her heel.

Nursing her hurt feelings, she'd already gone some distance when she remembered something.

'Oh, I forgot,' she said without turning around, 'the switchboard got a message from your friend Matt: he's been waiting for you for half an hour and he's starting to get impatient.'

Elliott dashed out of the hospital and hailed a passing cab. He had a lunch date with Matt and was very late.

Like love at first sight, there is such a thing as friendship at first sight. Matt and Elliott had met forty years before in very unusual circumstances. The two men apparently had nothing in common: Matt was French, extrovert, a lover of pretty women and life's pleasures; Elliott was American, rather reserved and private. Yet eventually they had bought a vineyard together in Napa Valley, 'the Périgord of California'. The wines they produced – a very drinkable Cabernet Sauvignon and a Chardonnay with flavors of melon and pineapple – had earned a good reputation through Matt's tireless efforts to promote them, not only across the States but in Europe and Asia as well.

For Elliott, Matt was the friend who would still be there when he had no other friends, the one he would call in the middle of the night if he ever had to dispose of a body.

Right now, though, Elliott was late and Matt was going to bawl him out.

The very exclusive Bellevue Restaurant where they frequently ate lunch was set above the Embarcadero and looked out onto the water. Glass in hand, Matt Delluca had been waiting for half an hour on the outside terrace overlooking the Bay Bridge, Treasure Island, and the downtown skyscrapers.

He was about to order a third glass when his cell phone rang.

'Hi, Matt, forgive me, but I'm running late.'

'Whatever you do, don't hurry, Elliott. I've gotten used to your very individual sense of punctuality.'

'Come on, you're not going to make a federal case out of it!'

'No, of course not; you're a doctor, and we all know that saving lives gives you special rights.'

'Just as I thought, you're mad at me.'

Matt couldn't help smiling. With his cell phone glued to his ear, he left the terrace and went into the main room of the restaurant.

'Do you want me to order for you?' he said, as he approached the display of shellfish. 'I have in front of me a quivering crab that would be honored to become your lunch.'

'I trust you.'

Matt hung up, and a sign to the waiter sealed the fate of the unfortunate crustacean.

'One grilled crab!'

Fifteen minutes later, Elliott hurried across the big room with its fine panelling and mirrors. After tripping over the dessert cart and accidentally bumping into a waiter, he finally joined his friend at their usual table. His first words were a warning: 'If you value our friendship, avoid using the words "late" and "again" in the same sentence.'

'I didn't say anything. We reserved the table for noon and it's one-twenty now, but I didn't say anything. So, how was your trip to Cambodia?'

25

Elliott had barely said a few words before he had a coughing fit.

Matt poured him a large glass of sparkling water.

'Aren't you coughing a lot?'

'Don't worry.'

'Even so . . . Shouldn't you be tested? A scan, or something?'

'I'm the doctor,' Elliott answered, opening his menu. 'So, what did you order for me?'

'Don't take this the wrong way, but you're looking terrible.'

'How long are you going to keep this up?'

'I'm just worried about you – you're working too hard.'

'I'm fine, I told you! It's just that Cambodia tired me a little . . .'

'You shouldn't have gone,' said Matt, making a face. 'I think Asia . . .'

'You're wrong, it was very rewarding. But a strange thing happened to me.'

'What?'

'I helped an old man and, like the genie of the lamp, he wanted to know my greatest wish . . .'

'What did you tell him?'

'I asked him for something impossible.'

'That you could finally win a golf match?'

'Well, if you're not interested . . .'

'No, tell me . . .'

'I told him that I would like to see someone again . . .'

At that point, Matt understood that his friend was serious, and his expression changed. 'And who would you like to see again?' he asked, already knowing the answer.

'Ilena . . .'

A wave of sadness swept over the two men, but Elliott refused to give way to melancholy. When the waiter brought the entrées, he went on with his tale, telling his friend the astonishing story of the bottle of pills and the nightmare he'd had the night before.

Matt tried to be reassuring. 'If you want my advice, forget this whole thing and ease off a little at work.'

'You can't imagine how disturbing the nightmare was, how real it seemed. It was so . . . so bizarre to see myself at thirty.'

'You really think those pills had that effect on you?'

'What else could it be?'

'Maybe you ate something that wasn't very fresh,' Matt suggested. 'I think you get too much Chinese takeout.'

'Stop it.'

'I'm serious. Never set foot in Chow's again: I'm sure his Peking duck is dog . . .'

The rest of the meal passed pleasantly. Matt had the rare gift of creating a kind of aura of good cheer. When he was with him, Elliott forgot his own dark thoughts and worries. The conversation had taken on a jocular tone and they were talking about more trivial things.

'Have you seen the girl near the bar?' Matt asked, taking a mouthful of flambéd bananas. 'She's looking at me, right?'

Elliott turned toward the bar: a pretty nymphet with endless legs and doe eyes was languidly sipping her dry martini.

'She's a call-girl, my friend.'

Matt shook his head.

'No way.'

'Want to bet?'

'You're only saying that because she's looking at *me*.'

'How old do you think she is?'

'Twenty-five.'

'How old are you?'

'Sixty,' Matt admitted.

'That's why she's a call-girl . . .'

Matt was shaken for a minute, but then he reacted vehemently. 'I've never been in better shape!'

'We're getting old, my friend, that's how it is, that's life, and maybe you ought to start accepting it.'

Matt dubiously considered this.

'Well, I'll say goodbye,' Elliott said, getting up from the table. 'I have a few more lives to save. And you? What are your plans for the afternoon?'

Matt glanced at the bar, and noticed sadly that the nymphet was talking with a young man. A few years earlier, he would have been able to steal the girl from this pretty boy, but now he felt out of his league, like a boxer about to fight one bout too many.

'My car's in the parking lot,' he said, catching up to Elliott. 'I'll take you back to the hospital. Since I'm so old, maybe I'll stop by for a check-up.'

THREE

*Sit down for an hour next to a pretty girl, and it seems
like a minute. Sit for a minute on a hot stove, and it
seems like an hour. That's relativity.*
                                          Albert Einstein

San Francisco 1976
Elliott is 30

'Isn't it perfect here?' asked Matt, stretching out on the sand
and looking across the huge bay ringed with hills spread
before them.

The two friends were free spirits. They wouldn't dream of
wasting time eating lunch in a restaurant; they would rather
meet on the beach and eat a hot dog before going back to
work.

It was a beautiful, light-filled day. In the distance, lightly
shrouded by fog, the Golden Gate seemed to float on a carpet
of milky clouds.

'You're right, this is better than prison,' Elliott agreed,
taking a bite of his hot dog.

'I have big news to tell you today,' Matt declared mysteriously.

'Really? What is it?'

'Wait a little bit longer. You'll get your surprise with dessert.'

Nearby, taking advantage of the last days of the Indian summer, a group of fashionably dressed young people were having fun: the men had long sideburns, flares and silky rollneck shirts, and the women wore long colorful tunics, deerskin jackets and lots of ethnic jewellery.

Matt turned on his transistor, and they heard the current hit, the catchy melody of 'Hotel California' by the Eagles.

Whistling the tune, he looked around the beach.

'You see the girl on your right, she's looking at us, isn't she?'

Elliott turned around discreetly. Stretched out on a towel, a pretty, sylphlike young woman was calmly eating an Italian ice. She crossed her long legs and made eyes at them.

'Seems like it.'

'What do you think of her?' asked Matt, looking back at her.

'May I remind you that there's *already* someone in my life.'

Matt brushed away the objection: 'Do you know that only five percent of mammals are monogamous?'

'So?'

'Why wait to join the ninety-five percent who don't complicate their lives with principles?'

'Because I don't know if Ilena would agree with you . . .'

Matt swallowed the last mouthful of his hot dog, giving his friend a worried look.

'Are you sure you're okay? You look lousy today.'

'Cut the compliments, you're embarrassing me.'

'It's just that I worry about you . . . you work too hard.'

'Work is good for the health.'

'I get it: you went to that Chinese place again, the one near you?'

'Chow's?'

'Yes. Have you tasted his Peking duck?'

'It's very good.'

'I've heard that it's cat.'

An ice-cream seller interrupted: 'What flavor will the gentlemen have – pistachio, caramel, coconut?'

Elliott relied on his friend, who was happy to order for two. As soon as the man was gone, the conversation picked up where it had left off. 'How did your weekend in Florida go? You seem preoccupied . . .'

'Something strange happened to me last night,' Elliott admitted.

'I'm listening.'

'I met someone at the airport.'

'A woman?'

'A man . . . of about sixty.'

Matt frowned as Elliott told him of his strange confrontation with the mysterious visitor who had ended up disappearing in the airport rest room.

Matt let a few seconds elapse, and then muttered: 'Yeah, it's worse than I thought.'

'I swear it's true.'

'Believe me, buddy, you should ease off a little at work.'

'Don't worry about me.'

'Why should I worry, Elliott? You tell me that another you

came back from the future to have a nice little chat. That's completely normal, right?'

'Okay, let's talk about something else.'

'How is the lovely Ilena?'

Elliott turned to face the ocean, and for a minute his gaze settled on the thin wisps of fog surrounding the metal pillars of the Golden Gate.

'She wants us to have a child,' he answered pensively.

Matt's face lit up. 'That's great. Can I be the godfather?'

'I don't want a child, Matt.'

'Really? Why?'

'You know very well: the world has become too dangerous, too unpredictable . . .'

Matt rolled his eyes. 'You're losing it, old man. You'll be there to protect your kid, and Ilena, and even I'll do my bit. That's what parents and godparents are for, right?'

'Easy for you to say: you fool around, change girls every other day. No sign of you starting a family . . .'

'Only because I haven't been lucky enough to come across a girl like Ilena. That's the kind of thing that only happens to you. There's only one like her on earth and you're the one who got her. But you're too stupid to realize . . .'

Elliott turned away and didn't respond. A breaker hit the beach and wafted spray in their direction. It only took a few minutes for their good mood to return and the conversation to switch to less important things.

When Matt judged that the moment for his 'surprise' had come, he dug a bottle of pink champagne out of his bag.

'What are we celebrating?' Elliott asked.

Matt could hardly conceal his excitement.

'I've done it, I've finally found it!' he said, popping the cork.

'Your ideal woman?'

'No!'

'The solution to world hunger?'

'Our land! Our future vineyard! An idyllic position on top of a hill with a big wooden farmhouse . . .'

When Matt had gotten his pilot's license a few years earlier he'd bought a hydroplane and now earned a good living ferrying tourists over the bay. But for a long time he'd been harboring the slightly crazy plan that he and Elliott would one day own a vineyard together in Napa Valley.

'I guarantee it's the right time to invest,' he enthused. 'Right now, there are only a few estates in the valley, but wine is the future of California. It's our red gold, you understand . . . If we start the business right away, we'll earn a fortune!'

Only partly convinced, but pleased by his friend's happiness, Elliott promised to come to see the land the following weekend and listened with amusement as Matt spoke of his grandiose dreams until the alarm on his watch called him back to reality.

'Okay,' said Elliott, getting up and stretching. 'A few more lives to save. What are your plans for the afternoon?'

Matt turned around to make sure that the beautiful girl hadn't moved. As though she'd been waiting for that, she gave him a suggestive wink.

Matt was beaming. He was young and handsome, his whole life ahead of him.

'Looks like Dr Love will be making a little house call . . .'

Stuck in traffic, the taxi was crawling down Hyde Street. Elliott paid the driver and slammed the door. The hospital wasn't very far; at this rate, he'd get there faster on foot. He lit a cigarette and walked rapidly down the street. He still felt a vague anxiety every time he drew close to the hospital. The same questions kept recurring in his mind. Would he measure up to what was expected of him? Would he make the right decisions? Would he lose any patients?

He was not yet of an age when he could harden himself against ordinary human feelings. He didn't have a protective layer, an inner armor to shield himself. Up to now, he'd had an impeccable career: a brilliant record at Berkeley where he'd skipped a year, training in Boston, four years of internship and several pediatric specializations for his clinical training. On each occasion he'd received excellent evaluations.

And yet, he was still not sure he was made for medicine. Of course, he had the gratification of taking care of others, of feeling useful. Sometimes, after a good day, convinced that he'd really made a difference, he left work with a feeling of euphoria. Then he got into his car and drove at top speed the length of the marina. He had fought for life and he'd won. On those nights, for a few hours, he felt almost godlike. But this blissful state never lasted very long. There was always the next day, and the day after that when a patient 'who wasn't supposed to die' slipped through his fingers.

He looked at his watch, put out his cigarette, and walked faster. The façade of the hospital rose up a hundred yards in front of him. *Am I really made for this?* Elliott asked himself again.

What kind of a doctor would be become? He had chosen the profession to keep an old promise, after an important event had occurred in his life. He didn't regret his choice, but some days he envied Matt his carefree existence. For ten years

Elliott hadn't had time for anything: to read, to play sports, to be interested in anything but his job.

He went into the hospital, picked up his coat, and went to the second floor. The mirror in the elevator reflected the face of a tired man. It had been ages since he'd slept eight hours in a row. Nights on call had taught him how to break up his sleep, to roll up in a ball and nap for stretches of ten minutes; now he could no longer stay in bed late.

He went through a door into a room with a bright tile floor where Ling, an emergency room intern, was waiting for him.

'I'd like your opinion about a pediatric patient, Dr Cooper,' he said, introducing him to Mr and Mrs Romano, the couple with him.

The man was short and dark, an Italian–American with a friendly air. She was taller, blonde, Nordic. An attractive marriage of opposites.

They were there for their daughter, Annabel, who had just been brought into the department and was lying motionless in bed.

'Her mother found her like that when she came home at noon. We think she didn't wake up this morning,' Ling explained. 'I've asked for a complete report and Dr Amendoza has done a tomography.'

This procedure used a new medical imaging device, a 'scanner', which was beginning to appear in hospitals around the world.

Elliott approached the comatose patient. Annabel was a fifteen-year-old girl who had inherited both her mother's fair hair and her father's open features.

'Has she recently suffered from headaches or nausea?'

'No,' answered the mother.

'Does she take drugs?'

'No!'

'Is it possible that she struck her head while sleeping or that she fell out of bed?'

Apparently not.

Even before touching his stethoscope to the girl's body, Elliott felt the life draining from it, and sensed death hidden in a corner of the room, waiting for its moment.

The examination began promisingly, however: Annabel was breathing well, and her heart and lungs were functioning normally. Nor was there anything abnormal in her corneal reflex.

But examination of the pupils told a different story. Moving his patient's head gently from side to side, Elliott observed that her eyes did not follow the movement of the head. Then, when he pressed on her sternum, her wrist contracted in a troubling manner.

'That's not a good sign, right?' asked Mr Romano. 'There's a problem with the brain?'

Elliott remained cautious. 'It's too soon to say. Let's wait for the test results.'

They came in a few minutes later. Even before Elliott put the X-ray on the light box, he suspected what he would see. As though they were in a teaching hospital, he allowed the intern to suggest a diagnosis.

'An edema in the cerebellum?'

'Precisely,' Elliott regretfully agreed, 'a hemorrhagic cerebellar edema.'

He left the dark room and went to see Annabel's parents.

'Well, doctor?' they asked simultaneously as soon as he'd crossed the threshold.

He was filled with compassion for them. He would have liked to say something cheerful, like: 'Everything's fine, she'll wake up any minute.' But that wasn't the case.

'I'm deeply sorry, but your daughter has had a cerebral attack and her condition is critical.'

There was a gap, a moment of silence that seemed to go on forever, as the words sank in. The mother stifled a sob, while the father was defiant. 'But she's breathing! She's still alive!'

'For the moment, but she has an edema that will grow until it affects her breathing capacity and she stops breathing altogether.'

'She could be put on a respirator!' said the mother.

'Yes, we could put her on a respirator, but that wouldn't change anything.'

Unsteady on his feet, the father approached his daughter's body.

'How . . . how could she have had a cerebral attack? She isn't even fifteen.'

'It can happen at any time and to anyone,' Elliott explained.

Bright sunshine streamed through the window, filling the room with sharp rays of light that seemed to caress the girl's golden hair. She looked to be asleep, that was all. It was hard to believe she would never wake up.

'But won't you even try to operate?' asked her mother in a disbelieving tone.

Her husband had moved closer. He took her hand. Elliott looked directly at her and said in a very soft voice: 'It's over, Mrs Romano, I'm sorry.'

He would have liked to stay with them longer, take on a tiny bit of their grief himself, find a few comforting words, even if he knew there were none.

But a nurse was already calling for him. He had an operation scheduled for three o'clock, and he was late.

Before leaving the room, he should have completed his professional duty by asking the parents whether they would agree to organ removal. A surreal discussion would then follow, during the course of which he would have to persuade them that the death of their daughter might help save other human lives. Yes, Elliott ought to have completed his professional duty to the bitter end, but today he didn't have the heart.

He left the room feeling downcast and full of barely contained anger. Before going up to the operating room, he stopped in the bathroom to splash water on his face.

'I'll never have children,' he swore to himself as he stared at his reflection in the mirror. 'I'll never have children, then they'll never have to die.'

Too bad Ilena didn't understand that.

Orlando, Florida 1976

Night was falling on Ocean World, the marine animal park. As the last glimmers of sunlight lengthened the shadows of the cypress trees, a scattered crowd was slowly leaving the nature preserve, delighted by encounters with dolphins, giant tortoises, and sea lions.

Ilena was leaning over the killer whale pool to cajole Annushka, the largest inhabitant, into coming to the edge.

'Hello, my pretty one.'

She grasped the whale's flipper and encouraged her to turn onto her back.

'Don't panic, it won't hurt you,' she said reassuringly,

before sticking a syringe into Annushka's rubbery flesh to take a blood sample.

This was always a delicate operation. While killer whales were the most intelligent of cetaceans, they were also the fiercest. Despite her friendly appearance, Annushka was still a monster eighteen feet long, weighing four tons, and capable of killing with a blow of her tail or severing a limb with one bite from the fifty sharp teeth in her jaw. For every one of her procedures, Ilena endeavored to secure the animal's voluntary cooperation, giving her treatment as though it were a game. Generally, this worked well. She had that special empathy with animals that made her an excellent vet.

'There, it's over,' she said, removing the syringe.

To reward the huge animal, she tossed her a pail of frozen fish and patted her sleek side.

Ilena was passionately attached to her job. As resident veterinarian, she was responsible for the physical and mental health of all the animals in the park. She supervised the maintenance of the pools and the preparation of food, and she also helped coach the trainers. To hold a position with so many responsibilities was unusual for someone of her age, particularly a woman. She had in fact fought tooth and nail to get it. Ilena had been fascinated by the world of the ocean, and particularly by cetaceans, ever since she was very little. In addition to her veterinary training, she had specialized in marine biology and taken advanced training in animal psychology. But in this area, jobs were very rare, and getting to work with killer whales and dolphins was about as easy as becoming an astronaut. But she had hung on to her dream and been rewarded because five years earlier, in 1971, Walt Disney had picked the small town of Orlando as the location for

Disney World, his huge amusement park. With the flood of tourists, Orlando had changed from a rural hamlet into Florida's biggest attraction. Ocean World had arrived in the wake of Mickey Mouse to become the largest marine animal park in the country. A year before the park's official opening, Ilena had already laid siege to the management, trying to get a position that had already been promised to an older veterinarian. They had agreed to take her on for a trial period, and finally she had been appointed instead of her colleague. This was the good side of America: competence finally beginning to win out over seniority, sex, and social origin.

She adored her job. She knew that her friends in Greenpeace disapproved of keeping animals in captivity, but they had to admit that Ocean World was not insensitive to the environment. In fact, Ilena had just got the company to agree to finance a huge protective program for manatees.

She left the pool area and went into one of the administration buildings. She labeled the tube holding the blood sample and took it into the small laboratory for analysis. Before getting down to work, she needed to go to the bathroom to throw cold water on her face. She had felt out of sorts all day.

As she looked into the mirror over the sink, she saw a tear running down her cheek. It had appeared without her even noticing.

'I'm such an idiot!' she said, rubbing her eyes with her forearm.

In fact, she knew perfectly well what was the matter: she couldn't stop thinking about her last discussion with Elliott. About his reaction when she'd talked about having a child. It was like that every time, and she didn't understand his hesitation, which she interpreted as a refusal to commit.

And yet, she didn't doubt his love for her for a second. Their relationship burned with an intense flame, nourished by their desire to surprise each other at every turn, to fill each other with delight.

But could such a love stand the test of time? Ilena was about to turn thirty. She glowed: men were constantly turning their heads to look at her, and she knew how attractive she was. But for how many more years? Her youth was gradually fading away. She already felt that she didn't have the same physique, the same strength, the same freshness as the kids of eighteen or twenty she saw on the beach or on the benches at the animal shows.

In itself, growing old didn't bother her a bit. But things were changing around her: people were talking about free love and the sexual revolution, and these changes unsettled her. She wanted to have a lasting relationship; had no desire to see the man she loved go off and try all the positions in the *Kama Sutra* with other women.

She took a sip of water and dried her eyes with a tissue.

Maybe she didn't show Elliott how deeply attached she was to him. She was modest by nature, and expressing her love in words was not her strong point. But when you're in love, there's no need to make speeches: you know it, you feel it, and that's that. And besides, when a woman asks a man to be the father of her children, that's clear enough, isn't it?

And it was purely because she loved Elliott that she wanted to have a baby with him. She was not one of those women longing to get pregnant who wanted a child at any price, entirely for themselves. She wanted to have one *with Elliott*, as the next chapter in their love story.

41

Only he obviously didn't agree.

And she didn't understand why.

She suspected that the desire to have a child was closely connected to every individual's personal and family history. Ilena had been fortunate enough to be raised by a poor but loving family in Brazil, and knew that she would flourish with motherhood. But Elliott had had a difficult relationship with his parents. Was that where the obstacle in him came from?

And yet, she had no doubt about his ability to make a child happy. She had seen him at work several times when she'd gone to pick him up at the hospital. He was a pediatric surgeon who knew how to deal with his young patients. He was solid and well balanced, neither immature nor egotistical like some of the men who had pursued her. She could easily see him as an affectionate father, listening attentively to his children. So much so that she had sometimes thought of stopping taking the pill without telling him, faking an accident and confronting him with a *fait accompli*, but if she had done that she would have felt she was betraying the trust between them.

So what was the problem?

She knew a lot of things about him: his determination, his altruism, his intelligence, his smell, the taste of his skin, the outline of his vertebrae, the dimple when he smiled . . .

But isn't there always one detail that escapes us about the person we love? And isn't it that single bit of mystery that makes our love last?

In any case, there was one thing she was certain of: the love of her life, the father of her future children, was Elliott, and no one but him.

She would have this baby with him or she would not have it at all.

San Francisco 1976

Elliott drove home feeling gloomy. There was no point in going fast this evening. He'd fought for life and he'd lost. He wasn't God, just an insignificant doctor.

Night was falling gently. Street lights and headlights went on in unison. Tired and distressed, the young doctor ran through the events of the last two days in his head: his disagreement with Ilena, his encounter last night with the strange man in the airport, and Annabel whom he'd been unable to save today.

Why did he always have the impression that his life was escaping him somehow? That he was not in control?

Lost in thought, he was a second late slowing down as he came to the intersection of Fillmore and Union Street. As the car veered slightly toward the sidewalk, he felt a kind of resistance, followed by a muffled sound.

A flat tire?

He switched off the engine and got out of the car to inspect the tires and the bumper – nothing there.

He was about to continue on his route when he heard a plaintive cry; a whimpering sound from the opposite sidewalk.

He looked up and saw a dog that had been thrown onto the other side of the street by the impact. 'That's all I need,' he said with a sigh.

He crossed over to the animal, a yellow Labrador lying on its side with its right front paw curled over.

'Come on, move!' he said to the dog, hoping he hadn't injured it.

But the dog didn't budge an inch.

'Get a move on!' he shouted.

Again the animal gave out a muffled cry that made it clear it was in pain. Its injured paw made it impossible for it to walk, but Elliott was unmoved. He had never been much drawn to animals. His business was with humans: men, women, children, old people . . . All the patients he treated in the hospital. But animals . . .

He shrugged his shoulders and turned his back on the Labrador. He wasn't going to waste his time with this mutt.

He got back into the car and turned the key.

In his place, of course, Ilena wouldn't have taken off like a thief. She would have been shaken, then she would have cared for the dog and gone out of her way to find its owner.

Of course, Ilena . . .

As though she were sitting next to him in the passenger seat, he could almost hear her whisper: 'Anybody who doesn't like animals, doesn't really like people.'

What a load of crap! he thought, shaking his head. Nonetheless he stopped the car twenty yards on and reluctantly retraced his steps.

Even three thousand miles away, that woman could do what she liked with him!

'Come on, fella,' he said, putting the dog on the back seat, 'let's get you fixed up.'

Elliott felt relieved when he got back to the marina. The row of houses bordering the ocean was built in an eclectic mixture of architectural style and period. Houses flanked with towers sat next to more modern buildings of glass and steel, all of it somehow magically producing an asymmetrical but harmonious whole.

It was completely dark now and the wind had picked up. Near the ocean, on the long strip of grass, a hippy was having fun flying a kite hung with little Chinese lanterns.

The doctor parked in front of his door and carefully lifted the dog out of the car. Carrying this fidgety burden, he headed toward a pretty Mediterranean-style house.

With a turn of the key he was in the house he had bought with the money from his inheritance. The place was unusual: it was about fifty years old but had been completely remodelled by the architect John Lautner, who specialized in futuristic dwellings, drawing inspiration from works of science fiction.

Elliott flicked a switch, and the interior of the house was bathed in an undulating bluish light, resembling the reflection of light off water.

Then he put the Labrador on the couch, picked up his medical bag, and examined the animal. Apart from a nasty open wound on its paw, the dog had only a few contusions. Oddly, it had no collar. It looked at him suspiciously when he checked.

'Listen, you don't like me and it's mutual. Even so, you need me, so you'll keep quiet if you want me to take care of you.'

Having dispensed this warning, he disinfected the wound and applied himself to making a bandage.

'There. Rest up tonight, and tomorrow it's off to the pound!' he said to the animal as he walked away from the couch.

He crossed the living room and went through the library

into the kitchen. These three spaces were part of a single huge room that overlooked an interior garden dominated by a cleverly illuminated yellow Alaskan cedar.

Elliott grabbed an open bottle of white wine from the refrigerator, poured a glass, and went upstairs to drink it. There, on the other side of a double bay window, a terrace roof stuck out like the prow of a ship about to plunge into the ocean.

Glass in hand, the doctor settled into a wicker armchair and let the wind buffet at him.

The face of Annabel Romano passed briefly through his mind.

What a rotten day, he thought, closing his eyes.

At that moment he had no idea that it was far from over . . .

FOUR

Hold on to your dreams . . .
You never know when you might need them.
Carlos Ruiz Zafón

San Francisco
September 2006
Elliott is 60

It was well past nightfall by the time Elliott got to the marina.
He parked in the driveway and went into the pretty Mediterranean-style house he'd been living in for thirty years. As he
came in a motion detector automatically activated the inside
lights, the undulating bluish glow creating the impression that
the room was surrounded by water.

The doctor went through the living room and library on his
way to the kitchen. Since his daughter had left for New York,
the house had been quiet and empty. Tramp, his old Labrador, had died twelve years earlier and no other animal had
taken his place. Elliott took a bottle of white wine out of the
refrigerator and poured himself a glass. The pain radiating

through his back made it hard for him to go up the flight of metal stairs leading to the floor above. He stopped for a moment in his bedroom, opened the night table drawer, and picked up the bottle of pills. He'd been thinking about them all day.

Then he went out into the terrace garden that had a spectacular view of the marina and the bay. He was pleased to hear the familiar hooting of the wave organ, a strange construction at the end of the dike that produced random sounds generated by the waves running through its pipes. *A gadget like that could only exist in San Francisco*, he thought as he settled into his old wicker armchair.

The wind in his face made him shiver. Just as he had that morning, Elliott looked at the nine pills in the bottle with a mixture of fascination and disbelief.

He had no idea what was in them, but he was very tempted to repeat the experiment of the night before. He didn't really have any illusions, though. The pills probably had nothing to do with last night's dream.

Even so, it was tempting to try again . . .

Slowly, he let one of the pills drop into his palm and hesitated for one final moment.

Suppose it was poison, or one of those nasty exotic substances that would blow his mind?

Possible, but what was he really risking? The cancer would soon finish him off anyway.

Sooner or later . . . he thought as he swallowed the pill with a gulp of wine.

At first, nothing happened. He settled more comfortably into his chair and waited. This disease was making him feel old and worn out.

He went over the last few hours in his head, thinking about his sudden painful decision to stop operating in a month's time.

A rotten day, he thought before closing his eyes and drifting off.

FIVE

Second Encounter

*The best evidence that time travel
is impossible is the fact that we haven't been
invaded by hordes of tourists from the future.*
Stephen Hawking

**San Francisco
September 1976**
Elliott is 30

'Relaxing, are we?'

Elliott opened his eyes, gave a start, and fell out of his chair.
Flat on the floor, he raised his eyes to the night sky. A dark
shape was outlined against the starlight: the man he had seen
the night before in the airport. With his arms crossed over his
chest, he was looking at Elliott with a slight smile, obviously
satisfied by his little prank.

'What the hell are you doing on my terrace?' the young
doctor fumed.

'Your house is my house . . .' his strange visitor retorted.

Torn between surprise and annoyance, Elliott sprang to his

feet. He moved toward the intruder with his fists clenched, and for a few seconds the two men eyed each other in silence. They were exactly the same height.

'Just what kind of game are you playing?' Elliott asked in a threatening tone.

The man evaded the question, answering quietly, 'You don't want to understand, do you?'

'Understand what?'

'The truth . . .'

Elliott shrugged his shoulders. 'And what is the truth?'

'The truth is that I am *you*.'

'The truth is that you're a raving lunatic!'

'And you, poor guy, are a little slow on the uptake.'

Elliott looked at the man in front of him a little more closely.

Tonight he wasn't wearing the rumpled pajamas of the night before, but cotton pants, a clean shirt, and a well tailored jacket. The guy had some presence, even a touch of charisma. Wild statements aside, he looked more like a businessman than someone who'd escaped from an asylum.

Elliott adopted his most persuasive tone to try to reason with him. 'Listen, I think you're not well. Maybe the doctor who's treating you . . .'

'*I'm* the doctor.'

This won't be easy, thought Elliott, scratching his head. What was he supposed to do in a situation like this? Call the police? An ambulance? A hotline for crazy people? The man didn't appear to be violent, but appearances might be deceptive.

'Your friends must be worried. If you tell me your name, I'll be able to find your address and take you home.'

'My name is Elliott Cooper,' the man stated calmly.

'That's impossible.'

'Why's that?'

'Because *I'm* Elliott Cooper.'

'You want to see my license?' the old man asked, and took his wallet out of his pocket. He seemed to find the whole thing amusing.

Elliott examined the document held out to him and couldn't believe his eyes: the license showed his name and his date of birth! Only the photograph showed the thirty-year difference.

It doesn't mean anything, he tried to reassure himself, *anyone could get a counterfeit license. But who would take the trouble and why?*

When he thought about it, there could be only one explanation: Matt was playing a practical joke on him. He held on to that idea for a minute, not fully convinced. Sure, Matt loved to have fun, and he had a slightly twisted sense of humor. But this was going too far. If he'd wanted to play a joke, he wouldn't have picked something so intellectual; he would have hit strictly below the belt.

For a joke, Matt would have sent a bevy of strippers or a high-class call-girl, Elliott thought, *not a sixty-year-old guy claiming to be me.*

Lost in thought, Elliott didn't notice the man getting close to him. His expression had become more serious. He grabbed Elliott by the arm and stared at him intently.

'Listen, as unbelievable as it seems, I've *really* found a way of going back thirty years in time.'

'Sure you have.'

'You *have* to believe me, for God's sake!'

'But what you're telling me doesn't make any sense!'

'If it doesn't make any sense, explain how I got out of the airport rest room without your seeing me?'

Elliott had no answer to that. This guy might be nuts, but he had an answer for everything.

'Mister . . .' he started to say, but the other man interrupted: 'Drop the "Mister", okay?'

At that point, they heard barking coming from the other side of the bay window. Elliott couldn't hide his surprise. God knows how the Labrador had managed to drag himself upstairs. Despite his injury, he was barking happily to announce his presence.

'Tramp!' the old man exclaimed, as though he had seen a ghost.

Trembling with happiness, the dog jumped into his arms and began licking his hands and sniffing everywhere, as though it was a ritual between them.

'You've already seen this mutt?' asked Elliott, even more puzzled.

'Of course, he's mine!'

'Yours?'

'Ours.'

He felt like tearing his hair out. The guy was really starting to get on his nerves. Maybe he needed to use a different approach; maybe he should pretend to go along with him.

Elliott let a few seconds pass, then asked with apparently complete seriousness: 'So, you really come from the future?'

'You could look at it like that.'

Elliott gave the impression of accepting that. He walked over and leaned on the railing. He stared at the street below, as though he were desperately looking for something. 'It's strange,' he said after a minute, 'I don't see your time machine. Did you park it on the street or in my living room?'

The other man couldn't keep from smiling a little.

'Pretty funny. You ever think of going into stand-up?'

Elliott was tired of pulling his punches. 'Listen, I don't know you, I don't know where you came from, but I do know you're playing some kind of game with me.'

'And why would I do that?'

'I don't have the damnedest idea, and to tell you the truth I couldn't care less. All I want now is for you to get out of my house, and I warn you, it's the last time I'll ask you politely.'

'Take it easy, I won't stay long.'

But instead of clearing out, the man sat down in the wicker chair and took a pack of cigarettes out of his pocket: it was red and white with a familiar black logo. Elliott recognized his own brand, but that didn't bother him: lots of people smoked Marlboros.

'You know,' the man said, and blew a smoke ring as he put his lighter down on the table, 'I can understand why you don't believe me. As you get older, you gradually become less sure of yourself, but I remember what I was like when I was your age: a man of science who believed in nothing without rational proof.'

'And what are you now?'

'A man of faith.'

A gentle breeze was blowing over the terrace. It was a beautiful early fall evening. The usual pollution seemed to have dissolved, leaving the sky unusually clear. They could see a magnificent display of thousands of stars and a full moon glowing with a bluish light. Seemingly absorbed by the moon-lit view, the man finished his cigarette and put it out in the ashtray in front of him.

'Maybe it's time for you to see me for what I am, Elliott: your ally.'

'A pain in the ass, that's what you are.'

'But I'm a pain in the ass who knows everything about you.'

Elliott exploded: 'Sure, you know everything about me because you *are* me. That's your crazy idea. But what do you really know about me? My brand of cigarettes, my date of birth . . . what else?'

He had lost his temper because he was afraid. He had the uneasy feeling that somehow the balance had shifted between them and the other man still had some weapons in reserve. As though to confirm his fears, the man spoke again in a serious voice: 'I know things you've never told anyone, not your best friend, not the woman you love.'

'What, for example?'

'Things you don't want to hear.'

'Go ahead, try me, just to see. I don't have anything to hide.'

'You think so?'

'What should we talk about?'

The man thought for a minute and said, 'You want to talk about your father?'

The question felt like a sudden slap in the face.

'What does my father have to do with anything?'

'Even though he would never admit it, your father was an alcoholic, wasn't he?'

'That's not true!'

'Of course he was. To the outside world, he was a respectable businessman, a loving husband, and a good father. But in your family, for your mother and you, it was a different story, right?'

55

'You don't know anything about it.'

'That's what you think. He calmed down a little bit when he got older, but when you were little, sometimes he really beat you, remember?'

Elliott said nothing, and the man went on. 'It came over him some nights after he'd had a few. When he was good and drunk, it didn't take much to make him mad, and when he hit you it calmed him down.'

Elliott felt like a boxer on the ropes. He took in what the man was saying without reacting.

'For a long time, you let him get away with it. Sometimes you even provoked him, didn't you? Because you knew that if he took it out on you, he wouldn't go after your mother.'

The man let a few seconds go by, and then he asked, 'You want me to go on?'

'Go fuck yourself!'

Instead he leaned toward Elliott and whispered in his ear as though he were telling him a secret: 'When you were ten, you got home from school one day and found your mother in the bathtub; she'd slit her wrists and was bleeding to death . . .'

'You son of a bitch!' Elliott exploded, and grabbed the man by the collar.

But he calmly finished what he had to say: 'You got there just in time to save her. You called for help, but she made you promise never to tell, so you didn't. You helped her break the glass in the shower stall, and she told the paramedics that she'd cut herself slipping on the wet floor. It was your secret. Nobody ever found out.'

The two men stood face to face, eyeball to eyeball. Elliott was shattered. He hadn't foreseen this airing of family secrets.

Not tonight, not like this. The memories were buried, almost wiped out, but still alive, still painful.

'At first, you thought you'd done the right thing, except two years later your mother jumped out of the window from the twelfth floor where you lived.'

Every word the man spoke had the impact of a body blow.

For the first time in a long while Elliott felt like crying. He felt vulnerable, punch-drunk, demolished.

'Since then, you haven't been able to stop thinking that you were partly to blame for her suicide, that things might have been different if you'd talked. Because she might have gotten therapy or been treated in a clinic. Should I go on?'

Elliott opened his mouth to protest, but no sound came out.

Even though he, too, seemed overcome with emotion, the man plunged back into the treacherous currents of truth. He had carefully prepared his final revelation, which he delivered like a *coup de grâce*: 'You tell anyone who'll listen that you don't want to have any kids because the world today is awful and the future looks worse, but that's not the real reason, Elliott . . .'

The young doctor frowned. He no longer knew what the man was getting at.

'You don't want to have any kids because you've always thought your parents didn't love you. And now you're afraid that you wouldn't be capable of loving your own children. Strange how the human mind works, isn't it?'

Elliott didn't deny it. It had taken three minutes for a man he'd never met to demolish everything he thought he knew, make him doubt it all. A miserable collection of little secrets, that's all any of us is.

A stronger gust of wind swept across the terrace. The man

57

turned up his collar, stepped toward Elliott, and put a hand on his shoulder, as though to comfort him.

'Don't touch me!' Elliott went over to the railing. He was gasping for air and his mind was in a whirl. Most importantly, he felt that he was missing something essential, the real purpose behind these revelations.

'Suppose that's all true,' he said, staring at his mysterious visitor, 'what do you want from me?'

The old man shook his head. 'I don't want anything from you. Sorry to disappoint you, but I'm not here for you.'

'But . . .'

'The reason I came back is to see *her* . . .'

He took out his wallet again, and this time he handed Elliott a faded photograph. A picture of Ilena in Central Park throwing a snowball, her face glowing and her cheeks flushed. It was his favorite photograph. It had been taken the winter before and it never left his wallet.

'How'd you get that? You go near Ilena just once and I'll beat you until . . .'

The man stood up without waiting for the end of the threat. As though it was time for him to leave, he stroked the dog and took a few steps toward the bay window. It was then that Elliott noticed him trembling the way he had the night before in the airport, just before he disappeared.

But this time he wouldn't let him get away. Elliott ran over to catch him, but it was too late. The man had already left the terrace and closed the sliding door behind him.

'Open the goddamn' door!' the doctor shouted, drumming on the glass.

It had a fluorescent coating that made it glow green at night. This architectural caprice changed the glass into a kind of one-way mirror. Now Elliott found himself on the wrong side, trapped on the terrace, blind and exposed.

'Open up!' he demanded again.

There was a silence, and then a voice on the other side of the glass murmured, 'Don't forget what I told you: I'm your ally, not your enemy.'

He couldn't let this guy get away. He wanted to know more. In desperation, he grabbed a wrought-iron chair and threw it as hard as he could at the sliding door, which shattered into a thousand glittering shards. Elliott ran into the house and down the stairs, searched through all the rooms, even went out into the street.

No one.

When he came back onto the terrace, the Labrador was howling at the moon.

'It's all right,' he said, comforting the dog, 'it's over.'

But deep down he knew differently. His troubles were only just beginning.

SIX

*I want you so much to remember the happy days when
we were friends. In those days, life was more beautiful
and the sun was brighter than it is today.*
Jacques Prévert and Joseph Kosma

1976
Elliott is 30

With the dog in his arms, Elliott dashed to his car. He had to
tell Matt what had happened to him. His first impulse had
been to call Ilena, but he'd hung up before she answered. How
could he tell her all this without making her think he'd gone
nuts? No, better to wait until he knew more before he
bothered her.

He opened the door to the Bug and put his new companion
on the passenger seat. He was starting to get attached to the
Lab, who seemed as disturbed as he was by the strange
adventure they'd just been through.

Elliott drove out of the marina into North Beach. It was
very late and traffic was light. He took Lombard Street and

negotiated the eight hairpin bends that had given it the reputation of being the most tortuous street in the world. The street was splendidly scenic and more than lived up to its reputation, but tonight Elliott was too preoccupied to admire the views of the illuminated displays of flowers at the roadside.

Eager to get to his destination, he sped through North Beach, passed in front of the Italian Cathedral, where Marilyn Monroe had married Joe DiMaggio a few years earlier, and came to the top of Telegraph Hill.

He was used to the steep streets of San Francisco, and he was careful to park at an angle at the top of the hill, with his wheels turned toward the sidewalk in accordance with the municipal regulations.

'Right, you stay here,' he ordered the dog.

The animal whined in protest, but Elliott was unmoved. 'Sorry, it's non-negotiable,' and he slammed the car door.

He went into a little alley surrounded by eucalyptus trees and down a flight of stairs adorned with flowers along the side of Telegraph Hill. The place was charming and unreal, as though a patch of countryside had popped up in the middle of the city. From here, the city was displayed at your feet, to Coit Tower in the distance glowing with white light. The colorful and luxurious vegetation provided a protective cover for countless birds: sparrows, wild parrots, mockingbirds. Elliott ran down the wooden steps, winding among rhododendrons, rose bushes, and bougainvillea, leading to the little art deco houses perched on the hillside. Halfway down, he came to a gate opening onto a neglected garden. He climbed over it as he always did and landed on the lawn of a painted wooden house. The sultry refrain of a Marvin Gaye song came from within. He was about to knock on the door, but it was already open. He went right in, eager to tell his friend about his worries.

'Matt, are you there?' he shouted as he came into the living room. 'You'll never guess what happened to me . . .'

He stopped dead. He had just seen two champagne glasses and an assortment of cookies on the table near the window. A whiff of exotic Indian incense drifted through the air. Elliott frowned and looked around the room. He saw a pair of high-heeled shoes near the fireplace, a pastel-colored bra on the couch, and a pair of lace panties hanging on a statuette. It looked as though Matt had company. At least, he hoped so, because if he wore that kind of underwear, he certainly wasn't the Matt Elliott knew. He was about to tiptoe out when he heard: 'Hi, you.'

He turned around as though he'd been caught doing something wrong. Standing in front of him, completely naked, was the girl from the beach.

'Um, good evening,' he muttered, turning away, 'sorry to . . .'

Feigning modesty, she held one hand over her breasts and the other below her stomach and walked languidly toward him.

'Matt didn't tell me that you'd be joining the party,' she said seductively.

'No, uh . . . that's not it. I just came to . . .'

'What the hell are you doing here now?' Matt interrupted as he came into the room wearing nothing but a sheet.

'Obviously interrupting something,' Elliott observed.

'Your perceptive, I see. Anyhow, let me introduce you to Tiffany. She's in town to audition for the part of the next Bond girl.'

'Pleased to meet you. Uh . . . I won't shake your hand since they're both busy.'

In exchange, Tiffany gave him a smile that showed off her gleaming white teeth.

Elliott turned to his friend. 'Listen, Matt, I need your help . . .'

'Right now? Can't it wait till tomorrow?' Matt asked. Couldn't his friend *see* what he was breaking up here?

'You're right, I'll call you tomorrow,' Elliott agreed, disappointed. 'Sorry I bothered you.'

He'd already taken a few steps toward the door when Matt, suddenly seeing that something important was worrying his friend, grabbed him by the shoulder. 'Wait a minute, tell me what happened.'

At the other end of the room, Tiffany sighed and picked up her clothes. When no one objected, she decided it was time to go.

'Okay, guys, I'll leave you to it,' she announced as she finished getting dressed. 'If you prefer games between boys . . .'

'No, no, no,' said Matt in a worried voice as he tried to hold her back, 'it's not *at all* what you think. Elliott is just a *friend*!'

'Don't worry, sweetie,' she reassured him as she walked out of the house. 'I know what it's like in San Francisco.'

Half naked, Matt pursued her through the garden, swearing by all that was holy that he wasn't gay, and begging for her phone number. The young woman, upset about being neglected, refused to give it to him. Matt persisted, but suddenly a gust of wind from the Pacific blew away the sheet. Naked as a baby, he grabbed the nearest flower pot – a flat-branched cactus – and held it in front of him. He continued to chase after Tiffany for a minute, determined to make her change her mind, but even in high heels she ran like a deer. In the house next door, a light came on and a shutter opened. Awoken by the rumpus, an old woman poked her head out the window. When he saw his neighbor's outraged face, Matt retreated, and hurried back to his house at top speed. He had almost reached the front door when he slipped on the top step of the porch and fell onto the lawn, the spines of the cactus embedded in the most sensitive part of his anatomy.

Howling in pain, he closed the door behind him and pointed an accusing finger at Elliott: 'I hope for your sake you have a *very good* reason for losing me that lay!'

'I think I'm going crazy, is that good enough?'

'Okay, okay. You're crazy, I'm out of my mind with pain . . . no, please, don't open your mouth.'

'I didn't say anything,' said Elliott, trying to keep from smiling.

'Just . . . give me a minute,' said Matt, and went into the bedroom. 'I'll get dressed and then we'll talk about your problem.'

Elliott drifted into the kitchen and put on some water for coffee. Despite his promise, he couldn't help calling out to Matt: 'You want a doctor's advice? Use tweezers.'

The atmosphere in the house was a little less tense. Matt had repaired the damage and put on jeans and a sweater. He looked as good as new when he sat down at the table with his friend.

'So, tell me,' he said, and poured himself a cup of coffee.

'He came back,' was all Elliott said.

'Let me guess – your time traveler, right?'

'Yes, he showed up on my terrace tonight.'

Matt took a sip of coffee, made a face, and added two lumps of sugar.

'He still says the same thing?'

'He claims that he's me, just thirty years older.'

'A weird symptom, wouldn't you say, doctor?'

'What's really disturbing is that he knows so much about me, intimate stuff, very personal things . . .'

'Is he trying to blackmail you?'

'Not at all. He claims he wants to see Ilena.'

'Well, if you come across your pal from the future again, don't forget to ask him for some tips on the races or the stock market . . .'

Matt took a sip of coffee, made another face, and put in three more lumps of sugar and a swig of milk, before finishing his sentence: '. . . so we could at least make a little money on the side.'

Elliott was annoyed. 'You don't believe me, is that it?'

'Sure, I believe there's a guy who's bothering you, but I don't believe he comes from the future.'

'If you'd seen the way he disappeared,' Elliott said in a pensive tone.

'You know what? Now I'm really worried about you. May I remind you that of the two of us, I'm the clown . . .'

Matt got up and dumped his coffee in the sink. 'Ugh! Your coffee tastes like sweaty socks.' He continued his diatribe: 'I'm the one who's a little nutty and extravagant, I'm the one who always pulls crazy stunts and tells stupid jokes. And you're the voice of reason and wisdom. So don't try changing places.'

'Okay, granted, but I still have a bad feeling about this guy.

He scares me. I mean, how do I know he won't do me some harm?'

'Then we have to find him and scare the pants off him.' Matt grabbed a baseball bat that was lying on the couch.

'Put that down,' Elliott said with a sigh. 'The guy is twice our age.'

'How do you suggest we get back at him then?'

Elliot thought for a minute and said, 'What the guy says is so off the wall that either he's mentally unbalanced . . .'

'Or?'

'. . . or he's telling the truth.'

'If you don't mind, let's stick with the first possibility.'

'In that case, we better contact all the hospitals and psychiatric clinics around here, to see if a patient has gone missing.'

'Okay, let's get going!' and Matt picked up his phone. 'If this guy exists, I promise you we'll find him.'

Elliott got the telephone directory off the bookshelf; the only other things on it were a complete collection of *Playboy* and a few books on wine growing.

'You know that wine and women are not the only important things in the world, don't you?' he couldn't help saying.

'Really?' asked Matt, only half joking. 'Because when I think about it, I don't see anything else.'

Once they'd made a list of numbers, they called all the institutions in California to see if the man they were looking for could be a missing patient. Psychiatric hospitals had been releasing a number of their inmates in recent years, partly because Governor Reagan had drastically reduced their budgets, something he planned to do on a larger scale if he ever became president.

Elliott and Matt spared no efforts, but after an hour they were forced to recognize that they had no leads. The job was too hard and it was the wrong time of day.

'This guy is the invisible man,' Matt said and dropped the phone. 'You want to keep going?'

'I think we're going about this the wrong way. All I want is some proof.'

'Proof of what?'

'Proof that this guy isn't me.'

'You're really losing it! This is the first time I've seen you like this, and I can tell you, I wouldn't like to have you operate on me. Relax, take a vacation, take Ilena to Hawaii for a week, and you'll see, everything will go back to normal.'

Matt collapsed on the couch and turned on the television in the middle of an episode of *Columbo*. On the screen, in between complaining about his wife, the detective neatly managed to trip up a criminal who'd made contradictory statements.

'Too bad he didn't leave something behind,' Matt said, and yawned.

'What do you mean?'

'Your time traveler, too bad he didn't leave something with his fingerprints at your place. Then we could have had it analyzed, just like in the movies.'

Elliott thought for a minute, going over the precise details of his conversation with his visitor, and then he grabbed his friend by the shoulders. 'Matt, you're a genius.'

'Of course. Too bad you're the only one who knows. By the way, why do you say that?'

'He left his lighter! I'm almost sure of it: he smoked a cigarette and put his Zippo on the table on my terrace.'

In a state of great excitement, Elliott picked up his jacket and his keys. 'I'm going home.'

'I'll go with you,' said Matt, catching up with him in the doorway. 'I don't want you driving in this state.'

'Thanks.'

'Besides, I'm not going to leave you by yourself just when things are getting interesting.'

The two friends left the house and climbed the wooden steps.

'Let's take my car,' said Matt. 'I've never liked your heap of junk.'

But when they got to his parking spot, they discovered that Tiffany had gotten to the magnificent Corvette first. Large lipstick letters covered the whole width of the windshield: BASTARD.

'Nice girl, your friend,' said Elliott.

'But you notice she also left her phone number,' said Matt, taking a calling card from beneath a wiper. 'There must be something irresistible about me.'

While his friend was wiping off the windshield, Elliott went to get the Labrador out of his car.

'You've got a dog now?' Matt said with surprise. 'I thought you didn't like animals.'

'Let's just say he's a special dog.'

Matt got in and fastened his seat belt. 'What's so special about him? He knows how to drive and you're using him as a chauffeur?'

'Yeah, and I even taught him to talk.'

'Seriously?'

'Come on, let's go. If you're good maybe he'll sing you the *Marseillaise*.'

Matt put his foot on the accelerator, and the Corvette drove off into the night. Elliott felt lighter, as though he'd been relieved of a heavy burden of anxiety. It had only taken a little while for him to recover his spirits. He had been afraid, and it was true that his visitor had upset him by digging up a few family secrets. But his confidence was restored now. He'd get the lighter and call a friend of his in the police. Analysis would show that the old guy's fingerprints were different from his and then everything would be back to normal. Then he could call Ilena and laugh with her about the whole story. In the meantime, he could needle Matt.

'You know, you don't always have to go out with girls that have the IQ of a snail.'

'What are you talking about?'

'The starlet I just saw you with didn't look like she could find her way out of a paper bag, if you know what I'm saying?'

Matt took this in calmly, then said, 'But did you ever see such a pair of . . .'

'Big tits aren't the only reason for going out with a woman,' Elliott interrupted. 'You're thirty years old, I thought you'd gotten over that stuff, but I guess I was wrong.'

Matt didn't give up. 'Physical attraction's important.'

'Sure, it's important for what's on your mind, but what about afterward?'

'After what?'

'You know, talking, being interested in each other, exchanging opinions . . .'

Matt shrugged his shoulders: 'If I want to talk, I call you. No need to go out with a rocket scientist for that.'

'In the meantime, you missed the turn to my house.'

'No, I didn't,' answered Matt, sounding annoyed, 'I'm just taking a shortcut you don't know.'

Unfortunately, the shortcut made the trip a few miles longer, and they didn't get to the marina for another ten minutes. Elliott was champing at the bit, but he was polite enough to say nothing.

The car had barely stopped in front of the house before he rushed inside and climbed the stairs four at a time to the terrace. He was afraid of only one thing; that the Zippo had disappeared.

Luckily it was still there, lying on the edge of the table.

'What happened here?' asked Matt, looking at the shattered glass all over the floor. 'You have a fight with King Kong?'

'I'll explain later. Right now I have to call someone.'

'Just a minute, night owl: it's two in the morning. San Francisco isn't "the city that never sleeps"; you're on the wrong coast. Right now, most normal people are in bed.'

'I'm calling the police, Matt.'

Elliott called police headquarters to find out if Detective Malden was on duty that night. He was, and they immediately connected him to the detective's desk.

'Good evening, Mr Malden, Elliott Cooper here. Sorry to bother you, but I need you to do me a big favor.'

The two friends waited for the detective on the terrace.

'I didn't know you had a friend who was a cop.' Matt looked surprised. 'How'd you meet this guy?'

'He's the one who investigated my mother's suicide,' Elliott mumbled. 'He helped me a lot at the time, and we've kept in touch. You'll see, he's a good guy.'

The two men had moved toward the table and were staring

70

at the windproof lighter left behind by the 'time traveler'. It was a silver-colored Zippo inlaid with shiny little stars, with the inscription 'Millennium Edition'.

'That's a strange expression,' said Elliott.

'Yeah,' Matt agreed, kneeling so he could study it more closely. 'It looks like it was manufactured in a limited edition to commemorate something like . . .'

'. . . the arrival of the year 2000,' Elliott finished the sentence, suddenly grasping the enormity of what he was saying.

'Nah, that's bull,' said Matt, and stood up.

A few minutes later a police car drew up in front of the house and Elliott hurried down to greet Detective Malden. He was a cop of the old school, a kind of aging Humphrey Bogart in a trench coat and fedora, but with a boxer's physique. He'd started at the bottom, learning his job on the streets. He'd been patrolling San Francisco for nearly forty years, and he knew all the city's secrets.

But the old policeman had not come alone. He introduced his new partner, Detective Douglas, to Elliott. Douglas was a young detective who'd just graduated from the police academy with a degree in criminology. Carefully coiffed and dressed, he was wearing a well-tailored suit and a neatly knotted tie, at two in the morning.

'What happened, Elliott?' asked Malden as he came onto the terrace, pointing to the shards of glass. 'Someone throw a rock through your window?'

'I'd like you to take some prints from this lighter,' he explained ingenuously, as though this were commonplace.

Like a dutiful student, Douglas had already taken out his pen and notebook. 'Has there been a break-in or a burglary?' he asked.

71

'Not exactly,' Matt answered. 'It's a little more complicated . . .'

'If you're not filing a complaint, we can't do anything for you,' said the young detective, with a touch of annoyance.

'Take it easy, Douglas,' said Malden.

Elliott was beginning to understand that he was going to have trouble avoiding an explanation. On the pretext of making some coffee, he brought the older cop into the kitchen with him so he could speak to him in private.

'Now, Elliott, explain to me what happened,' said Malden as he lit up a cigarillo.

When he remained silent, Malden remembered their first meeting. Even though it was twenty years ago, he recalled it as if it had been yesterday.

One rainy night he had been called to investigate the suicide of a woman who had jumped from a downtown apartment building. He'd found identification on the body – her name was Rose Cooper – and had taken it on himself to break the awful news to her husband and her son.

When his mother committed suicide, Elliott was barely ten. Malden remembered him as an appealing child, intelligent and sensitive. He'd also met the kid's father, a businessman, who hadn't seemed particularly upset by the news of his wife's death. Malden remembered too the marks and the bruises he'd seen on the boy's arms.

In fact, he'd guessed at rather than actually seen those marks. Perhaps it was this kind of intuition that made him a good cop: he sensed things. And in this case, he sensed them all the better because his own father had regularly beaten him with a belt when he got home from his day at the factory.

Of course he could have turned a blind eye; people didn't

pay too much attention to that kind of thing in those days. But he'd come back to see Elliott the next day and the day after that. He'd taken the opportunity to drop a few hints to the father, to show him that he knew and that he intended to keep an eye on the kid. As time progressed, Malden kept in touch with Elliott and took an interest in his education. He had an old-fashioned view of his job, seeing himself as a policeman who cared about people in general, rather than just about arresting criminals.

Now the policeman took the cup of coffee Elliott handed him and rubbed his eyes to dispel the memories. He had to focus on the present.

'If you don't tell me anything,' he insisted, 'I won't be able to help you.'

'I know that, but . . .'

'But what?'

'When my mother died, you asked me to trust you, and you promised that when I needed help, you'd be there for me . . .'

'It's still true, kid.'

'Well, today I need you. I need not only the policeman but also the friend: the policeman to analyze those prints, and the friend to trust me even if I can't explain anything right now.'

Malden sighed. 'Those are fine words, but I can't do a fingerprint analysis just like that. I need authorization, I'd have to prepare a report. We'd have to get a team from the lab on it. Besides, it could take several days, maybe even weeks . . .'

'But I need a result right away!'

Malden thought for a while, scratching his head. His star had been waning for a while at headquarters. Officially, he was criticized for disregarding the chain of command and using unorthodox methods to get results. In fact, he hadn't been forgiven for going a little too far in a corruption investigation that had tarnished the reputations of some important municipal figures. Malden knew that he was now on a tight leash and that his new partner was there primarily to keep an eye on him and wait for him to make a mistake. All of this should have made him cautious, but he had a promise to keep. A promise he had made twenty years before to a kid who had just lost his mother.

'Maybe I've got an idea about how to get those prints without going through the usual channels,' he said suddenly.

'How?'

'You'll see,' he said, looking mysterious. 'It's not regulations, not by a long shot, but it might work.'

Back in the living room, he sent Douglas out to buy a tube of super glue.

'And where am I supposed to find that at two in the morning?' Douglas complained.

Malden gave his partner the address of a camera shop that was open all night and sold the glue, which was manufactured by Kodak.

While Douglas was doing that, Malden kneeled and scrutinized the inscription on the lighter. 'Millennium Edition? What does that mean?' he asked, turning to Matt.

'We don't know any more than you do,' he said, opening a can of Coke.

'You didn't touch it, at least? If you did, no prints . . .'

'We're not that dumb!' Matt protested. 'We've seen the cop shows.'

Malden gazed balefully at him and then said to Elliott, 'I need a cardboard box.'

'How big?'

74

'A shoebox will do.'

Elliott rummaged in his bedroom closet and came up with a shoebox.

In the meantime, Malden had picked up the lamp from the table, taken off the shade, and put his hand on the lit bulb to judge its temperature.

Douglas got back a few minutes later, proudly brandishing a tube of super glue. At first he had taken Malden for a has-been, but he'd been forced to acknowledge that the old cop's ingenuity surprised him more and more every day. In fact, he'd learned more in a few weeks with Malden than in his three years of training.

'Everything's ready,' Malden announced. 'Let the show begin.'

'You're going to take prints with a cardboard box and a tube of glue?' asked Matt incredulously.

'Exactly. And you've never seen *that* on the cop shows, my boy.'

Malden asked Matt to give him the Coke can he'd just drained. The policeman took a penknife out of his pocket and used it to cut out the bottom of the aluminum can. He squeezed the contents of the tube of glue into this little improvised dish and set it next to the lighter. Then he picked up the lamp and used the heat radiating from the bulb to heat the glue. A nasty smell soon filled the room. Malden covered it all with the cardboard box and turned to his audience with a satisfied look on his face.

'Just a few more minutes, and it'll be ready,' he said with a smile.

'What exactly did you do?' asked Matt, looking more and more dubious.

With one eye on the box, Malden adopted a professorial tone and explained: 'The chemical name of super glue is cyanoacrylate . . .'

'Well, what do you know?' said Matt.

Malden gave him a black look which meant that he didn't want to be interrupted, and Matt got the message.

'The heat causes the cyanoacrylate vapors to be drawn to the amino acids and lipids, the basic ingredients of human perspiration carried by the prints.'

'And polymerization will take place,' said Elliott, who was beginning to understand.

'Poly what?' asked Douglas, who felt completely lost.

'Polymerization,' explained Malden. 'That means that the super glue vapors will settle on the fingerprint, which is invisible to the naked eye, and form a kind of protective shell that will make it possible to bring out the print and to preserve it.'

Matt and Douglas looked at the old policeman doubtfully. They were in fact witnessing a pioneering experiment that would revolutionize the work of investigators around the world within a few years.

Elliott kept on staring at the box, anxious to find out what it would reveal.

After a minute, Malden decided that enough time had passed and picked up the box. A solid white deposit had settled on three spots on the lighter, revealing the distinct traces of three fingerprints.

'And there you have it,' he said, bending over. 'At first sight we have a fine thumbprint on one side, and on the other, I'd say . . . the tips of an index finger and a middle finger.' He carefully wrapped the evidence in a handkerchief and slipped it into his trench coat pocket.

'If I understood you right,' he said, turning to Elliott, 'you want me to compare these prints with the ones we have on file.'

'Not exactly,' the doctor corrected him. 'I want you to compare them with mine.'

Matching his words with action, he took a fountain pen out of his pocket, dripped a little ink on the table, pressed each finger into it, and set down his own prints on a blank piece of paper.

Malden took the sheet of paper and looked Elliott in the eye. 'Even though I don't understand what this is all about, I'll do it anyway, because I trust you.'

The young doctor nodded silently; his way of thanking the policeman. Matt finally dared to ask another question: 'Will it take long to compare the two sets of prints?'

'I'll get right on it,' Malden assured him. 'Since the prints are good, I hope for some quick results.'

Elliott showed the two policemen out. While Douglas went to get the car, Malden promised, 'I'll call you as soon as I'm done.'

Then, after hesitating a moment, he asked: 'By the way, are you still with your Brazilian, Ilena?'

'Still?' answered Elliott, a little surprised by the question. 'Well, with us it's . . .'

Held back by shyness, he didn't finish his sentence, but Malden had gotten the point. 'I understand,' he said and lowered his head. 'When a person comes into your heart, it's forever . . .'

Elliott was moved as he watched the old policeman walk off. He knew that for the last few years he'd been living with his wife's losing battle with Alzheimer's, and that the bell for the final round was about to ring.

It was three in the morning, but Elliott wasn't sleepy. He'd gone back with Matt to pick up his VW, and stopped at a gas station on Market Street. As he was filling his tank, lost in thought, a toothless woman started yelling at him. She was pushing a shopping cart full of rags and old junk and seemed to be drunk or drugged. He didn't pay any attention to her stream of insults. He worked two days a month as a volunteer doctor at the Free Clinic, a municipally-run center for the needy, and he knew that the city at night was a different place. In tourist guides and movies, San Francisco always appeared at its best, with its colorful neighborhoods, housing for the most part confined to two or three storeys, and numerous green spaces. And there were the constant reminders of the city's hippy fame.

It was true that San Francisco had had its moment of glory in the sixties when, in the wake of Janis Joplin and Jimi Hendrix, hundreds of flower children had moved into the Victorian houses of Haight–Ashbury. But the summer of love was long gone. The hippy movement was slowly dying out, undermined by its own excesses. Joplin and Hendrix had both died at twenty-seven, Hendrix drowning in his own vomit after stuffing himself full of sleeping pills, and Joplin from a heroin overdose.

By the end of 1976, most people seemed to have lost interest in free love and communal living. Drugs, in particular, had done incredible harm. Supposed to open minds and free people from their inhibitions, LSD, methamphetamine and heroin had instead caused addiction and slow death. Elliott had seen the terrible effects for himself at the clinic: overdoses, hepatitis from dirty needles, pneumonia, bad trips that made people jump out of windows.

Piled on top of this was the problem of the Vietnam veterans, many of whom had joined the ranks of the growing army of homeless people in the city. American troops had withdrawn from Saigon the year before, and many traumatized veteran returnees now lived in slums or out on the streets of San Francisco.

Elliott paid for the gas and drove through the city with his windows open, thinking of the strange conversation he'd had earlier that night. After leaving Matt, he felt alone and vulnerable again. He was forced to concede at last that everything his visitor had said to him was true, from the beatings his father had given him to the guilt he had felt when his mother committed suicide.

Why had he never talked about all that with Ilena? Why had he never considered showing his weaknesses to the woman he loved?

And Matt? He hadn't told him anything either. Simply out of male reticence? The truth was that it was easier. With Matt, everything could be kept light-hearted and frivolous. His company was a comfortable way for Elliott to protect himself from the harsh realities of the world and to recharge his batteries when the responsibilities of his job became too burdensome.

But even though there was nothing better than love and friendship to make life bearable, in the final analysis there were some situations you could only deal with on your own.

A few miles away, Detective Malden was busy in his office at police headquarters. He'd just quarreled with his young partner who'd criticized him for doing private work while he was on duty. Malden knew that Douglas was ambitious; he barely concealed his hope that Malden would be fired so he could get a fast promotion. When the little bastard had threatened to file a report, Malden had chewed him out and sent him off to an office in another part of the building. It was too bad: Douglas could have been a good cop; he had all the necessary qualities, but he'd picked the wrong way to go about it. In Malden's day, you didn't try to succeed at any cost by pushing other people out of your way. But maybe he was getting old. Maybe the younger generation had different values: more ambition, more individual initiative, the kind of things Reagan talked about on television.

Malden finished his mug of coffee. This time he was sure Douglas would follow through on his threats. Too bad. If the top brass finally did do him in, well, he'd quit the job and spend even more time in the hospital with Lisa. Anyway, retirement age was not far off. In the meantime, he would help Elliott one more time by doing what he'd asked.

He began by staining the prints that had shown up on the lighter with a fluorescent dye. Then he took a set of photographs that would have to be developed and enlarged. Only then would the real analysis begin. He looked at his watch anxiously. He had some tedious work ahead of him, and the night was not long enough.

Before going home, Elliott stopped at an all-night grocery on Van Ness, where he bought cigarettes and a box of dog food.

'Hello, Tramp,' he said as he opened his door.

He'd barely come onto the terrace before the Labrador ran up and licked his hand just as he'd licked the stranger's hand a few hours earlier.

'You don't have to overdo it,' said Elliott, and poured the dog food into an improvised bowl.

He stood watching the Lab for a while, surprised to discover that he appreciated the company. He swept up the glass and smoked a few cigarettes, staring into space, his mind wandering back to his childhood. Every five minutes he anxiously looked over at the telephone, waiting for the verdict on the fingerprint analysis. Even if this whole thing didn't make sense, he couldn't help feeling overwrought, as though he were waiting for the results of some medical tests that might reveal the existence of a fatal disease.

Assistant Detective Douglas tore up the report he'd just finished typing. He stood up and went downstairs to the room they used for breaks. Tonight the station was unusually quiet. Douglas made two cups of coffee, went back to the third floor, and knocked on Malden's office door.

The only answer he heard was a grunt, which he decided to interpret as an invitation.

'Need a hand?' he asked, sticking his head in the doorway.

'Maybe . . .' the old cop said gruffly.

Douglas handed him a cup of coffee and glanced around the room.

Pinned to the wall were about ten greatly enlarged photographs offering a view of the labyrinth of fingerprints. Cops loved fingerprints; 'the only snitches that never lie' was the common saying. Placed end to end, the photographs seemed to make up a strange tapestry resembling a huge topographical map: gently sloping lines, bifurcations, crests, and little islands that might be combined in an infinite number of patterns. A fingerprint is a unique work of art that takes shape in the months before birth. In the mother's womb, the fetus goes through a myriad of little stress situations which randomly shape the fingers' flesh. Everything happens before the sixth month of pregnancy; after that, the shapes become fixed and remain the same for life.

Douglas had learned at the police academy that every finger had about one hundred fifty characteristic points. To decide whether two prints were identical, you just had to identify correspondences between these characteristic signs. A dozen common points were needed for authentication to have legal validity.

'Let's get to work,' he said to his boss.

Douglas had sharp eyes. Malden had patience. The two of them made a good team.

At dawn, Elliott decided to take a shower. He put on fresh clothes and left the house for work at the hospital. On the way, he had to turn on his headlights and wipers. In a few hours, the weather had completely changed. The sky that had been so clear the night before was now full of clouds, promising one of those rainy mornings that were a sign of the coming of winter.

He turned on the radio to listen to the news. It was all disturbing: a deadly earthquake in China, military repression in Argentina, an oil spill off the coast of France, a massacre in Soweto in South Africa, while in Houston a maniac barricaded in his house was taking potshots at the public.

Meanwhile, in post-Watergate America, the presidential

contest between Ford and Carter was in full swing. Disillusioned, Elliott changed the station and finished his trip listening to the Beatles singing 'Let It Be'.

He had just entered the hospital lobby when the guard stopped him: 'A call for you, doctor.'

Elliott took the phone that was handed to him.

'I have your results,' said Malden.

He took a deep breath and asked, 'What do they say?'

'The prints are identical.'

'You're sure about your results?'

'Certain. We verified them several times.'

But Elliott wasn't yet ready to accept the evidence.

'In absolute terms,' he asked, 'what are the chances of two different people having identical fingerprints?'

'One in several billion. Even twins have different prints.'

Since the doctor didn't seem to be reacting, Malden made his conclusion even clearer: 'I don't know what your problem is, Elliott, but the two sets of prints come from the same person. There is no possible doubt, that person is you.'

SEVEN

*I keep death at bay by living, suffering,
fooling myself, taking risks, giving, and losing.*

Anaïs Nin

September 2006
Elliott is 60

The blinds were slanted so that the sunlight hit the walls
before washing over the walnut floors. Wearing an old pair of
jeans and a cable-knit sweater, Elliott went down the metal
staircase leading to the kitchen. It was his day off and he was
determined to take his time eating breakfast. After a shower
and shave, he felt refreshed. This morning he was feeling no
pain, as though the extraordinary events of the night before
had driven the specter of death a little further away.

He poured a glass of orange juice, fixed a bowl of muesli
and went into the garden to eat. It looked like it was going to
be a beautiful day. A few fleeting images from his nocturnal
adventure were still running through his head. He felt more
elated than puzzled. He still didn't know what was in the pills,

but so what, they really worked! Most importantly, this second journey had enabled him to clear up several points. He thought he now had a better grasp of the mechanics of his time traveling.

First, the time interval had been the same on each occasion: thirty years to the day. The first time he'd noticed the date on a display at the airport, and last night he had seen it in a newspaper on the table.

Next, he could obviously transport objects into the past, because his clothing had gone with him on both trips. And he could also bring objects back to his own time: the blood-stained napkin was the best evidence of that.

But there was something that still bothered him: his time in the past was so short. Twenty minutes each trip wasn't very much. Just enough time to exchange a few words with his 'double', and then he was shaking, which meant he was about to return to the future.

But maybe it was too soon to find the real reason for this pattern. In any case, one thing was certain: dreams were what made it possible for him to travel through time.

Back in the house he sat down in front of his computer. He was a surgeon, of course, but what did he really know about sleep and dreams? Not much, in fact. He had absorbed tons of knowledge as a medical student, but forgotten a lot of it. To refresh his memory, he spent the next hour consulting an online medical encyclopedia.

Sleep is made up of different phases that succeed one another and repeat throughout the night.

Okay, he remembered that. What else?

Light sleep corresponds to the phases of Slow Wave Sleep and deep sleep to the phases of Paradoxical Sleep.

Paradoxical Sleep? That reminded him of something . . .

This expression designates the phase of sleep in which brain activity is most intense, whereas the body is completely atonic, with relaxation of all muscles from neck to toe.

Fine, but where did dreams come in?

We spend about twenty-five years of our life sleeping and about ten dreaming. That amounts to somewhere between 100,000 and 500,000 dreams.

Elliot pondered that number for a little while. So human life was filled with hundreds of thousands of dreams. That was both fascinating and disturbing. Sensing that he was on the right track, he allowed himself to light a cigarette and kept reading:

Periods of Paradoxical Sleep occur approximately every ninety minutes and last for a full fifteen minutes. It is during these phases that the most complex dreams occur.

The last detail made him fidget in his seat. Everything fit together: last night he'd gone to sleep at around ten and 'reappeared' thirty years earlier around eleven-thirty. His journey had thus lasted ninety minutes: the same length of time it took to reach the first phase of Paradoxical Sleep! So that was how it worked: during that period of brain activity, the substance in the pill provoked in him a return to the past. It might all seem completely off the wall, but he'd reached a stage in his life when, since he no longer believed in anything, he was ready to believe almost everything.

With a few clicks of the mouse, he continued exploring this mysterious continent and discovered that while science had discovered many things about *how* people dreamed, it didn't have much to say about *why*. In many respects, dreaming was still a mystery. Like any programmed activity of the body or mind, dreaming had to have a function, a purpose . . . But what was it?

No one had yet provided a scientific answer to that question.

Of course, there were all those esoteric theories going back to ancient Egypt that saw dreams as signs sent by the gods or by some invisible world. But who could believe such nonsense?

Elliott was considering the possibilities when his thoughts were interrupted by the phone. He answered and recognized the voice of Samuel Bellow, the lab technician he'd asked to analyze the residue in the pill bottle. 'I have the results of your analysis,' Bellow said.

1976
Elliott is 30

At the same time of day, thirty years earlier, Elliott was finishing his coffee in the break room at Lenox Hospital.

For the tenth time that morning, the young doctor was scrutinizing the fingerprint photographs that Malden had sent him by messenger. At this point, he was compelled to believe the unbelievable: somewhere in the future, another him had found a way to travel in time so as to pay him a few visits.

But as for figuring out how he did it, that was another story.

Elliott had never been much of a science fiction fan, but he had studied Einstein's theory of relativity. And what did he have to say about time travel? That it was entirely possible, provided you could exceed the speed of light. Elliott had trouble imagining his strange visitor orbiting the earth at 200,000 miles a second, like some aging Superman, though.

It seemed he had to look elsewhere for the answer.

Maybe it had something to do with black holes. He'd seen a documentary on television about them: dying stars with gravitational fields that were able to bend space–time. It was theoretically possible to imagine a body being sucked into one of those black holes and projected into another time, another universe.

Sure, but no one had yet been able to observe a black hole, and it was hardly likely that a human body could go through one of them without being torn to bits.

Besides, what about all the temporal paradoxes that spiced up all the novels and movies about time travel? Suppose when you went back into the past you prevented your future mother and father from meeting? Suppose you killed your parents before you were conceived? Then you were trapped in a vicious circle of existence and non-existence:

I killed my ancestor.

Therefore, I wasn't born.

Therefore, I didn't kill my ancestor.

Therefore, I was born.

I killed my ancestor . . .

Elliott sighed. There was no question: if you accepted the possibility of time travel, you agreed to violate a dozen physical laws and you denied all principles of causality and logical consistency.

And yet . . .

And yet, the photos he had in his hands were in fact proof that the whole story was true. 'Definitive scientific proof', he thought, remembering that every individual's fingerprints were unique.

His mind wandered as he fiddled with the windproof lighter that Malden had given back to him, setting off a little shower of sparks. He snapped the Zippo shut and quickly stood up. He felt unable to keep still. In the last few hours he must have drunk a dozen cups of coffee. The fear he'd felt the night before hadn't gone away, but it was mingled with the excitement of experiencing something that eluded his grasp. He was an ordinary man and something extraordinary was happening to him. Where was all of this leading? He didn't have the slightest idea. From this point on he was entering into the unknown and wasn't sure he could face what was coming.

He poured another cup of coffee and opened the window facing the street. He was alone in the room so he nervously lit a cigarette which he puffed on carefully, to avoid setting off the smoke detector. For the last few minutes a question had been gnawing at him. Could he communicate with his other self living in the future? Why not? But how should he go about it, and what message should he send?

He thought about it for a while without coming up with any obvious solution. Like a comet from out of nowhere a wild idea came to him then, but he rejected it. No, he couldn't do just anything, he had to calm down, put all of this aside for a while and get back to work.

Full of good intentions, he sat down at a table in front of a stack of patient files to complete his surgical reports. But after a couple of minutes he gave up pretending. How could he concentrate after what he'd just been through? He looked at his watch: he had a good two hours before his next operation, and with a little luck he'd find someone to replace him on call. He took off his white coat, picked up his jacket, and walked out. Five minutes later, he left the hospital.

As he was leaving the parking lot, a FedEx truck was coming in. Intoxicated by what he was experiencing, Elliott looked at it with a smile of defiance. He'd show FedEx and UPS. He, Elliott Cooper, was going to send a message thirty years into the future.

2006
Elliott is 60

'I have the results of your analysis,' said Bellow.

'What do they say?'

'Well, it's something botanical: a compound of mulberry and medlar leaves essentially.'

Elliott couldn't believe his ears. 'Nothing else?'

'No. If you want to know what I think, this medicine can't do much: it's just a placebo.'

Stunned, the doctor hung up. So there was no magic ingredient in his pills. The old Cambodian, the idea that he could 'make a wish', the hope of seeing Ilena again: that was all a joke. The cancer must have spread to his brain. The encounter with his double thirty years earlier must have happened only in his head: at the end of his life, his mind was wandering.

This was it, then, the purpose of dreams. He should be thinking about psychoanalysis, not science. Dreams were nothing but representations of repressed desires, a kind of safety valve that let the unconscious express itself without endangering psychological equilibrium. Elliott had knocked at Einstein's door, but it was Freud who had answered.

So, a simple phone call had brought him back to earth. The magic had disappeared and in the harsh light of morning, what had seemed so real to him the night before was revealed as nothing but a mad illusion. He had so much wanted to believe in it, but no . . . This splendid adventure, this brief journey in time, was purely an invention of his own mind. Illness and imminent death had driven him to fantasize about a possible return to a crucial moment in his past.

The truth was that he was scared to death. He refused to accept that his life was almost over. Everything had happened so fast: childhood, adolescence, youth, maturity . . . A few blinks of the eye, and it was already time to go? Jesus, sixty was too young! He didn't feel like an old man. Before he'd been diagnosed with cancer, he'd been in great shape. When he went on humanitarian missions, he'd trek through mountains, leaving young guys of thirty or forty behind. And Sharika, his Indian intern, a real beauty – she'd wanted to go out with him, not with one of the pretty boys who were just starting out.

But that was all over, finished and done with. He had nothing to look forward to but death and fear.

The fear of seeing his body grow weak.

The fear of suffering and losing his independence.

The fear of dying all alone in a bare hospital room.

The fear of leaving his daughter at the mercy of this uncertain world.

The fear that in the end his life had had no meaning.

And the fear of what was waiting for him afterward. Once he'd given up the ghost and gone over to the other side.

Oh, shit . . .

He wiped away a tear of rage from his cheek.

Right now, a fierce pain was ripping through his guts. He went into the bathroom, rummaged in the medicine cabinet for a painkiller, and splashed some water on his face. The man he saw in the mirror had glittering, bloodshot eyes.

How much time did he have left? A few days, a few weeks? As never before, he felt the need to live, to run, to breathe, to talk, to love . . .

You couldn't say he'd made a mess of his life: he had a daughter whom he adored, he'd been useful, he'd traveled, known many pleasures, and had good times with Matt. But there had always been something missing.

Ilena . . .

Since her death thirty years ago, he'd somehow lived a detached life, more like a spectator than a participant in his own existence. And it was true that for the last few days he'd come to believe in the idea of time travel, for the slightly crazy hope of being able to see Ilena again before he died.

But now the illusion had faded and he was angry with himself for being taken in. 'You'll stop hurting when you stop hoping,' that was what people said.

And Elliott wanted to stop hurting.

So, to permanently extinguish the last glimmer of hope still lingering in his heart, he threw the little bottle of pills down the toilet.

He hesitated for a minute . . . and then he flushed.

1976
Elliott is 30

Elliott parked his Bug on Valencia Street in the Mission District. At this time of day, the Hispanic neighborhood was already humming with activity. The inexpensive stores and the taco and fruit stands made Mission one of the most picturesque parts of the city.

The doctor walked down the street in the middle of a noisy, vibrant crowd. The façades of all the buildings were decorated with brightly colored murals. Elliott stopped briefly to look at these fascinating paintings that reminded him of the style of Diego Rivera. But he wasn't there as a tourist. He carried on, walking a little faster. The place had a harsh, charged atmosphere that some people found enticing, but it also had its bad aspects, like the Chicano gangs that insulted passers-by and ruined the convivial atmosphere of the neighborhood.

At the intersection of Dolores Street, after a row of salsa clubs and stores selling religious articles, he finally saw the sign he was looking for:

BLUE MOON: JEWELRY AND TATTOOS

He pushed open the door and came face to face with a poster of Freddie Mercury in drag. The singer from Queen was blatantly miming a sex act. On the turntable near the cash register, a reggae tune by Bob Marley was playing at full volume, made popular by Eric Clapton's cover of 'I Shot the Sheriff' the year before.

Elliott sighed. This was not really his scene, but he put on a brave face.

'Kristina?' he called out, heading toward the back of the store.

'Doctor Cooper! What a surprise!'

The tall blonde woman in front of him looked tough: she was wearing motorcycle boots, leather hotpants, and had an outrageous tattoo at the base of her spine.

Elliott had met her at the hospital six months before when he'd operated on her son for a defective kidney. Since then, he'd been regularly monitoring the baby, a Chinese boy that Kristina was raising with her partner Leila, a surgical nurse he worked with. From their first meeting, Elliott had been intrigued by the free spirit of this woman, a Berkeley graduate with a degree in Asian studies who'd decided to open a tattoo parlor instead of teaching in a university. Kristina lived the way she wanted and openly displayed her homosexuality. That wasn't a problem in San Francisco: the gays had taken over from the hippies as the presiding group in the city a few years before. Drawn by the city's tolerance, tens of thousands of homosexuals had moved into the Castro and Noe Valley neighborhoods.

'I'll be with you in a minute,' she said, offering him a seat.

The doctor sat down next to a transvestite from South America who was having his ears pierced. Elliott felt a little embarrassed, and asked if he could use the phone to call Matt with his latest news. When he told Matt about the fingerprint analysis, his friend didn't seem overly troubled.

'Nobody but you has ever seen this guy,' he pointed out. 'If you want to know what I think, this whole thing happened in your head.'

'What do you mean, in my head?' Elliott was annoyed. 'And the Millennium Edition lighter with my fingerprints, that's in my head?'

'It must be something you bought, but don't remember buying, that's all.'

Elliott was devastated: 'So you don't believe me?'

'No,' Matt admitted, 'and I hope that if I told you a story like that, you wouldn't believe me either and you'd try to get me to see reason.'

'Thanks for your support!' Elliott replied, and hung up, very angry.

'So, doctor, what can I do for you?' asked Kristina, motioning him into a chair. 'What would you say to a Hell's Angels tattoo or a big dragon on your back?'

'Neither one,' he said, and rolled his shirtsleeve all the way up. 'I just want a little inscription there, at the top of my shoulder.'

'You wouldn't prefer something more artistic?' she said as she prepared a needle. 'Look at that one.'

Kristina turned her leg a little, revealing a kind of Japanese devil beneath the mesh of the stocking on her upper thigh.

'That's a real work of art,' Elliott conceded, 'but it's not quite my style.'

'A pity. You're not bad-looking and there's nothing sexier than a tattoo on your lover's body.'

'I don't think my girlfriend would agree.'

'Women can sometimes surprise you.'

'There I have to agree with you.'

He took a pen out of his jacket pocket and wrote a few words on the back of a magazine.

95

'That's what I want,' he said, and handed it to Kristina. The young woman frowned. 'Is that some kind of code?'

'Let's just say it's a personal message to an old friend.'

Kristina checked her tattooing needles. 'It'll hurt a little at the beginning, and then the pain will fade. You won't regret this?'

Elliott closed his eyes for a second. Could there really be interaction between present and future? It seemed absurd, but he had to try. To give himself courage, he imagined the expression on his double's face thirty years in the future, if he got this message.

'No, I won't.'

The strident noise of the machine filled the room, and Kristina said, as though she were reciting a creed: 'The body is one of the last places where we can be free.'

2006
Elliott is 60

After flushing the pills down the toilet, still feeling disappointed, Elliott stretched out on the living room couch. He had a date with Angie at noon, and he didn't want to turn up looking like a zombie. With his eyes closed, he listened to his own breathing. He wanted it to be free and regular, but it was halting and congested. He felt as though he were suffocating, unable to catch his breath. The disease fiercely at work inside his body contrasted with the gentle light filtering through the clerestory windows. Outside, he could hear birdsong and the sound of the sea. Outside, life went on, but he was no longer part of it. Despite the sunlight, he started to shiver; probably a fever starting. At the same time he felt a tingling in his upper arm, just where it met the shoulder. It wasn't really a pain, more like something being stuck in his flesh. He rubbed the stiff muscle with his hand, but that had no effect. He stood up, took off his sweater, and rolled up the sleeve of his T-shirt.

At first, he couldn't see much: a vague mottled spot, bottle green in color, that seemed to be spreading out across his shoulder. Intrigued, he stood in front of the large bathroom mirror. As he watched, he understood that the strange blotches were in reality letters taking shape one by one.

He stood there stunned for a moment, wondering what was happening. Then he finally understood . . .

'The little bastard!'

His weary heart was beating like mad, but he was relieved. No, he wasn't crazy. Everything was not just in his head. Thirty years earlier, the kid was trying to send him a message by getting a tattoo.

'Not so dumb,' he thought, and drew closer to the mirror.

He stared at his eyes and saw that they were glittering. It was stupid, but he was weeping for joy. Sure he would die soon, but he wasn't senile yet.

On his shoulder a short phrase was displayed in dark letters:

WAITING FOR
YOUR NEXT VISIT

Yes, sure, there'd be another visit, except that . . . he'd been stupid enough to get rid of the pills!

Panicked, he kneeled in front of the toilet, and stuck his hand as far down as he could, hoping but not really believing that the bottle hadn't been flushed away.

97

No, he had to stop kidding himself.

He got up and tried to think calmly. Where did the water flow to? He didn't really know; he'd never been much for tinkering, not to mention plumbing. So he ran down to the garage below and looked up at the ceiling, where he saw a tangle of pipes. He followed the main line to a cast iron plate: the waste trap. With a little luck, the bottle was stuck there. He lifted the metal lid and rummaged around in the sludge, but he found nothing.

This was the end of the adventure. The bottle must have gone on its way to a water purification plant, and he would never find it again.

Damn it, he'd ruined everything with one angry gesture.

What else could he try? In sheer desperation, he went outside and rang the bell of his nearest neighbors, an old couple full of hormones and Viagra, all their wrinkles removed by plastic surgery, who were obsessed with exercise and nutrition.

'Hello, Nina,' he said on the doorstep.

'Hello, Elliott, what brings you here?' she asked, and looked him up and down, wondering why his hands and arms were covered with smelly mud.

She didn't like me very much already, he thought, *a criminal who smokes, drinks real coffee, and eats meat that's full of cholesterol . . .*

'Could I borrow a few tools from Paul?'

'Paul's gone swimming, but let's see if you can find something in the shed.'

Elliott followed her into the shed where he found exactly what he needed in the form of a fire axe.

'Um . . . Are you sure everything's okay, Elliott?' she asked as she saw him take hold of the weapon.

'Just fine, Nina,' he assured her, giving her a smile like Jack Nicholson's in *The Shining*.

He went back to his garage, where he began methodically to demolish everything that bore even the slightest resemblance to a pipe. The operation took a good half hour, and the whole place was soon flooded. Every time he knocked down a pipe, he checked to make sure the bottle was not stuck in an elbow.

Leave nothing to chance. Keep going as long as there's some hope.

That's what he'd always done in his profession, and in thirty-five years on the job, he'd sometimes managed to save desperate cases.

So why not today?

Axe in hand, up to his knees in water, it would have been easy to mistake him for a madman. *If the police came now, I'd probably be locked up*, he said to himself as he feverishly chopped down another pipe.

And besides, maybe that's what he was: a madman. But *the madman thinks he's wise and the wise man realizes that he's nothing but a fool*. Who said that? Shakespeare? Jesus? Buddha? Whoever it was, he was damn' well right.

And even if he was crazy, at least he felt alive.

Alive.

ALIVE.

A last blow of the axe destroyed what was left of the pipes.

Elliott had no strength left. He fell to his knees in the icy water.

He stayed there for a while, exhausted and beaten. So, it was over. The pills were gone for good.

And then, all of a sudden . . .

It appeared: a little glass bottle bobbing on the surface.

Elliott threw himself on it as though it were the Holy Grail. He trembled as he wiped his hands dry on his shirt and opened the tightly closed bottle. The eight pills were still there, completely dry.

Collapsed in the foul water, half-crazed, with his fist clutching the frail container, Elliott let out a sigh of relief.

Maybe he only had a few weeks to live, but he had just found the most important thing again.

Hope.

EIGHT

You can do anything, think or believe what you like,
have all the knowledge in the world, but if you don't
love someone, you are nothing.
Marcelle Sauvageot

2006
Elliott is 60

Elliott was looking out the window, waiting for the taxi he'd called. He had thought he'd never be able to rid himself of the stench of the sewage in his garage, but a hot shower and fresh clothes had made him look civilized again. He'd had to shut off his own water to stop the flooding, and been forced to use his neighbors' bathroom. The only other thing he had to do was call a plumber, but that could wait a few hours. His immediate priority was to go downtown to meet his daughter who was coming in from the airport.

He looked at himself in the mirror. From the outside, the illusion held, but inside everything seemed to be crumbling:

pain in his chest, stiff muscles, twinges in his lower back . . .
Slowly but surely, the cancer was working away.

He needed something to cheer him up, so he rummaged in
the drawer of a lacquered chest and took out a half-smoked
joint. He went through his pockets for his lighter, a Zippo
that his daughter had given him to mark the millennium, but it
was nowhere to be found. He was annoyed, and went into the
kitchen to get a match to light his joint. He wasn't much of a
dope smoker, and he wasn't a militant defender of the medical
benefits of cannabis, but today he allowed himself this self-
medication. He took a few puffs and felt a little stronger.
Then he closed his eyes and let his mind go blank until the
beeping of the taxi's horn woke him from his meditation.

He got to Lori's Diner, his daughter's favorite restaurant, a
few minutes early. He went upstairs and a waitress showed
him to a little table by the window, looking out on Powell
Street. Sitting on his stool, Elliott was diverted by the choreography of the cooks grilling steaks, frying eggs, and cooking
slices of bacon on a huge grill. It was an unusual spot with a
fifties décor that served generous portions of traditional
American food, before all the low-cholesterol diets. It was
the kind of food it was fashionable to criticize but that
everyone secretly loved: burgers, home fries, ice-cream sodas
and milk shakes. The juke box in the middle of the room
played one Elvis song after another, and at one end an
authentic Harley-Davidson was suspended from the ceiling
by a tangled mass of wires above a row of pinball machines.

When he came here, Elliott always felt like he was in *Back
to the Future*, and every time the door opened he almost
expected to see Marty McFly and Doc Brown walking in,

followed by the faithful Einstein. This very scenario was running through his mind when a customer walked in. But it wasn't Marty . . .

It was a young woman with straight blonde hair who seemed to light up the room around her.

A young woman of twenty.

A girl.

His girl.

Angie.

He watched her coming and for a minute he looked at her without her noticing him.

There was no denying that she was attractive, with her long, tight cashmere sweater, a cotton skirt – which he thought was too short – black tights with a glossy sheen, and leather boots. But he wasn't the only one looking at her: at the next table, a little jerk was going into raptures in front of his friends about the 'blonde bombshell' walking in their direction. Elliott gave him a dirty look. As a father, he cursed all testosterone carriers, without exception, who looked at his daughter as a sexual object.

Angie finally saw him and happily waved hello.

As this radiant creature walked toward him, he was filled with the conviction that having his daughter was unquestionably the best thing he had ever done. He was obviously not the first parent to have that feeling, but it had a different meaning now that he was racked by pain, and death was about to win the last battle.

And to think that for a long time he hadn't wanted to have children . . .

He had grown up in a dysfunctional family, what with his father's alcoholism and his mother's mental instability. It was not the kind of childhood to make someone want to be a father. Even now, the most vivid memories he had of that time were images of violence and fear, and he knew that they had blocked his way to fatherhood for a long time. It was hard to explain why: probably fear of being unable to love and of causing pain himself.

But one thing was certain: the idea of becoming a father reminded him so strongly of his own childhood suffering that he had refused to have a baby with the only woman he'd ever loved. And when he thought about that, it broke his heart.

Then Ilena had died and the next ten years had been nothing but an endless nightmare. He'd sunk into despair, able to keep his head above water only because of Matt and his work, to which he'd clung as though it were a life-preserver.

He had of course met other women, but they'd passed through his life without stopping for very long, and for his part he'd been careful never to hold on to any of them. But one day, at a medical conference in Italy, he'd met a cardiologist from Milan. It had been just a brief affair, a weekend, and they hadn't kept in touch. But nine months later, she'd told him that she'd just given birth to a baby girl, and that the child was his. This time he was faced with a *fait accompli*. There was no way he could get out of it, especially because the cardiologist didn't really have any maternal instincts and had no intention of raising the child on her own. Three months after the birth, Elliott had gone to pick Angie up in Italy and, by mutual agreement, the child saw her mother afterward only during vacations.

So, without preparation, he'd become a father and his life had been transformed. After a season in hell, his life finally had meaning. From then on, every night before going to bed, the last thing he did was to make sure that his daughter was peacefully asleep. The word 'future' was once again in his vocabulary, in a prominent place next to 'bottle', 'diaper', and 'baby formula'.

Of course, there was more pollution than ever, the ozone layer was deteriorating, the world was going to hell, consumer society was becoming increasingly unbearable, and his work didn't leave him a free moment. But this all seemed suddenly unimportant faced with a baby weighing only a few pounds, with her bright eyes and her fragile smile.

Now, as he watched her walking toward him in the restaurant, he remembered those early years when he'd raised her on his own, with no woman to help him. At first he'd thought he wouldn't make it. He'd panicked for a little while. How did you go about being a father? He had no idea and it wasn't explained anywhere. Sure, he was a pediatric surgeon, but that didn't help very much in everyday life. If she'd needed to have a ventricle sewn up or a quadruple bypass, he would have been useful, but that wasn't the problem.

Then he'd understood the great secret: you're not born a father, you become one. By improvising along the way the course you guess to be right for your child.

He'd waited forty years to find out that there was no answer, no solution, just love.

It was what Ilena had always told him, and he'd always answered, 'If only it were so easy.'

When all the time it was.

'Hi, Dad,' said Angie as she bent over to kiss him.

'Hello, Wonder Woman,' he answered, looking at her short skirt and thigh-high boots. 'How was your flight?'

'Great, I slept the whole way.'

Angie sat down on the opposite stool, and put a large keyring and a tiny chrome-plated cell phone on the table.

'I'm as hungry as a bear,' she said, and picked up the menu to make sure her favorite burger was still on it.

Once she had reassured herself, she started talking enthusiastically, telling hundreds of stories about her medical studies and her life in New York. She was smart and generous, very idealistic, and always wanted to do her best at everything she undertook. Elliott had not especially pushed her to become a doctor, but she cared about other people, and said she got that from him.

To him she looked relaxed, glowing, magnificent.

Mesmerized by her outbursts of laughter, he wondered how he'd be able to tell her about his disease. It wouldn't be easy for a twenty-year-old girl to suddenly find out that her father had terminal cancer and had only two or three months to live . . .

Elliott knew his daughter well. Even after she'd left for New York, they'd stayed very close. Despite her appearance and her woman's body, Angie was still emotionally a child and he was sure she wouldn't react calmly to what he was going to tell her.

In his profession, several times a week he had to tell tearful people that their child, their spouse, or their parent hadn't survived an operation. It was always a hard moment, but with time he'd come to accept that aspect of his job.

Yes, as a doctor, he was faced with death every day, but it was the death of others, not his own . . .

Of course, he was a little afraid of what was going to happen to him. He didn't really believe in eternal life or any form of reincarnation. He knew that what awaited him was not only the end of his life on earth, but the end of his life, period. His body would go up in smoke in an incinerator, and Matt would probably scatter his ashes in a pleasant place, and that would be it. End of the road!

That's what he would have liked to be able to explain calmly to his daughter, that she shouldn't worry about him because he'd be able to deal with the situation. Besides, if you thought about it objectively, his dying wasn't such an outrage: he wouldn't have turned his nose up at another few decades, but he'd had enough time to savour life, experience its joys, sorrows, and surprises . . .

'How are you doing?' asked Angie out of the blue, breaking into his train of thought.

He looked at her tenderly as she brushed her hair out of her piercing blue eyes.

He felt his throat tighten and was overcome with emotion.

Damn it, this is not the time to break down!

'I have something to tell you, sweetheart . . .'

Angie's smile imperceptibly faded, as though she already knew bad news was coming.

'What is it?'

'I have a tumor in my lungs.'

'What?' she said, as though she didn't understand.

'I have cancer.'

She let a few seconds go by in stunned silence and then asked in a tight voice: 'You're, you're going . . . to recover?'

'No, sweetheart, it's metastasized everywhere.'

'Shit . . .'

Overwhelmed, she held her head in her hands for a minute and then looked at him. A tear was running down her cheek, but she hadn't given up all hope.

'But . . . have you consulted specialists? There are new techniques to treat small-cell cancer. Maybe if . . .'

'It's too late . . .' he interrupted, in a tone of finality.

She wiped her eyes with the sleeve of her sweater, but it was no good: the tears kept flowing and she couldn't stop them.

'How long have you known?'

'Two months.'

'But . . . why didn't you say anything?'

'To protect you, to keep from hurting you . . .'

She was annoyed. 'So, for the last two months, every time we talked on the phone, you let me blabber on about my little problems and you didn't bother to tell me that you had cancer!'

'You were starting your first year of clinical study, Angie, it was a stressful time for you and . . .'

'I hate you!' she shouted and stood up.

He tried to hold her back, but she pushed him away and ran out of the restaurant.

By the time Elliott came out it was pouring. The sky was black with clouds and thunder was rumbling. The doctor regretted having neither a raincoat nor an umbrella because his linen jacket was soaked through in less than two seconds. He very quickly realized that he would have trouble finding Angie. Traffic was backed up, buses were full, and taxis were all taken.

At first he thought he'd go to the cable car terminal at the corner of Powell and Market, but soon gave up that idea: the rain hadn't discouraged the tourists who were crowded around the spot watching the operators work the cars with muscle power. He thought the wait would be too long and headed for Union Square, hoping he could catch a car on the way. The first two that went by were so full that he didn't even try. But he did manage to jump on the third just as it started the steepest part of its climb.

He stayed on the car to the last stop: Fisherman's Wharf, the city's old fishing port, now taken over by tourist restaurants and souvenir shops. Shivering with cold, Elliott walked past the seafood stands, where fish-sellers were shelling live crabs and plunging them into huge pots on the street. It was raining even harder when he got to Ghirardelli Square. He passed the old chocolate factory and arrived at Fort Mason.

Soaked to the skin and shivering, he kept moving fast. The howling wind drove the rain straight into his face. The physical effort had brought back the burning sensation in his lungs and his lower back, but that wouldn't keep him from finding his daughter. He knew where she would go when she was upset.

He finally came out onto the sandy beach between Marina Green and the former air base at Crissy Field. The sea was raging, and huge waves were throwing spray for dozens of yards. Elliott squinted: Golden Gate Bridge had almost disappeared, swallowed by fog and low-lying cloud. The beach was deserted, veiled with a heavy curtain of rain. He took a few steps and shouted at the top of his lungs: 'Angie! Angie!'

At first only the wind answered. His eyes misted over with tears and he felt weak and vulnerable, almost at the end of his rope.

Then he sensed her presence, not knowing exactly where she was, and he heard: 'Daddy!'

Angie was running toward him through the streets of rain. 'Don't die!' she begged. 'Don't die!'

He hugged her tightly and they stood locked together for a long time, soaked, exhausted, shattered by grief.

As he consoled his daughter, Elliott swore to himself that he would fight death with all his strength to delay it as long as possible.

Then, when the last moment came, he would depart in peace, because he knew that something of himself would persist beyond the nothingness.

And he understood that this, too, was perhaps one of the reasons why men had children.

NINE

When it comes to books and friends,
it is best to have only a few but all good ones.
Popular saying

1976
Elliott is 30

When Elliott left the hospital after his night on call, he felt the chill of the early morning. Lost in thought and preoccupied by his worries, at first he didn't notice the little crowd in the parking lot. In among the ambulances and next to a fire truck, Matt was putting on a show for a small group of nurses. Torn between amusement and annoyance, Elliott looked on: with his cream-colored cotton suit and his wide-collared shirt open to the navel, Matt looked odd. A Travolta before his time, he was dancing to disco music coming from his car radio. It was still dark, but his improvised show was lit by the headlights from his Corvette.

'You should be dancing,' he sang in falsetto, imitating the Bee Gees.

His gap-toothed smile gave him a boyishly attractive air, and in a way Elliott couldn't help admiring his adventurous and free-spirited side.

'What are you doing here?' he asked when he got near the car.

'You should be dancing!' Matt repeated and took his friend by the arm.

He tried to pull Elliott into his dance, but the doctor refused to play along: 'Have you been drinking?' He could smell the alcohol on Matt's breath.

'Give me a minute to thank my audience and I'll explain everything.'

Elliott frowned and climbed into the Corvette while Matt did a last pirouette. Won over by his charm, the nurses willingly applauded his performance and then went back to work.

'It was an honor, ladies,' he said with a bow.

Then, intoxicated by his little triumph, he jumped over the car door and miraculously landed in the driver's seat.

'And now fasten your seat belt,' he said, turning to Elliott.

'What are you up to?' Elliott replied irritably.

Matt didn't answer, but shifted into reverse and turned the car 180 degrees to face out of the lot.

'I stopped at your place to pack your bags,' he explained, pointing to a suitcase stuck behind the seats. 'By the way, your whiskey bottle's empty . . .'

'What are you talking about?'

'Your plane takes off at nine.'

'What plane?'

The tires squealed as Matt roared out of the parking lot. After a few turns, they were on Van Ness, and a little pressure on the pedal pushed the V8 past 70.

'You ever hear of speed limits?' said Elliott, hanging on to his seat.

'Sorry, but we don't have much time . . .'

'Will you at least tell me where we're going?'

'I'm not going anywhere,' Matt answered calmly. 'But you're going to Florida to see Ilena.'

'What?'

'You make up with her, you propose, and you have two or three beautiful children . . .'

'Are you nuts?'

'Right now, I think you're the one with a screw loose, Elliott. Admit it, this story about a so-called time traveler is bothering you.'

'It's bothering me because it really *happened*.'

Matt refused to get into an argument and tried to be reassuring. 'Talk to Ilena, put things back together between you, and you'll see that everything will work out.'

'But I can't take off just like that! I've got several operations scheduled this week and . . .'

Matt cut him off: 'You're a surgeon, not God! The hospital will find someone to take your place.'

Elliott was suddenly very tempted by the prospect of seeing the woman he loved. He felt he needed to see her, but he still wasn't ready to let his feelings win out over his professional conscience. What's more, he was going through a bad patch; his head of department, the fearsome (and feared) Dr Amendoza, was harshly critical of his work and delighted in putting him down at every opportunity.

'Listen, Matt, thanks for trying to help, but I don't think it's such a good idea. I've only been working at the hospital for a few months and I have to prove myself. On top of that, my department head thinks I'm a screw-up. So if I miss a few days, he'll make me pay for it, and I'll never get a permanent appointment.'

Matt shrugged his shoulders. 'I've talked to Amendoza, and he agreed to give you until next Monday off.'

'You're shitting me! You talked to Amendoza?'

'Sure.'

'Sure you're shitting me, or sure you talked to Amendoza?'

Matt shook his head. 'This boss of yours realizes you haven't been all there the last few days. And for your information, he thinks highly of you.'

'You're joking . . .'

'The nurses told me. Amendoza tells everyone in the hospital that you're an excellent surgeon.'

'Everyone except me . . .'

'Yes, and that's why I'm here: to straighten you out when you need it.'

The clouds were slowly fading on the horizon, giving way to a rosy light that promised a beautiful day. Matt rummaged in his jacket pocket and pulled out an airline ticket.

'Trust me, I know what's good for you.'

Elliott felt his defenses crumbling, but he tried to resist one last time.

'And Tramp?'

'Don't worry about your mutt. I'll feed him every day.'

Out of arguments, he finally accepted the ticket gratefully, aware of how lucky he was to have a friend like Matt. For a moment, he recalled the strange circumstances of their meeting ten years ago, in a tragic episode that they never talked about. This morning, he would have liked to say something to Matt to express his gratitude, but as usual he couldn't find the words, and the Frenchman was the one who broke the silence.

'If I hadn't met you, you know where I'd be now?'

Elliott shrugged his shoulders and didn't answer. Matt said simply: 'I'd be dead.'

'Don't be stupid.'

'But it's true, and you know it.'

Elliott looked at his friend out of the corner of his eye. Matt's rumpled clothes and eyes red from lack of sleep revealed he'd been up all night. And that wasn't the only thing that bothered Elliott: his reckless driving, his intoxication, and his repeated references to death and the ghosts of the past . . .

It was staring him in the face now: Matt, too, was going through a rough time. The good humor he displayed in every situation concealed his own dark side and pain, the way his cheerful disposition sometimes gave way to black thoughts and depression.

'Let me tell you something,' Matt said. 'Every morning when I get up, I look at the sky and the ocean and I tell myself that the only reason I'm still here to take advantage of them is you.'

'You're drunk, Matt.'

'Sure I'm drunk,' he admitted. 'You save lives, I get drunk. Because I can't do much of anything else except pick up girls and put on a show . . .'

He let a few seconds pass, then said, 'But you know what? Maybe that's my mission on earth: to take care of you and help you any way I can.'

He'd spoken solemnly. To try to mask his feelings and to keep the silence from growing too heavy, Elliott started talking about trivial things. 'Your radio's not bad,' he said, looking at the newly installed high end radio-cassette combination.

'Yeah, it's got a ten-watt amplifier,' Matt explained, relieved to change the subject.

'You bought the last Bob Dylan?'

Matt chuckled. 'Dylan's finished. *This* is the future,' he said, and rummaged in the glove compartment for a cassette with a striking black and white cover.

'Bruce Springsteen?' Elliott read. 'Never heard of him.'

Matt told him everything he knew about the unusual young rock star who was growing more and more popular, singing about working class lives in New Jersey.

'You'll see,' he said, and put the cassette in. 'This stuff is dynamite.'

'Born to Run' started playing as the sun rose. For the rest of the drive, the two friends let themselves be carried by the music, each of them lost in thought; elsewhere, but together . . .

The airport finally appeared in the distance. Matt got on the approach road to the terminal and pulled up in front of the departure building with a squeal of tires.

'Let's go, hurry up.'

Elliott grabbed his suitcase and ran toward the glass doors. He'd gone about ten yards before he turned around and yelled to Matt: 'If my plane crashes and I get to heaven first, do I keep a spot for you?'

'Sure,' Matt agreed, 'a warm spot next to Marilyn Monroe . . . and not too far from you.'

TEN

The strongest bond between
two people isn't love, it's sex.
Tarun J. Tejpal, *The Alchemy of Desire*, p. 11

The strongest bond between
two people isn't sex, it's love.
Tarun J. Tejpal, *The Alchemy of Desire*, p. 670

1976
Elliott is 30

'Ladies and gentlemen, we are about to begin our descent to
Orlando. Kindly return to your seat, place your seat back in
the upright position, and make sure that your seat belt is
fastened.'

Elliott stopped looking out the window and turned toward
the aisle. The plane was half empty. His friend could be as
skeptical as he liked, but Elliott had no more doubts about the
reality of what he'd just been through. For the duration of the
flight he hadn't stopped examining the passengers, wondering

whether he might see his sixty-year-old double among them. Since the fingerprints had confirmed the identity of his strange visitor, he had been waiting for the next visit with a mixture of anxiety and impatience.

The plane landed smoothly. Elliott quickly retrieved his suitcase, rented a car, and headed for Ocean World. After a night on call and a six-hour flight during which he'd been unable to sleep, all his limbs felt stiff and he was dropping with fatigue. He rolled down the window of the Mustang to breathe in a little sea air. It was much warmer here than in San Francisco. Fall had not yet come to Florida. He got onto International Drive, lined with lush lawns and brand new hotels. The town seemed to be on a perpetual vacation. It might all seem artificial, but he decided to play along.

After he'd parked in the huge lot at Ocean World, he couldn't decide whether or not to call Ilena from a phone booth. Finally he decided he'd surprise her and bought a ticket like any other tourist.

The marine park was a little town in itself, covering almost 150 acres and employing several hundred people. Since he was familiar with the park, he knew the spot where he would find Ilena. To get there he walked through the hilly garden with its pink flamingos surrounding the tropical aquarium and came out onto the little man-made beach where the giant tortoises lazed. From there he continued alongside an enclosure in which a handful of alligators were basking in the sun, and finally reached the tank containing the killer whales.

The place was impressive: the six killer whales in Ocean World lived in a tank that was thirty-five feet deep and held twelve million gallons of sea water. It was currently between shows and the stands were almost empty. Unnoticed, Elliott took a seat and watched the trainers busy with the whales. It didn't take him long to spot Ilena: she was the only woman in the group. Wearing a diving suit, she was playing dentist, drilling a tooth for one of the whales, which was facing her with its jaw wide open. Elliott shivered and thought about those circus performers who put their head in a lion's mouth, even though he knew Ilena wouldn't appreciate the comparison . . .

This tall, slender creature from the sea was as beautiful as a siren, shining like a diamond on a heap of glass marble. Sometimes when they went to a store or a restaurant, he let her go in first, and people momentarily wondered what kind of man could be accompanying such a fabulous woman. When their eyes finally turned to him, he always thought he could read a little disappointment in them.

Two trainers near the pool were sticking close to Ilena as though hypnotized by her striking beauty. She laughed at their jokes like a good sport, but kept them at arm's length.

Could he measure up to a woman like that? Had he managed to make her happy?

He had avoided these questions for a long time, content to live in the moment, but today he was ready to face them.

They still loved each other, of course, but life and work had separated them a little. Because of the distance between them and their careers, their relationship was now conducted in fits and starts.

He often wondered what his life would be like if he hadn't met her ten years ago. There was no doubt that she had made him a better person: she had had something to do with his calling as a doctor, she had given him confidence, and she had opened his eyes to the realities of the world. But what about him? What had he done for her? What had he given her? Maybe she'd wake up one morning and realize that she'd wasted her time staying with him.

Then he'd have to accept losing her.

'Losing you . . .' he murmured from his detached position, as though she could hear him.

In any case, he was sure of one thing: he would do everything he could to make sure that day never came. As for what he could give her . . . Would he agree to leave his job in the hospital and his life in San Francisco to come and live with her in Orlando? He couldn't bring himself to answer that question, and yet he felt he could give his life for her, which had to reveal the strength of his feeling.

Invigorated by this thought, he got up from the stands, thinking it was time to interrupt the mating dance of the two pretty boys hovering around Ilena.

'Hey, kid!' he called out to a teenager selling helium balloons.

'Yessir.'

'How much for the balloons?'

'Two for a dollar.'

Elliott gave him twenty dollars, which more than paid for the whole bunch. Concealed behind it, he approached the tank noiselessly.

'This area is not open to the public!' one of the trainers interjected.

Elliott knew some of the employees, but he'd never met this one. He glanced at him and saw the aggression in his face.

Now there's the kind of guy who'd have a pissing contest, he thought, and kept going despite the warning. *Well, I won't let this jerk spoil my surprise.*

But the trainer had other ideas. 'Are you deaf, or what?' he yelled and pushed him.

Elliott nearly stumbled and was forced to let go of the bunch of balloons to keep his balance. 'Asshole!' he said angrily to the guy.

The young trainer blocked his way, his fists clenched.

'What's going on here?' asked Ilena, walking in their direction.

'This guy thinks he's at home!' explained the trainer, pointing to Elliott.

As the helium balloons rose upward, Ilena was astonished to discover the face of the man she loved and remained speechless for an instant.

'It's okay, Jimmy, I'll take care of it,' she said when she recovered from her surprise.

Regretfully the trainer turned away from Elliott, murmuring, 'Little shit!'

'Big asshole!' Elliott replied in the same tone.

As the trainer moved off, grumbling, Elliott and Ilena stood six feet apart, looking at each other in silence.

'I was in the area, so . . .'

'Sure. Admit it, you can't live without me.'

'What about you?'

'Me? I'm surrounded by men here . . . You ought to be worried . . .'

'I *am* worried, that's why I'm here.'

She looked at him defiantly. 'By the way, I liked your tough guy routine . . .'

'Sorry about the fight with Jimmy.'

'Don't be sorry: I like it when you fight for me . . .'

He pointed upward. 'I bought those for you.'

She looked up: driven by the wind, the balloons were floating off into space.

'If that's your love, it's flown away.'

He shook his head. 'Love doesn't fly away so easily.'

'Better be careful, though, it can't be taken for granted.'

As the sun went down behind the palm trees, Elliott moved toward Ilena. 'I love you,' he said simply.

She threw herself into his arms and he whirled her around as though they were twenty again.

'I've had a thought . . .' he said as he put her down.

'What?' she said, still clasped in his arms.

'Suppose we have a baby?'

'Here? Right now?' she answered, remembering the answer Elliott had given a few days earlier at the airport. 'In front of the whales and the dolphins?'

'Why not?'

Ilena parked the Thunderbird at the end of a gravel driveway leading to a charming pink brick house framed by white pillars and with a covered terrace on the upper floor. She'd been renting that floor for the last few months from Miss Abbott, a disagreeable old lady who was heiress to a rich Boston family but spent most of her time in Florida where the climate seemed to be good for her rheumatism. Miss Abbott was a relic of the old school and insisted that her tenants be 'members of good society'. She had warned Ilena several times that she was absolutely forbidden to have men in the house, which 'was not a brothel.'

Ilena put her finger to her lips to tell Elliott not to make any noise. The house seemed still and quiet and Miss Abbott was a little hard of hearing, but they had to be careful. They got out of the car without slamming the doors and went up the narrow fire escape single file to get into the apartment without going through the main entrance.

Elliott went first, grumbling, none too happy about playing the role of an adolescent violating curfew. Behind him, Ilena was finding the whole thing amusing until she heard, 'Ilena, is that you?'

The front door had just opened and Miss Abbott had already come out onto the porch.

'Hello, Miss Abbott, nice day, isn't it?' Ilena said lightly.

'What are you doing there, Ilena?' the landlady asked, frowning. Suspicious, she moved away from the house so she could see the whole staircase, but Elliott had already had time to slip into the apartment.

'I . . . I thought you were asleep and I didn't want to disturb you,' Ilena explained.

The old woman shrugged her shoulders and asked in a gentler tone: 'Won't you have a cup of tea with me?'

'Um . . . well . . .'

'I made some cookies I think you'll like. They've just come out of the oven.'

'Well, you see . . .'

'It's an old recipe I got from my grandmother. I'll write it down for you if you like.'

'I wouldn't want to deprive you.'

'Not at all,' she said, drawing Ilena into the house. 'It's my pleasure.'

And from the tone of this statement, Ilena guessed that Miss Abbott may not have been fooled by her ruse.

✳   ✳   ✳

123

Alone in the little apartment, Elliott was beginning to grow impatient. He slipped out of the room on tiptoe and tried to get a glimpse downstairs. He was dismayed to find that Ilena had been trapped by the landlady. Sitting on a rocking-chair with a cup of tea in her hand, she was listening distractedly as Miss Abbott listed the ingredients for her special cookies.

He understood that Ilena was stuck for a while and went back inside, patiently enduring the wait by examining the large room that smelled of incense and cinnamon. The place was cheerful, with candles everywhere, brightly colored cushions, and a few Indian trinkets. In a corner were an acoustic guitar, a tambourine, and sheet music for Joan Baez and Leonard Cohen songs. On the wall was a poster for *Jules et Jim* that Matt had brought back for Ilena from his last trip to Paris. On the night table, along with books about animal psychology, Elliott saw the latest Agatha Christie and a novel with an eye-catching cover by a writer he didn't know: *Carrie* by Stephen King. Distractedly, he read the blurb on the cover.

Another writer who'll be forgotten in five years . . . he thought as he put it down.

Continuing to roam, Elliott noticed an odd device: a kind of printed circuit enclosed in a koa wood case connected to the television set. Ilena had bought it the previous summer in the Byte Shop in San Francisco for the tidy sum of six hundred dollars. She had a scientific mind and was fascinated by the new machines called micro-computers. Elliott didn't know much about them. In the not too distant future, she had assured him, computers would be as common in houses as refrigerators or washing machines. Thinking about the whole thing, he couldn't keep from shrugging his shoulders.

Even so, driven by curiosity, he skimmed a few pages of the manual on the desk. The machine was apparently fairly simple, having just a keyboard and cassette player, but Elliott couldn't figure it out at all. In fact he would have been incapable of saying what a thing like that was actually for. The only fact he could pick up was the bizarre name its creators had chosen for their company: Apple Computer.

You'll never get anywhere with a name like that, guys! he thought, not even daring to turn on the machine.

Instead, he threw himself on the bed, picked up the Stephen King book, and started flicking through it while he waited for Ilena. Within a half hour, he'd devoured nearly one hundred pages.

It's really not bad . . . he admitted almost against his will, as someone opened the door to the bedroom.

The trees outside the window showed their autumn colors, bathing the room in a mellow gentle light.

Smiling and looking mischievous, Ilena studied Elliott, apparently amused by what she saw. She was wearing faded bell-bottom jeans, a cheesecloth shirt, leather sandals, and a turquoise bracelet on her wrist.

'I hope you at least brought me some cookies,' he said jokingly. 'I'm starting to get hungry.'

'And I hope you've gotten some rest,' she retorted, as she undid two buttons on her shirt.

'Why do you say that?'

'Because you're going to need all your strength.'

She clicks the door closed with her foot and goes over to the window to pull the curtains together; he takes hold of her and tries to draw her onto the bed. First she pushes him off, only to draw him to her and press him against the wall.

He frames her face with his hands. Ilena's hair is still wet and smells of salt water. She loosens his belt and pulls his jeans down his thighs. He takes off her shirt, paying no heed to the buttons. She tastes the sweetness of his tongue as their lips part. She puts her arms around his neck and he lifts her up as she wraps her legs around him.

After a struggle with her bra, he lets his fingers run over her breasts, down to her bare stomach, lower still. A moan. You and me. His name whispered in his ear. Cold hands caressing his sides and moving up his spine.

They brace themselves against the back of a chair, knock it over, kneel on the rug, and then both fall against the wall. She rears above him, but he brings her back against his body. She holds her breath, tightens, and feels an icy shiver and then a burning wave sweep over her. Her body trembles and then completely relaxes.

Outside, the wind has risen. A gust shakes the window, and one of the shutters flies open, hitting an earthenware vase that shatters on the ground. In the distance, a dog barks and someone shouts something.

But they care nothing for the world outside, for people or dogs.

Nothing else has any importance but the intoxication of losing themselves in one another, the vertigo of slipping into an abyss, and the fear of breaking the bond.

Now she hangs onto anything she can: his hair, the odor of his skin, the taste of his lips. Her heart is beating so fast that it almost hurts, but she doesn't want the moment to end.

Then there is something like a void, a hollow in her stomach, and something breaks inside her.

Now, she has the feeling that she is outside time, no longer on earth, that she is eternal.

With another feeling of being projected a great distance.

To another place.

Out of this world . . .

They lay stretched out in silence in the darkened room, pressed against one another, legs tangled and fingers interlaced. Night had fallen and it had grown colder, but they were in their own warm and cozy cocoon.

They were even starting to drift into sleep when the phone rang suddenly. Ilena instantly shook off her drowsiness, wrapped a sheet around herself, and picked up the receiver.

There was a silence, then: 'Okay, I'll be right there.'

She hung up and turned to Elliott. 'Sorry, baby . . .'

'Don't tell me you have to leave.'

'It's an emergency.'

'Who was it? A dolphin? A whale who needs you to sing a lullaby so he can get to sleep?'

'We're short a trainer for the show, and I'm the only one who can replace him.'

She joined him on the bed and massaged his shoulders.

'What show? It's seven at night.'

'Until the end of the season, there's a night show.'

'It's almost October. The season is over.'

'Not here, darling. This is Florida and the weather's still good.'

She gave him a last kiss and got up.

'You can stay here if you want. Don't worry about Miss

Abbott: she goes to bed early, and if you want my opinion, she knows very well that you're here . . .'

'I'd rather go with you,' he answered without hesitation.

'Afraid someone will try to pick me up?'

'No, but I just remembered seeing a pretty girl behind the souvenir counter. I'll keep her company while you do your show.'

'If you do that, I'll kill you,' she warned, and threw a pillow at him. In the blink of an eye, Ilena put on her clothes and fixed her hair.

'Sounds kind of extreme,' Elliott observed as he put on his shirt.

'That's the way it is. And don't think love will conquer all. If it has to be that way then maybe this was the last time we'll ever sleep together . . .'

'Anyhow, it was good.'

'And that was stupid.'

'What?'

'What you just said!'

'I don't have the right to say it was good?'

'No.'

'Why?'

'Because it breaks the spell!'

Women . . . would he ever understand them?

'All the moments we spend together,' he said, as he put on his jacket, 'I store in my mind like images from a film.'

'That, on the other hand, was nice,' she said, and closed the door behind her.

Playing along with Miss Abbott, Elliott used the fire escape to get back to the car. When Ilena could no longer hear him, he muttered to himself, in a joky tone: 'Short films that I would play in my head if I were in a retirement home one day, old and impotent. Just to remember how happy we were, the two of us.'

And on this point, at least, he had no idea how right he was . . .

ELEVEN

Third Encounter

> *Yesterday, I was still twenty,*
> *I have been massaging time . . .*
> Charles Aznavour

> *Yesterday, love was such an easy game to play.*
> John Lennon and Paul McCartney

1976
Elliott is 30

The Aquatic Café provided a spectacular view of the whale tank a few yards below, allowing visitors to the park to have a drink while they watched the show. In less than fifteen minutes the killer whales and their trainers would begin their display of choreography and spectacular feats.

From his table, Elliott watched the sparsely populated stands gradually fill up for the last show of the day. A waiter brought the bottle of Budweiser he had ordered, and he nodded his thanks.

The place was softly lit. Near the bar a singer accompanied

by an acoustic guitar was performing the hits of Carole King, Neil Young, and Simon and Garfunkel.

Lulled by the sound of the guitar and still feeling as though he were holding Ilena, Elliott didn't notice the man who had just sat down at the table next to his.

He took a sip of beer and automatically lit a cigarette.

'So you're the one who took my lighter.'

As though he'd been caught doing something wrong, he immediately turned toward the man who'd just spoken to him. Sitting on the leather banquette next to his, the man – who, he now knew, was himself grown older – was looking at him with a glint of amusement in his eyes.

Elliott was not surprised by this new appearance – he had prepared himself for it, and it confirmed his conviction that he had not dreamed what had happened.

'I know everything,' he said in a shaky voice.

'What do you know?'

'I know that you were telling the truth. I know that you are . . . me.'

The man got up from the banquette, took off his jacket, and sat down opposite Elliott.

'Pretty clever, your tattoo idea,' he said, rolling up his sleeve so the letters were visible.

'I knew you'd appreciate it.'

Seeing that he had a new customer, the waiter came up to their table.

'What'll you have, sir?' he asked the older man.

'The same thing,' he said, pointing to the bottle of Bud. 'My friend and I often share the same tastes.'

The two men couldn't keep from smiling, and for the first time, in this dimly lit café, an odd complicity seemed to bring them together. A full minute passed in silence. Each of them was appreciating in his own way the strange intimacy they now shared. It was a bizarre sensation, like finding a family member who had been missing for years.

Finally, Elliott exclaimed: 'Damn it, how do you do it?'

'Time travel? If it makes you feel any better, it surprises me as much as you.'

'It's crazy!'

'Yes,' he agreed, 'it's crazy . . .'

Elliott took a puff of his cigarette. His head was spinning.

'How is it there?'

'You mean in 2006?'

'Yes . . .'

'What do you want to know?'

He had lots of questions – ten, a hundred, a thousand . . . Starting with this one: 'What's the state of the world?'

'No better than it is now.'

'The cold war . . .'

'Over long ago.'

'Who won, the Russians or us?'

'If only it were that simple . . .'

'There was no third world war? No nuclear bomb?'

'No, but we have other problems: the environment, globalization, terrorism, and all the consequences of September 11 . . .'

'September 11?'

'Yes, something happened on September 11, 2001, at the World Trade Center in New York.'

'What?'

'Listen, I don't know if it's such a good idea for me to tell you about it . . .'

Too eager to find out everything he could, Elliott asked about something else: 'And how am I doing?'

'You do what you can.'

'Did I become a good doctor?'

'You already *are* a good doctor, Elliott.'

'No, what I mean is . . . am I tougher? Have I gotten used to some of the patients dying? Have I been able to establish some emotional distance?'

'No, you never get used to patients dying. And it's precisely because you decided not to "establish emotional distance" that you kept on being a good doctor.'

For a moment, Elliott had such a sense of the uncanny that he got goosebumps. He'd never looked at things in that way.

Then he had the vague sense that time was limited and he wouldn't be able to ask all the questions tormenting him, so he refocused on the important things: 'Do I have children?'

'A daughter.'

'Ah . . .' he said, not knowing whether he should be happy about it. 'Am I a good father?'

'I think so.'

'And Ilena? How is she?'

'You ask too many questions.'

'Easy for you to say: you have all the answers.'

'If only that were true . . .'

His visitor took a sip of beer and he, too, took out a Marlboro.

'Should I give you back your lighter?' Elliott offered, bringing the flame of the Zippo up to the old doctor's cigarette.

'You can keep it. It'll be yours anyhow one of these days . . .'

133

At the bar, the musicians had started the Beatles song 'Yesterday', which made Elliott think of a less weighty question: 'What kind of music do you listen to in the future?'

'There's nothing better than that,' and he tapped his foot in time to the music.

'Did they get back together?'

'The Beatles? No, never, and they can't now: Lennon was assassinated, and Harrison died a few years ago.'

'And McCartney?'

'He's still going strong.'

The room suddenly grew quiet, indicating that the aquatic show was about to start. The two men both turned toward the whale tank as the trainers entered to the applause of a large audience.

'That's her, isn't it? That's Ilena?' asked the old man, squinting.

'Yes, she's replacing one of the trainers.'

'Listen, I can't stay very long. In a few minutes I'm sure I'll disappear again. So don't take this the wrong way, but in the time I have left, all I want to do is look at *her*.'

Not really knowing what this was all about, Elliott watched his double get up and leave the café to head for the stands.

Elliott is 60

Elliott went down the center aisle to reach the front. The tank was the largest one ever built anywhere and was divided into three sections, with the main pool connected to two smaller ones: one for medical care and one for training. The large bay window that extended for nearly two hundred feet made it possible to see the whales performing underwater during the show.

And the show itself was impressive. The whales moved their vast bulk with amazing grace, jumping, breaching the surface and splashing. But Elliott had eyes only for Ilena, who was directing them underwater, guiding the giant beasts the length of the window.

Seeing her after all these years had a violent effect on him. He found her unbelievably beautiful, like an angel seen in a dream. For thirty years he had looked at the few photographs he had of her thousands of times. But they did not convey her startling beauty.

Overcome by emotion, he felt everything rushing back to him at once: his regret for not having loved her more, not having understood her better, not having been able to protect her. And, as always, the feeling of helplessness and fury at having to surrender to the tide of time that submerges everything in its wake.

Elliott is 30

Still overwhelmed by what he'd just been through, Elliott sat nailed to his seat while his older double watched the show from the stands.

Far from satisfying his curiosity, everything he'd just learned had only sharpened it.

The old man had left his jacket hanging on the back of his chair; Elliott couldn't stop himself from going through the pockets. Oddly, he felt neither ashamed nor guilty: the normal rules clearly didn't apply here. He managed to find a wallet and two little cases.

The wallet didn't tell him much that was new, except that he found a photo of a pretty young woman of about twenty.

'My daughter?' he wondered, idly.

He looked for any resemblance to Ilena, but couldn't find any. Upset by that, he put the photo back where he'd found it and concentrated on the other two objects.

The first was a tiny black and silver case with a little screen and buttons with numbers on them. He read the word NOKIA above the screen, but it didn't mean anything to him. Probably the name of the company that made the device. He turned it every which way, unable to figure out what it could be used for, and then it started to ring. Taken aback, he put it down, not knowing how to make it stop.

As the ringing got louder, every customer in the café turned toward him, their looks of surprise mingling with disapproval. He suddenly understood, with a flash of insight, that this was a telephone, and even if the call wasn't for him, it seemed logical to press the green button in order to answer it.

'Hello,' he said, holding the tiny device to his ear.

'It took you long enough!'

The voice yelling at him that seemed to be coming from a great distance was the voice of . . .

'Matt?! Is that you, Matt?'

'Yeah, of course.'

'Where are you?'

'On the estate, where do you think I am? Somebody has to work to keep the vineyard running.'

'The vineyard? You mean *our* vineyard? We already bought it?'

'Uh . . . You know we bought it thirty years ago. I guess you're still not doing so well, huh?'

'Matt?'

'Yeah?'

'How old are you now?'

'Okay, I know I'm not twenty any more. You don't have to repeat it every day!'

'Just tell me how old you are.'

'Same as you, old man, sixty . . .'

Elliott paused to get his thoughts together. 'You'll never guess what's happening to me.'

'With you I expect the unexpected. Where are you anyhow?'

'In 1976 and . . . I'm thirty.'

'Sure . . . okay, I'll let you go. I have problems at work. For your information, the cases of wine for France won't be able to leave on time: those bastards are always on strike,' he grumbled and hung up.

Elliott couldn't help smiling, both touched and flabbergasted by this bizarre conversation. But he hadn't had the last of his surprises. He picked up the other device and saw that there was a plastic cord wrapped around it. He unwound the cord and saw two little buttons hanging at the end. The indications *right* and *left* gave him a clue: *Earphones?*

He put the two buttons in his ears and then looked at the device more carefully. The case, which was barely thicker than a coin, had a color screen and a kind of dial in the middle. He turned it over and read the label:

iPod

Designed by Apple in California – Made in China

He turned the dial and saw on the screen a list of names he'd never heard of: U2, R.E.M., Coldplay, Radiohead . . .

Finally he found something he knew: The Rolling Stones. He smiled in satisfaction. Here, he was on familiar ground. He confidently turned the volume up to maximum and pushed the button marked *play* . . .

The first guitar chords of 'Satisfaction' blasted his eardrums, as though a Boeing were going through his head.

He let out a scream, dropped the device, and pulled off the earphones. Shaken, he hurriedly put the wallet, telephone, and iPod back into the jacket pockets which they never should have left.

The future certainly looked like it would be complicated . . .

Elliott is 60

The show was nearing its end. In the middle of the tank, two huge whales, launched like torpedoes, were cutting through the water at startling speed. When they reached the end of the pool, they made a coordinated turn, leaped into the air, and landed with an enormous splash that sprayed the spectators in the front rows with water and foam.

Elliott got a little salt water on his face but he was so hypnotized by Ilena that he barely noticed.

For the grand finale, she climbed to the top of the crossbar above the tank, holding a fish between her teeth. For a few seemingly interminable seconds, the audience held its breath until Annushka, the dominant whale in the tank, heaved her enormous bulk out of the water and delicately seized the fish.

Ilena bowed to the thunderous applause. As she looked across the audience, her gaze lit fleetingly on the old man and she was disturbed: *He looks like someone* . . .

She gave in to a spontaneous impulse and threw him a radiant smile, full of confidence and warmth. For a moment time stood still. Drowning in that smile, Elliott knew that this was the memory he would take away with him.

So now he had what he had asked for from the old Cambodian: he'd seen the only woman he'd ever loved again before he died. His wish had just been fulfilled, and he'd have to be satisfied with that.

Then he felt a rush of blood in his throat and his mouth was filled with a metallic tang. He was suddenly out of breath as the trembling that announced his return to the future took hold. He immediately left the stands and headed for the café.

When he got to his double's table, he had just enough time to warn him.

'This time, I'm leaving for good, Elliott. Forget everything I've told you and everything you've seen. Keep on living your life as though you'd never met me.'

'You're not coming back?'

'No, this was the last time.'

'Why?'

'Because your life has to resume its normal course. And because I've gotten what I came for.'

He was shaking more and more, but he was fully aware that he couldn't just let himself vanish in the middle of the room. Elliott helped him put on his jacket and went with him to the bathroom.

'What did you come for?'

'I wanted to see Ilena again, that's all.'

'Why?'

'Your questions are starting to bug me.'

But the young doctor was not about to give up. He'd taken

hold of the old man by the shoulders as though to keep him from leaving too soon.

'Why did you want to see Ilena again?' he shouted, pushing him up against the bathroom wall.

'Because she's going to die,' he was forced to admit.

'What do you mean, she's going to die? When?'

'Soon.'

'She's twenty-nine. You don't die when you're twenty-nine!'

'Stop being stupid. You're a doctor, you know it can happen at any time.'

'But why did she die so young?'

His eyes full of tears, the other man said nothing. Then just before he disappeared, he said the worst thing possible: 'Because you killed her . . .'

TWELVE

*We are all looking for the one person who
will give us what we're lacking in this life.
And if we don't manage to find him
we can only pray that he will find us . . .*
                                        Desperate Housewives

Florida 1976
Elliott is 30

They'd gotten on the road at dawn.

There was a strong north wind that had cleared the sky and
carried off the first fall leaves. At the wheel of the Thunderbird, Elliott was heading toward Miami, while Ilena lay asleep
in the passenger seat.

She had managed to arrange two days off and they had
decided to spend a long weekend in Key West, where Ilena's
paternal uncle lived. It was a getaway they'd promised
themselves for years, but they'd always put it off. *We always
think we have time . . .*

For the tenth time in five minutes, Elliott turned his head

and made sure that nothing was disturbing Ilena's sleep. He looked at her as if she were a fragile and precious object that he had to take care of. Her steady, peaceful breathing contrasted sharply with the worry gnawing at him.

He should have taken full advantage of his vacation and the renewed intimacy with the woman he loved. And yet his mind was elsewhere, completely absorbed by what his double had revealed to him. He could still hear those threatening words echoing in his head: '*Ilena will die soon . . . because you killed her.*' It all seemed absurd, but for the moment unfortunately he had to admit that everything else the man had told him had turned out to be true.

He'd thought about it all night, and one thing had intrigued him: if Ilena was going to die, why hadn't his time traveler given him the information that would help him save her? Above all, why had he said that it was the last time he'd come back?

'Keep your eyes on the road, not on me!' Ilena warned, opening her eyes and stretching.

'The problem is, you're better looking than the road . . .'

As she leaned toward him for a kiss, he was suddenly tempted to tell her everything: *Listen, I've met someone from the future who told me that you were going to die soon. And get this: this person is me in thirty years.*

He opened his mouth, but no words came out. He couldn't tell her something like that, simply because it didn't make any sense. You can ask a friend or a lover to believe the unbelievable, within certain limits. But this time things had gone far beyond any limits. Like Matt, Ilena couldn't be his ally in this battle. He was going to have to fight it alone, and he didn't feel up to it. He felt crushed by the weight of what was happening to him, and once again he had doubts about his own sanity.

But this spell of depression didn't last. Of course he had an ally: his double! He just had to find a way of forcing him to come back and give a hand. Last time, he'd had the idea of the tattoo to send a message into the future. This time, he'd have to figure something else out.

But what?

San Francisco 2006
Elliott is 60

After two long days of rain, the sun was shining on San Francisco once more.

Elliott and his daughter had decided to spend the day together. They rented bikes, rode across the Golden Gate Bridge, and wandered all morning in rural Marin County. They said not a word about the disease. They were living each moment with a feeling of urgency, determined to savor to the full this treacherous life that can only be fully appreciated when you are about to leave it.

They stopped in Sausalito at noon and spread a blanket out on the beach to picnic near the ocean. They spoke little, content merely to be in each other's company. Now nothing had any importance beyond the fact that they were together.

After eating they got back on their bikes and rode along the coast to the little town of Tiburon, where they stopped at a stand that rented jet-skis. Angie was dying to have a go but she was feeling nervous. Just as she had when she was a little girl, she needed her father's encouragement to overcome her fears.

As he watched his daughter climb onto the vehicle and cautiously steer it away from the jetty, Elliott thought over what had happened to him the night before.

Thanks to the third pill, he'd been able to see Ilena again, a few weeks before she died . . . Up to that point everything had seemed simple. He'd returned to the past, he'd seen Ilena, and everything was fine; but far from satisfying him, this last trip back in time had disturbed him and had revived old wounds, guilt, and regret. Most of all, he was mad at himself for having talked too much and now he was worried about the possible repercussions of what he had said. He should never have warned his double about Ilena's death. And he must never surrender to the temptation of going back to the past to change the course of events. And yet, that temptation was great. If he took just one more pill, he could save Ilena from death.

Except that you can't change the past with impunity. That much he was sure of. Until now he'd managed to limit the damage by behaving as a mere spectator from the future, but if he started trying to interfere in the events of his past life, things could become complicated. Everybody knew about the butterfly effect in chaos theory: through a series of chain reactions, an insignificant event could bring about a large-scale catastrophe; the flapping of a butterfly's wings in Japan could cause a hurricane in Florida . . .

He had seven pills left, but he promised himself he wouldn't use them.

For if Ilena didn't die, then the Elliott of 1976 would live his life with her. They would buy a house and surely have children, but Elliott would never meet Angie's mother, which would amount to forfeiting his daughter's life.

No matter which way he looked at the problem he always came to the same conclusion: saving Ilena meant condemning Angie.

And there was no way he would take that risk.

Elliott is 30

The sun was already high in the sky when they got on the Overseas Highway running from Miami to Key West.

It felt like they'd reached the end of the earth. A string of islands stretched for 150 miles in a turquoise sea that looked like a Polynesian lagoon. Elliott and Ilena were in heaven, astonished by the pelicans flying just over their heads and intoxicated by the impression that they were sailing over the ocean at the wheel of their car.

The long straight causeway ran over crystal clear water, sweeping island to island via dozens of bridges built on stilts. They'd put the top down in the Thunderbird and had found a station playing classic rock. They drove fast, intoxicated by their speed and the magical landscape.

They stopped on Key Largo at a fisherman's shack that had been turned into a restaurant. Surrounded by coral reefs, they feasted on crab cakes, conch, and shrimp.

Just before they got back on the road, Elliott stopped at the post office. 'I want to call Matt to remind him to feed my dog.'

'Okay, handsome. While you do that I'll buy some sun lotion.'

Elliott went into the building, which was decorated with navigation charts, fishing nets, and models of boats. He'd mulled it over all morning and thought he'd come up with a new way of sending a message to the future. He went up to the window and said he wanted to send two telegrams to San Francisco.

The first began:

Matt,
Thanks for everything, but I still need your help.
  Please don't try to understand what I'm going to ask you to do. One day I'll explain everything. In the meantime, trust me . . .

San Francisco 1976
Matt is 30

The golden light of the late afternoon filtered through the linen curtains. On his guitar, Matt was playing Tiffany a ballad he told her he'd written himself: he'd 'borrowed' some chords from Elton John, along with the words, which he'd only changed in order to incorporate his current conquest's name and make the song his own.

'That cheesy stuff still works?' asked Tiffany, not taken in for a minute.

Stretched out on the couch she looked at him with eyebrows raised, sipping a drink.

Matt put down his guitar and walked toward her, smiling.

'Okay, I admit it – I'm no James Taylor.'

She took another sip of her drink and smiled back at him.

Even when he apologizes, this guy turns on the charm, she thought to herself as she sat up. *And the worst thing is that it works.*

She had reached a point in her life when she no longer expected anything from men, though that still didn't stop her from falling in love with them.

Matt sat down next to her, mesmerized by the perfection of her legs and her devastating cleavage.

Not only is this girl a knockout, but she's smarter than she looks.

There was something just a little bit frightening about that. Matt was always afraid that he wouldn't measure up in such matters. He hadn't gone to college and he felt inferior because of his lack of education, even though he was too proud to admit it.

He leaned toward Tiffany and kissed her on the lips. *Okay, Matt, don't get distracted. Just concentrate on one thing: sex.*

He'd gone to a lot of trouble to persuade Tiffany to give him another chance. It hadn't been easy, but he was about to reach his goal. Taking his time, he prolonged the delicious moment, put his hand on her thigh, and slid it slowly toward . . .

'ANYBODY HOME?'

Matt jumped to his feet. Unbelievable!

'Western Union!' yelled a voice on the other side of the door. 'I have two telegrams for Matt Delluca.'

While Tiffany straightened her dress, Matt grumbled and opened the door, collected his messages, and gave the telegram man a tip.

'They're numbered,' he said. 'You have to read them in order.'

Matt feverishly ripped open the first envelope. In his mind, telegrams were associated with bad news: death, illness, accident . . .

He unfolded it and read the few lines typed on little strips of blue paper.

It was a message from Elliott, fairly long and muddled, but two sentences caught his attention: 'Trust me,' and a little further on, 'Go to my place <u>as soon as possible</u>.'

'I'm terribly sorry, but I have to leave,' he told Tiffany.

As though she'd been expecting as much, she got off the couch, picked up her shoes, and stood in front of him. 'If you walk through that door, you know you'll *never* sleep with me . . .'

He looked at her intently. The last rays of sunlight made her dress transparent, showing off her mesmerizing curves.

'It's an emergency,' he explained.

'What about me? I'm not an emergency?'

She stared back at him and sensed that beneath his playboy exterior, there was more to him than there appeared on the surface. She would have liked to have held on to him, but there was no way she was going to let this go a second time. 'You'll regret it as long as you live,' she said, casually unfastening a button on her dress.

'That I'm sure of,' Matt agreed.

'Well, too bad.'

She picked up her purse and left. 'You poor sap!' she said and shut the door behind her.

Florida 1976
Elliott is 30

Elliott and Ilena reached Key West just as the sun was setting the horizon ablaze. They had reached the end of their journey, the southernmost point in the United States, where America began and ended . . .

148

With its narrow streets, tropical gardens, and colonial houses, the place seemed to be outside time. They parked the Thunderbird near the shore and walked a few steps along the beach amidst the herons and pelicans; then they went to a little café where the regulars liked to chew the fat and solve the problems of the world. They had arranged to meet Roberto Cruz, Ilena's uncle, a long-time resident of the island who'd been Hemingway's factotum when the writer had lived on Key West in the 1930s. Since then, the town had bought the house and turned it into a museum, and Roberto worked there as the caretaker. With his Hawaiian shirt and graying beard, he was cultivating a resemblance to the famous writer. He lived in a small building next to the museum and he insisted that Elliott and Ilena stay with him rather than in a hotel. They accepted and followed him home.

'Welcome to Hemingway's house!' he said as he opened the iron gate to reveal a handsome Spanish colonial house.

As he went into the garden, Elliott was wondering if Matt had gotten his telegrams.

San Francisco 1976
Matt is 30

'Hello, Tramp!' said Matt as he opened the door to Elliott's house.

The Lab ran up barking, delighted to have the company. Matt scratched the dog's head and took him out to the garden after he'd filled his dish. Lost in thought, he stood for a few minutes leaning against a tree, reading and rereading the telegram from his friend.

Matt was worried. For the last several days, Elliott's behavior and what he said had seemed completely illogical, and he reproached himself for not managing to dispel his friend's fantasies. He'd thought all he had to do to get Elliott's feet back on the ground was to get him on a plane to Ilena, but it hadn't worked. From the very beginning, he'd thought this whole time traveler business was trouble. As the days had gone by, he'd been plagued by the feeling that something serious was going to happen to his friend.

Despite his skepticism, he carried out to the letter the instructions in the telegram. Elliott may have been losing his marbles, but Matt had decided to stay loyal to his friend, who was his only family, the one person who kept him steady. Matt was an orphan. He'd spent his childhood and adolescence in the Paris region, shunted from family to family. He'd left school at fifteen without qualifications. After a series of dead-end jobs he got involved in some shady deals. Several times he'd found himself mixed up in brawls that had turned nasty, and he'd spent a few nights in the police station. As he was beginning to be 'known to the police', he'd decided to leave France and take his chances in America. Since he had nothing to lose, he'd sold everything he owned and bought a one-way ticket to the 'New World'. Many people in his situation would have given up long before, but he was resourceful and had a gift for friendship. First in New York and then in California, he'd immediately felt at home in this open society that attached little significance to diplomas or social origin.

As the first telegram had promised, Matt found a large atlas in the library. It was old, but still magnificent, with its detailed plates protected by tissue paper. Without opening the second telegram, he slipped it between pages 66 and 67 and put the book back on the shelf.

Then he went into the garage, rummaged in the toolbox, found an old soldering iron, and went back into the house with it. He plugged it in in Elliott's office, let it heat up for a minute, cautiously picked it up, and applied the reddened tip to the heavy wooden work table.

San Francisco 2006
Elliott is 60

It had been dark for a long time when Elliott got back to the marina. He was coming from the airport, where Angie had taken the last flight to New York. As he opened the door to the house, a feeling of intense dejection and solitude set in. Lost in thought, he moved toward the window in his office, looking at the lights of the port glowing in the darkness without really seeing them. The house was like him: sad and icy freezing and desolate. Trembling with cold, he rubbed his arms to warm them up. As he drew near the radiator, he came to a stop. On his office table was a clumsily written inscription made with a soldering iron:

LARGE ATLAS
PAGE 66

He was flabbergasted and moved closer. This horrible graffiti hadn't been there that morning. Yet it already seemed to have a patina of age.

Who had decided to have fun . . .?

It didn't take him long to answer the question. After the

tattoo, the jerk was now trying to send him another message. He just had to figure out what it meant.

Large atlas? It took him a minute to figure out the reference. The only atlas he'd ever owned was a gift his mother had given him only a few days before her suicide. He'd faithfully kept the book in his library, but he'd never opened it. He went over to the shelves and climbed on a chair so he could reach it.

Page 66?

He hastily turned the pages.

Could it be that after so long . . .

A pale blue envelope fell onto the floor.

A telegram?

He hadn't seen one in years. He picked it up, and, not even examining it, frantically tore it open along the perforations.

Inside were a few typed lines that had traveled through time and waited thirty years for someone to set eyes on them:

Surprised?

You think you're all-powerful, don't you? Because you've found a way of making return trips into the past, you think you're entitled to drive other people mad with anxiety and leave with no questions asked?

Well, it doesn't work like that . . .

Because, if you think about it, you may know my future, but I'm the one who controls your past. You can't do anything against me, but the consequences of my actions influence your life.

Now I've turned the tables and I'm running the show.

I want some explanations and I want them now.

I'll be waiting for you.
Tonight.

Terrified by what he'd just read, Elliott set the telegram on the table. He'd opened Pandora's box and his worst fears were coming true . . . He thought about the situation for a few seconds and then, resigned, took hold of the bottle of pills that he always kept with him and forced himself to swallow one.

There was a flash of lightning and a rumble of thunder outside. The living room window threw back at him the gaze of the man who was now his worst enemy: himself.

THIRTEEN

Fourth Encounter

> *We go through the present blindfolded . . .*
> *Only later, when the blindfold is removed and we*
> *examine the past, do we realize what we've been*
> *through and understand what it means.*
> Milan Kundera

Key West, Florida
2 A.M.
Elliott is 30

The raging storm had knocked out all the power on Key West. Elliott was unable to sleep. Without waking Ilena from her deep slumber, he lit the oil lamp and decided to explore Hemingway's house.

Lit by lightning, the house seemed to be shaken by rain and wind like a ship in a storm at sea. As Elliott was mounting the central staircase, a powerful thunderclap made all the windows rattle. The young doctor shuddered and thought for an instant of going back, but he shrugged his shoulders and pressed on.

Even so, he had had a fright . . .

At the top of the stairs he walked across the creaking floor to the study. He was carefully opening the door when something hissed and struck him in the face.

A cat!

He remembered having read that Hemingway adored cats and had owned fifty of them. He touched his face: the cat had given him a deep scratch on the cheek as it flew past.

Really, me and animals . . .

He took a few steps into the study, admiring the personal objects of the great writer: his old typewriter that had been with him in Spain during the civil war, a ceramic given to him by Picasso, a collection of fountain-pens, a threatening-looking African mask, dozens of press clippings and photographs . . .

There was a magical atmosphere in the room. There was no denying that between fishing jaunts and drinking bouts, Papa Hemingway had taken the time to write some masterpieces in Key West, among them *A Farewell to Arms* and 'The Snows of Kilimanjaro'.

Not a bad track record, thought Elliott, as the lights finally came back on.

He blew out the lamp and went over to an old record-player. He carefully put the first record that came to hand on the turntable, and a few seconds later the sounds of a violin and a guitar filled the room: Django Reinhardt and Stéphane Grappelli, the best jazzmen of the thirties . . .

But the record suddenly stopped, the lights sputtered, and the room was plunged into darkness again.

Just my luck, thought Elliott again, *why did I blow out that lamp?*

He wanted to light it again, but he'd left his lighter in the bedroom.

It was hard to see anything in the study except for the streams of rain running down the windows. He remained motionless in the dark for a few minutes, hoping that the lights would come back on at any moment.

He suddenly felt a presence, heard breathing then a metallic sound.

'Who's there?' he asked in an anxious voice.

The only answer was the flame of a lighter that sprang up a few yards in front of him. He recognized the glowing eyes of his double, staring back at him in the darkness.

'You want some explanations? All right, I'll give them to you . . .'

The old doctor lit the wick on the oil lamp, settled into a brown leather armchair, and turned to Elliott.

'Tell me what's going to happen to Ilena!' Elliott shouted with youthful impatience.

'Sit down and stop yelling.'

Fidgeting impatiently, Elliot grudgingly agreed to take a seat on the other side of the desk. The old doctor reached into an inside jacket pocket and took out a photograph.

'Her name is Angie,' he explained, handing over the picture. 'She's twenty and she's the most important person in the world to me.'

Elliott studied the photograph attentively.

'Is her mother . . .'

'No, her mother is not Ilena,' the old man cut him off, anticipating the question.

'Why?'

'Because when my daughter was born, Ilena had been dead for ten years.'

Elliott took in the information without blinking.

'Why should I believe you?'

'Because I have no reason to lie to you.'

The young doctor then asked the question that had been tormenting him since the night before: 'Suppose that's true, why do you say I'm the one who killed her?'

The man facing him paused as though he were weighing each word before stating: 'You killed her because you love her badly.'

'I've heard enough crap from you!' Furious now, Elliott got to his feet.

'You love her as though you have your whole life before you . . . That's not the way to love.'

Elliott considered this argument briefly and rejected it. This wasn't the real problem. Right now he had to get as much information as possible, not philosophize about love. He turned the conversation back to the only thing that really interested him.

'How is Ilena supposed to die?'

'She's going to have an accident.'

'An accident? What kind of accident? And when?'

'Again, you ask! You can't expect me to tell you.'

'Why?'

'Because I don't want you to save her . . .'

For a few seconds Elliott remained silent and motionless, staring at the curtain of rain covering the window. He felt this conversation was getting away from him and he no longer had a grasp on what it meant. 'But it's now or never . . . You found a way to go back in time and you intend to let the woman you love die?'

'Don't think for one minute that I'm doing this willingly!' The older man sounded exasperated. He pounded his fist on the desk. 'I've been thinking of nothing else for thirty years! If *only* I could save her, *if only* . . .'

'So, stop thinking about it. Do it!'

'No!'

'Why not?'

'Because if we save Ilena, you'll live your life with her.'

'So?'

'So, then you'll never have Angie . . .'

Elliott wasn't sure he understood. 'Where's the problem?' he asked, shrugging his shoulders, 'I'll have other children . . .'

'Other children? But I don't give a damn about your other children. I don't want to lose my daughter! I don't want a world where Angie doesn't exist!'

'And I won't let Ilena die,' Elliott answered with determination.

Impelled by their anger, the two men had stood up. They were now only a few inches apart, facing each other, ready to try one last bluff. 'Maybe you think you have the upper hand because you're younger, but without me you'll never know how Ilena died and you won't be able to do anything to save her.'

'Yeah, well, if Ilena dies, don't count on me to be the father of your Angie!'

'When you're a father, you'll understand me, Elliott: you don't abandon your child, even to save the woman you love . . .'

They stood like that for a long time, staring at each other, neither one budging. The complicity that had brought them together at their last meeting had been replaced by antagonism. This was the struggle of a man against himself at two different ages. They were each ready to fight to the end: one to save his woman, the other not to lose his daughter.

The conversation was at an impasse when the older man glimpsed a way out: 'How far are you prepared to go to save Ilena?'

'As far as necessary,' Elliott answered, not batting an eyelash.

'What are you prepared to give up?'

'Everything.'

'Then maybe I have an idea . . .'

The rain was still coming down in torrents.

The two men had ended up sitting next to each other on the walnut bench next to the desk. Through the window behind them the beacon from the Key West lighthouse shone at regular intervals, casting their shadows on the wall and the floor.

'You want to save Ilena, and that's understandable, but you can only do it if you promise to respect three conditions . . .'

'Three conditions?'

'The first is that you speak to no one about what's happening to us. Not to Ilena, of course, but not even to Matt.'

'I trust Matt,' Elliott protested.

'It's not a question of trust, it's a question of danger. Listen, I'm convinced we're making a mistake, a terrible mistake, by trying to go against fate, and we'll pay dearly for it sooner or later. I'm ready to take the risk with you, on condition you do not involve anyone else.'

'What's the second condition?'

'If we manage to save Ilena, you'll have to leave her . . .'

'Leave her?' Elliott asked, completely incredulous.

'Leave her and never see her again. She stays alive, but you'll have to live your life as if she were dead.'

Elliott took a while to grasp the enormity of this. He opened his mouth, but was unable to speak.

'I know very well that I'm asking you something terrible,' the old doctor acknowledged.

'And what's the third condition?' he finally managed to croak.

'In nine years, on April 6, 1985, at a surgical conference in Verona, you'll meet a woman who will show interest in you. You'll respond to her advances and spend a weekend with her, during which our daughter will be conceived. This is how you'll have to act because it's the only way to save both Ilena and Angie.'

More ominous growls of thunder rumbled through the sky.

When Elliott still didn't answer, his double explained: 'This is the price you pay for changing destiny. But you're free to refuse.'

The old man stood up and buttoned his coat as though he were about to go out in the rain.

Elliott understood then that he had no choice but to accept the pact. In a fraction of a second, the happy years he had lived with Ilena flashed before his eyes. At the same time, he understood that this happiness would soon be at an end. To save her, he had to be ready for the misery of losing her.

As his double was about to leave the room, Elliott put out his hand to detain him.

'I accept!' he said emphatically.

His double did not turn around; he merely answered: 'I'll be back soon,' and closed the door behind him.

FOURTEEN

Fifth Encounter

Everything that must happen will happen,
whatever your efforts to avoid it.
Everything that must not happen will not happen,
whatever your efforts to bring it about.
Râmana Mahârshi

I have noticed that even people who assert that everything
is predestined and that we can change nothing about it
look both ways before they cross the street.
Stephen Hawking

San Francisco 1976
Elliott is 30

October, November, December . . . three months with no
news from the future!

On the surface, life had returned to normal. Elliott treated
his patients at the hospital; Ilena worried about her whales;
Matt had not seen Tiffany again, but he was working hard to
make a go of the vineyard he'd bought with Elliott.

Although he tried to distract himself, the young doctor was in a constant state of anxiety, worrying about the slightest detail to do with Ilena, and constantly expecting his double to reappear.

But he hadn't shown his face again.

So on some days, Elliott started to hope that he'd dreamed the whole business. Suppose the encounters had happened purely in his head? After all, that wasn't impossible: more and more people were suffering from burnout caused by stress and overwork that could lead to depression and delusions. Maybe he'd been a victim of that syndrome. Maybe, now, things were back to normal and the episode would turn out to be nothing but a bad memory.

He would dearly have loved to believe it . . .

Winter had settled on San Francisco, blanketing the city in a cold gray mantle with only the Christmas lights cheering things up.

Elliott was in a good mood when he got to the hospital on the morning of December 24. It was his last day on call before vacation. Ilena was supposed to meet him that night, and the next day they would leave together for Honolulu for a week of lounging under the palm trees.

The sun had not yet risen when an ambulance came roaring into the hospital parking lot. In it was a stretcher bearing a woman with severe burns.

It had all begun a half hour earlier when firefighters had gone to put out a blaze that had just started in a building in Haight–Ashbury. It was an old, decrepit place that junkies sometimes used to crash in. At five o'clock, a young woman in the middle of a bad heroin trip had poured gasoline on her body and struck a match.

Her name was Emily Duncan. She was twenty years old and had only a few hours left to live.

With the emergency services requiring a surgeon, Elliott was called to help immediately. When he examined the patient he was shocked by the severity of the burns.

Her entire body was covered with lesions, third-degree burns that disfigured her legs, her back, her chest . . . Almost all her hair had burned off, and her face could barely be identified through the wounds. A wide burn seemed to be compressing her chest to the point of strangulation.

To make it easier for her to breathe, Elliott decided to make two lateral incisions, but as he held the scalpel over her body, he felt his hand draw back. He closed his eyes for an instant, trying to clear his mind and regain concentration. His professionalism finally overcame his emotions and he could begin operating without shaking.

For a good part of the morning the medical team struggled over Emily, doing everything possible to give her the best care and to soothe the intense pain she was suffering.

It soon became obvious, however, that the young woman could not be saved. Her burns were too extensive, her lung capacity too weak, and her kidneys no longer functioning. They decided just to stabilize her and wait . . .

When Elliott came into Emily's room in the early afternoon, he found her covered with bandages and surrounded by drips. He was surprised by the strange calm pervading the room, the prologue to a wake disturbed only by the beeping of the heart monitor.

Elliott approached the bed and looked at the young woman. Her blood pressure was still worrying, although the effects of the heroin had worn off and she seemed to have recovered consciousness.

Enough perhaps to understand that she was doomed . . .

He sat down silently on a stool near this woman whom he did not know and for whom he could no longer do anything. No family had been found, and no one was there to be with her for her last battle. Elliott would have preferred to be somewhere else, but he did not avoid the desperate gaze that she fixed on him. He saw in it terror, but also questions to which he had no answer.

At one point, she tried to whisper something to him. He leaned over, lifted up the oxygen mask, and thought he heard 'It hurts.' To ease the pain, he decided to increase the dose of morphine. He was going to write the order when he suddenly understood that Emily had not said 'It hurts' but 'I'm afraid.'

What could he say to that? That he, too, was afraid, that he was sorry he wasn't able to save her, that on a day like today life didn't seem to have any meaning?

He would have liked both to take her in his arms and to shout out his indignation. Why had she done such a crazy thing? What chain of circumstances leads you to a dilapidated crash pad, drugged to the eyeballs? What inner pain could justify sprinkling yourself with gasoline and setting yourself on fire when you're barely twenty?

He would have liked to shout all that at her. But that's not what doctors are supposed to do in hospitals.

So he just stayed with her, giving her all the compassion he could, because there was no one else to do it. It was Christmas

Eve, the hospital was short-staffed, and above all the system wasn't prepared for this: the system was set up for treatment, not to provide support.

Emily was having more and more trouble breathing and couldn't stop shivering.

Elliott knew she was suffering horribly in spite of the morphine. He also knew that he would never forget her eyes desperately staring into his.

You always think you've seen everything in this job, but it's not true. You think you know the worst, but the worst is always yet to come. And something still worse is just around the corner.

One hour, then another went by. At three, when Elliott's shift was officially over, he got up quietly. 'I'll be back,' he promised Emily.

He went out into the corridor and pressed the button for the elevator. He had to tell Ilena, explain that he couldn't pick her up at the airport, and that he would probably get home in the middle of the night.

He went to the phone booth in the lobby and dialed the number for Ocean World, hoping that she hadn't already left. The receptionist answered, and he asked to be connected with the veterinarian's office.

He heard Ilena's voice say, 'Hello.'

'Hi . . .' he started before realizing he was talking to no one.

He turned his head: someone had put their hand on the hook and cut off the conversation.

His double.

'It's today . . .' the old man informed him.

'Today?'

'Ilena is to die today.'

Together the two doctors went up to the roof of the hospital. At different ages, they'd come here to smoke without having to endure the critical looks of their colleagues. Here, at least, they knew they would be left in relative peace.

As Elliott was pacing restlessly, eager to know more, his double grasped him firmly by the shoulder. 'You must not make that call.'

'Why?'

'Because Ilena will not understand.'

'What?'

'That you're neglecting her to stay with a patient after your shift is over. You haven't seen her for three weeks: she's expecting you to pick her up at the airport and that you'll spend the evening together.'

Elliott tried to justify himself: 'That young woman . . . what's happened to her is terrible. She has no one and . . .'

'I know,' the old man sympathized. 'Thirty years ago I stayed up with her all night, and I've never forgotten her.'

His voice full of emotion, he went on, 'But in the early morning, when I left the hospital, some terrible news was waiting for me: the woman I loved was dead.'

Elliott didn't understand. 'What's the connection between this patient and Ilena's death?'

'I'll tell you everything,' the old man promised. 'I just want to be sure our agreement still holds.'

'It does,' Elliott assured him.

'Then this is what will happen if you make that phone call.'

The old doctor began his story. He talked for a long time in an agitated voice tinged by regret.

Elliott had closed his eyes to concentrate on listening. Pictures ran through his mind like a movie . . .

Ilena: Hello.

Elliott: Hi, it's me.

Ilena: It won't do you any good, you won't find out what your present is until tonight!

Elliott: Listen, darling, I have a problem . . .

Ilena: What's the matter?

Elliott: I can't come and get you at the airport . . .

Ilena: I thought you finished at three o'clock?

Elliott: That's true, my shift is over . . .

Ilena: But?

Elliott: But I have to stay with a patient. A young woman who tried to commit suicide this morning in a crash pad . . .

Ilena: An addict?

Elliott: What difference does it make?

Ilena: If I understand correctly, you're telling me that you're spending Christmas Eve in the hospital with a junkie you've known for only a few hours?

Elliott: I'm only doing my job.

Ilena: Your job! You think you're the only one who has a job?

Elliott: Listen . . .

Ilena: I'm tired of waiting for you, Elliott.

Elliott: Why are you reacting like this?

Ilena: Because I've been waiting for you for ten years and you don't even see it.

Elliott: *We'll talk about all this tomorrow morning . . .*
Ilena: *No, Elliott. I'm not coming to San Francisco. Call me back when you're sure you want to spend your life with me.*

Elliott stood in the phone booth for several minutes. Three times, he picked up the receiver, ready to call Ilena back, apologize, and try to patch things up. But he didn't do it, because he could not abandon the young woman dying two floors above him.

Ilena waited in front of the telephone for half an hour, then when she understood that Elliott would not call back, she furiously ripped up her airplane ticket and threw it in the wastebasket. She also threw away the gift she'd bought and that he'd never see: a watch engraved with his initials.

She left the office completely demoralized and took refuge in the park's private gardens where she cried her eyes out in front of the indifferent gaze of the flamingos and the alligators.

Then she decided to cancel her vacation and go back to work. She spent the end of the afternoon following her usual routine, as though nothing had happened. It had been dark for some time when she ended her inspection with a visit to her favorite whale.

'Hello, Annushka. You're not doing so well either, are you?'

For the last few days, the matriarch of the Ocean World whales had been depressed, refusing to eat or to participate in the shows. Her fin was flaccid and her gentleness had given way to aggression toward her trainers and the other whales in the tank. The cause of her behavior was not hard to guess: her eight-year-old daughter Erica had been taken away from her to participate in a whale breeding program in Europe. A twenty-hour plane trip in an iron box without even a trainer to comfort her.

What had they been thinking of?

Ilena had done everything she could to oppose the transfer, emphasizing the traumatic consequences of the separation, explaining that the members of a pod never parted in the wild. But for financial reasons, management hadn't followed her recommendations. The truth was aquatic parks were expecting that capturing whales would soon be prohibited, and were trying to increase births in captivity.

'Come on, baby!'

Ilena had leaned over the water to encourage the whale to approach the edge, but Annushka did not respond to her calls. The whale was swimming in circles, distraught, emitting plaintive whistles.

Ilena was afraid that her immune system had been weakened: despite appearances, these giants were fragile, at the mercy of any passing microbe. Kidney and lung infections were common. Joachim, the dominant male in the tank, had had that bitter experience six months earlier when he was struck down by septicemia. This was what sometimes happened to these giants, they were conquered by something minuscule.

Ilena was beginning to feel increasingly uncomfortable about keeping whales in captivity. Imprisoned within four walls, splashing around in chemically treated water, fed with vitamins and antibiotics, dolphins and whales in aquatic parks did not have the ideal life that was presented to visitors.

As for the shows, they were certainly impressive, but weren't they a kind of insult to the species, whose cognitive capacities were not very different from those of humans?

Suddenly, for no apparent reason, Annushka started to charge, violently striking her head against the metal rail around the tank.

'Stop that!' Ilena ordered, and quickly plunged a pole in the water to drive the animal off.

She'd seen whales with suicidal tendencies before, and it was clear that Annushka was trying to injure herself on purpose. Ilena was worried, and threw her a few fish to distract her.

'Calm down! Calm down, lovely!'

Gradually, the animal's assaults grew less powerful and Annushka seemed to recover her calm.

'That's good, Annushka,' said Ilena, a little reassured . . . until she saw a long trail of blood staining the surface of the water.

'Oh, no!'

From banging into the rail so many times, the whale had wounded herself.

The young veterinarian leaned over the water. At first glance, the wound seemed to be on the animal's jaw.

Ilena should have followed the trainers' golden rule: never approach a whale when it's aggressive, and never get into the water with one if you're not certain of its cooperation.

She should have set off the alarm.

She should have alerted her colleagues.

She should have . . .

But still feeling the effects of her quarrel with Elliott, Ilena had let her guard down.

She dove into the tank, where Annushka had resumed her frenetic circling.

When she sensed that Ilena was coming toward her, the whale leaped on her at once, opening her mouth as though to bite, and dragged her toward the bottom.

Ilena fought back, but the whale was much stronger. Every time Ilena came back to the surface, the animal forced her underwater, giving her no rest.

Ilena was a skilled swimmer who was able to hold her breath for several minutes.

But you can't struggle for long against an animal that weighs four tons and measures eighteen feet . . .

At one point, when she had given up hope, she managed to reach the surface and take a breath. She made a desperate attempt to swim to the edge of the tank, and she was almost there when . . .

She turned around.

In an instant of horror, she had time to see the enormous tail fin coming down on her with phenomenal speed.

The shock was terrible and the ensuing pain so intense that she almost lost consciousness. She sank without a struggle, allowing herself to be drawn to the bottom. In a final moment of lucidity, as her lungs were filling with salt water, the young woman wondered why Annushka, whom she had been training for years, had reacted so violently. There was probably no answer to that question. Maybe in the long run, life in a tank makes you crazy . . .

Her last thought was for the man she loved. She'd always been convinced that they would grow old together and here she was, going first, not even thirty years old.

But you don't choose your fate. Life had decided for them like it always does.

Gripped by panic and terror, plunged into darkness, Ilena was seized by a deadly current. As she was finally floating over to the other side, she regretted only that they'd left each other in the middle of a quarrel, and that the last image Elliott would have of her would be tainted with bitterness and resentment.

The wind blowing on the hospital roof felt like icy breath.

As though waking from a nightmare, Elliott opened his eyes as his double was coming to the end of his terrible story.

The two men stood in silence, one terrified by what he had just heard, the other still dazed by the story he had told.

Elliott shook himself, opened his mouth to speak, and then hesitated. Anticipating his doubts, the old doctor took a yellowed clipping out of his pocket. 'If you don't believe me . . .' he began.

Elliott practically tore the paper out of his hands. It was an old article from the *Miami Herald*.

Despite its yellowed appearance, the clipping was dated the next day, December 25, 1976.

His hands shaking, Elliott read through the article, which was accompanied by a large photograph of Ilena.

Young Veterinarian
Killed By Whale!

In a terrible accident last night at Ocean World in Orlando, a killer whale attacked its trainer for unknown reasons.

It took only a few minutes for the whale to overpower and drown the woman who was trying to help it: Ilena Cruz, the park veterinarian. While the precise circumstances of the accident remain unclear, it seems that the veterinarian did not follow all the safety procedures. Pending further investigation, the park's management has declined to comment.

When Elliott looked up from the article, he saw the old doctor walking off into the fog. 'Now it's up to you,' he said, opening the metal door and disappearing.

Feeling abandoned, Elliott stayed on the roof for a little while longer, disturbed, and chilled by the cold, disbelief and indecision. Then he stopped asking himself questions: the time had come to take action.

What happened tomorrow didn't matter.

He didn't care about the price he'd have to pay.

He was going to save the woman he loved.

And nothing else mattered.

He stormed into the lobby like a guided missile and pushed his way past several colleagues in his rush toward the phone. He dialed Ilena's number.

A couple of rings . . . The seconds seemed like minutes, then finally he heard a voice:

Ilena: Hello.
Elliott: Hi, it's me.
Ilena: It won't do you any good, you won't find out what your present is until tonight!
Elliott: Listen, darling . . .
Ilena: What's the matter?
Elliott: Nothing . . . I'll come and get you at the airport later as we planned.

Ilena: I can't wait to see you . . .
Elliott: Me neither.
Ilena: Your voice sounds funny. Are you sure you're all right?
Elliott: Now I'm fine.

After he hung up, Elliott couldn't bear to go back to the room and face Emily's gaze as she died her slow death. He asked one of the nurses on duty to check on her regularly, then put on his coat and went out into the parking lot.

Did what he'd just done make any sense at all? Had he really changed his and Ilena's future? Is one sentence instead of another all it takes sometimes to change your whole life?

All these questions were jumbled together in his head as he walked toward his car. Automatically, he lit a cigarette and put his hands in his pockets to warm up. He felt the newspaper clipping in one of them, and suddenly had a flash of inspiration. If he had changed the future, Ilena had not had her accident, and a reporter had not written the article, so that article didn't exist.

Intrigued, he took the yellowed paper out of his pocket, unfolded it, and turned it in every direction. Unbelievably, the content was not the same. As though by magic, Ilena's photo was gone and, instead of the article relating the death of the young veterinarian, there was another front-page story.

Ocean World: Death of a Whale
Annushka, the matriarch of the killer whales in Orlando's Ocean World, died last night from a jaw wound caused by a collision with the metal

shell of the tank. The wound seems to have been self-inflicted.

Park management acknowledged that depression may have accounted for the whale's actions: the park had just transferred her daughter to another zoo.

Ocean World will open as normal today.

No member of staff was hurt.

FIFTEEN

Sixth Encounter

He was my North, my South, my East and West . . .
W. H. Auden

San Francisco 1976
Elliott is 30

It's Christmas Day.

On this December morning, California's mild weather has been replaced by gray skies and cold. San Francisco looks a little like New York, and it almost seems as though it's about to snow.

The house is silent, bathed in the pale light of dawn. Snuggled against Elliott's shoulder, Ilena is sleeping peacefully. But the young doctor has the deathly look of someone who hasn't slept all night.

Elliott turns toward Ilena, kisses her tenderly, careful not to wake her, and looks at her for several minutes, aware that these are their last moments together. One last time, he breathes in the aroma of her hair, moves his lips over her velvety skin, and listens to the rhythm of her heartbeat.

Then he notices his silent tears falling on the sheet. He puts on a sweater and a pair of jeans and leaves the room without making a sound.

He cannot bring himself to believe that he's going to leave her. He knows he made an agreement with his double, but now that Ilena is saved, what could stop him from staying with her? How could that bastard retaliate to force him to honor his part of the contract?

Crushed by despair, he drags himself from room to room, hoping, without really believing it, that he'll come across his other self so he can let fly all his anger and indignation. But his double doesn't show his face. The sixty-year-old Elliott has fulfilled his side of the bargain and now it's up to his younger self to keep his promise.

Elliott goes into the kitchen and collapses on a chair. Near the door stand their bags ready for a trip to Hawaii that neither he nor Ilena will ever take. Because he knows that he has no choice but to leave her. He feels a force inside him, a voice impelling him to follow that course. He is nothing but a puppet whose strings are being pulled by an unknown power offstage.

The glass table reflects his face back at him, emaciated and disheveled. He feels empty, defeated, as though he has lost all self-confidence and any sense of how the world works.

From the very first day he met his double, he has had the impression he's living in a universe that follows no known laws. Gripped by fear of the unknown, he can no longer sleep, he doesn't eat, and he's tormented by all kinds of impossible questions. Why is this happening to him? Is this encounter a blessing or a curse? Is he still completely sane? Having no one to talk to about his problem is killing him.

Suddenly, he hears a sound: the floor creaks and Ilena comes into the room wearing nothing but panties and a shirt tied at the waist.

She gives him a mischievous smile and hums an Abba tune. He knows it's the last time he'll see her happy. She is beautiful beyond belief and they have never been more in love.

And yet, in a few seconds, everything is going to come apart . . .

Ilena approaches Elliott and puts her arms around his neck, but she soon realizes that something's wrong. 'What's going on?'

'We have to talk. I can't go on playing games.'

'What games?'

'The two of us . . .'

'What . . . what are you talking about?'

'I've met another woman.'

There it is, it only took two seconds: two seconds to destroy a love that lasted ten years. Two seconds to separate the two sides of a single coin . . .

Ilena rubs her eyes and sits down in front of Elliott, still thinking it's a stupid joke, or she's not really awake, or she misheard . . .

'You're kidding?'

'Do I look like I am?'

She looks at him, devastated. He has red eyes and drawn features. It's true that for several months she has felt that he's been deeply worried. Then she hears herself ask him: 'Who is this woman?'

'You don't know her. She's a nurse who works with me at the Free Clinic.'

It still seems unreal, so much so that now she thinks she's dreaming. It's not the first time she's had this kind of nightmare. That's it, it's a horrible nightmare that will soon be over. And yet, she wants to know: 'How long have you been seeing her?'

'A few months.'

Now she doesn't know what to say. All she understands is that what she's built up for the last ten years has suddenly just crumbled. Meanwhile, Elliott continues his demolition work. 'It hasn't been working for us for a while now,' he says.

'You never said anything . . .'

'I didn't know how to talk to you about it . . . I tried to get you to understand gradually . . .'

She would like to cover her ears, not to hear. Innocently, she still hopes that this whole discussion will go no further than the confession of an infidelity.

But Elliott has decided otherwise. 'I want us to separate, Ilena.'

She wants to answer, but it's too painful. She feels helpless tears running down her cheeks.

'We're not married, we don't have kids . . .' Elliott goes on.

She wants him to stop talking because his words are like knife wounds to her heart and she won't be able to take this for much longer. Forgetting pride or self-respect, she bursts out: 'But you're *everything* to me, Elliott: my lover, my friend, my family . . .'

She moves closer as though to fall into his arms. He steps back.

She gives him a look that tears him apart. When he thinks he can say nothing more, he nevertheless opens his mouth and manages to announce: 'You don't understand. *I don't love you any more*, Ilena.'

It's still early on Christmas morning.

After an unusually late start, San Francisco is slowly waking up. In this city that's constantly on the move, the streets are almost deserted and most stores are closed.

In many houses, people are celebrating: children are already up, eager to open their presents, and music and sounds of happiness can be heard. In other places, though, it's a hard day to get through, a day when solitude weighs more heavily than usual. The bums are spread out on the public benches near Union Square. In Lenox Hospital, after a troubled night, a young woman of twenty has died from burns. Somewhere in the marina, a couple has just separated . . .

A taxi arrives at the glass house and takes Ilena to the airport.

A little later, Elliott leaves the neighborhood. Shattered by sadness and shame, he drives around the city, nearly causing several accidents. The stores are open in Chinatown. Elliott parks, enters the first restaurant he comes across, and goes straight to the rest room.

As he heaves his guts into the toilet, he suddenly senses a presence behind him. A presence he has now learned to recognize and to fear . . .

He turns suddenly and gives his double a hard punch that sends him hurtling into the tiled wall. 'All this is because of you!'

Stunned by the blow, the old doctor collapses against the wall. He struggles to his feet, and rubs his chin for a minute as Elliott launches another verbal assault: 'It's your fault that she left!'

Cut to the quick, the old man rushes him, grabs him by the neck, and knees him in the groin.

Then the two man stand side by side, catching their breath in an atmosphere filled with anger and sadness.

Elliott is the first to break the silence, sobbing, 'She was my whole life . . .'

'I know that . . . That's why you saved her.'

His double puts his hand on Elliott's shoulder and, trying to console him, says, 'Without you, she'd be dead.'

Elliott lifts his head and looks at his other self in front of him. It's odd: he still can't think of him as anything but a stranger. Compared to this man, in whom he has trouble recognizing himself, he's only lived half his life. The other one has thirty years on him: thirty years of experience, thirty years of encounters and friends . . .

But maybe also thirty years of remorse and regret.

He already feels that his time traveler is about to leave. He recognizes the characteristic trembling and the nosebleed.

And the old doctor does indeed grab a paper towel to staunch the bleeding. This time he would have liked to stay longer, because he knows that his younger self is about to go through some hard years. He regrets he didn't find the right words to help him, knowing very well that words hold little weight in the face of suffering and adversity.

Most of all, he deplores the fact that every one of their encounters has ended with a confrontation and a misunderstanding, like a father–son relationship that never got past the stage of primal conflict.

Yet he refuses to leave without giving Elliott something more than a knee in the balls. Convinced that it's the last time he'll see himself at this age, and remembering the sadness he'd endured at that time, he tries to offer some words of comfort: 'At least you'll live knowing that Ilena is alive, somewhere. I lived with her death on my conscience. And, believe me, that makes a hell of a difference . . .'

'Go fuck yourself,' is all he gets for an answer.

It's certainly not easy to communicate with yourself! he thinks as he's drawn into the labyrinth of time.

And the last picture his brain registers is his double giving him the finger.

SIXTEEN

Men no longer have the time to learn anything.
They buy things ready-made in stores. But since no
one sells friends, men have no more friends.

Antoine de Saint-Exupéry

San Francisco 1976
Elliott is 30

Elliott came out of the rest room feeling furious. What had he done to deserve this?

Since Ilena left, he'd been haunted by the way she'd looked at him when he claimed he no longer loved her. He'd felt her terrible hurt, and despite that he'd persisted in humiliating her.

Of course, he'd done it *for her*, to save her life, except she'd never know anything about it. She'd spend the rest of her life hating him . . .

And that was exactly the way he felt at that moment: he hated himself and wished he could be someone else.

Depressed and exhausted, he sat down at the bar and asked for a glass of rice wine that he drank in one gulp. He felt like dying. He lit a cigarette and ordered another drink, and another.

So this was it; he was going to do what his father used to do, get falling-down drunk.

Usually Elliott drank only occasionally, most of the time just to gratify Matt, who was a real wine connoisseur. He was the son of an alcoholic, and he'd had firsthand experience of the damage drinking could do. For him, it would always be associated with the beatings his father had given him when he was out of control.

But that was exactly what he was after now: he wanted to lose control, become someone else. When he asked for another drink, the bartender hesitated a second before serving him, seeing that his customer was not in his normal state.

'Give it to me!' Elliott yelled as he grabbed the bottle and dropped a ten-dollar bill on the bar.

He went out into the street, hugging the bottle to his chest. He got behind the wheel of his car and took another gulp.

'Look at me, Dad, I'm just like you!' he yelled as he drove off. 'I'm just like you!'

And this was only the beginning . . .

It wasn't very hard to find drugs in San Francisco. Elliott had seen so many addicts at the hospital and at the Free Clinic that he knew their habits and the places where they hung out.

So he headed to the Tenderloin, a disreputable neighborhood where he knew he'd easily find what he wanted. For ten minutes he walked up and down the streets of this devastated neighborhood, a real human sewer, before he found a dealer he knew, a guy who looked Jamaican and called himself Yamda.

Elliott had filed two complaints against him, because he

often tried to sell his stuff inside the Free Clinic to patients in detox. The two men had come into serious conflict on several occasions, the last time even coming to blows.

It's true that Elliott could have found another dealer – there were enough of them around – but when you decide to hit rock bottom, humiliation is part of the deal.

When he caught sight of Elliott, the dealer initially looked worried until he understood that his visitor was there as a customer.

'So, Doc, are you looking for a big thrill?' he snickered.

'What do you have to offer?'

'How much you got?'

Elliott fumbled in his wallet: he had seventy dollars, enough to buy a large quantity of any kind of junk.

'Choose your poison,' said Yamda, cheerfully. 'Hash, speed, LSD, heroin . . .'

On calm days, you always think you've conquered them.

You think that in the end you've finally done them in.

That you've gotten rid of them for good, now and forever.

But that seldom happens.

Most of the time, the demons are still there, lurking somewhere in the shadows.

Tirelessly waiting for the moment when our guard drops.

And when love goes away . . .

When Elliott got home, he ran up the stairs four at a time, heading for the bathroom. Overjoyed to see his master again, the Lab ran up to greet him, but . . .

'Get lost!' the doctor yelled, aiming a kick in the dog's direction, half missing because he was drunk.

Tramp stifled a sharp yelp, and despite the hostile greeting, tried a new approach by following Elliott. It did him no good; Elliott grabbed him by the scruff of the neck and unceremoniously shoved him outside.

When he was alone, Elliott shut himself up in the bathroom and opened the medicine cabinet, looking for a syringe. His hands shook as he took the bricks of heroin Yamda had sold him out of his pocket.

Quick, let him inject something to blow his mind. He didn't want to get high, or to liberate his spirit like those dumb hippies. What he wanted was to get completely out of it, to blank it all out. Anything to make him forget. Anything to go somewhere else. Somewhere where he would not be haunted by his double or by the memory of Ilena.

A place where he would no longer be himself.

He put the brick in a glass saucer and added a little water. Using his lighter, he heated the bottom of the saucer and filtered the liquid through a piece of cotton wool. He stuck the needle in the cotton wad, drew out the dope, and injected it into a vein in his forearm.

As a burning wave swept through his body, he let out a cry of deliverance. He felt as though he had embarked on a journey into the depths of his being, prepared to confront the darkest aspects of himself.

San Francisco 1976
A few hours later
Matt is 30

This Christmas, Matt was feeling really down.

For the last few weeks, he'd been working relentlessly to

restore his vineyard, and the business was now up and running. But when he'd got up this morning, his life had seemed empty because he had no one to share it with. Swallowing his pride, he'd picked up the phone to do what he'd continually been putting off: call Tiffany and apologize for the way he'd behaved. Unfortunately, the number she'd given him had been disconnected. She'd apparently left town without telling him and without trying to see him again.

That's what happened when you put off until tomorrow . . .

In the early afternoon, he got into the Corvette to drive over to the marina. Elliott must have already taken off for Hawaii, but he could always feed Tramp and take him for a walk on the beach.

When he got to the street beside the water, he immediately noticed Elliott's VW up on the sidewalk.

Strange . . .

He got out of the car and went up the porch steps. He rang the bell and waited.

No answer.

He'd brought the keys Elliott left with him when he went out of town. He put the key in the lock, but realized that the door was open.

'Hello,' he said, 'anybody home?'

When he went inside and saw the dog cowering, Matt immediately understood that something was wrong.

'You all alone, Tramp?'

The dog was barking and running to the stairs. Elliott appeared at the top of then, looking like death warmed over.

'What are you doing here?' Matt asked, his eyes wide. 'You didn't go to Hawaii?'

'I'm the one who should be asking what the hell you're doing in my house.'

'Take it easy. You don't look so hot,' said Matt, ignoring the hostility. 'What happened?'

'You wouldn't understand,' said Elliott, as he took a few steps down.

'Why? Because I'm too stupid?'

'Maybe.'

This time Matt felt hurt. This kind of aggression wasn't like Elliott; he was obviously not himself.

'Where's Ilena?'

'There is no more Ilena! It's over!'

'Come on, what are you talking about?'

'I've left her.'

Matt was stunned. This was the last thing he was expecting.

Elliott collapsed on the couch. The drugs had not yet worn off. His head was spinning and he felt nauseous. He had a splitting headache that felt like invisible drills piercing his skull.

'Wait a minute, Elliott, you can't leave Ilena.'

'I just did.'

'But she's your whole life . . . She gives you your bearings, she's the best thing that ever happened to you.'

'Stop with the fancy phrases!'

'But I'm just saying what you used to say. And you also said that thanks to her you'd found your place, in the world.'

And it was true.

'If you let her leave, you'll spend the rest of your life regretting it and hating yourself.'

'Leave me alone, will you!'

'Did you have a fight?'

'None of your business.'

'It is my business because I'm your friend and I won't let you ruin your life!'

'Why don't you go back home and screw yourself senseless – and leave me in peace!'

Elliott closed his eyes, overwhelmed by what he'd just said. He couldn't go on insulting his friend. He had to tell him what was happening to him and how grief-stricken he felt.

Except that he couldn't. That was part of the price he had to pay: not to tell anyone what had happened.

Even though Elliott's insults had deeply wounded him, Matt tried to be conciliatory one more time: 'I don't understand what's happening to you, Elliott, but I do know you must be very unhappy to say things like that. And I don't think you can solve your problems on your own.'

Elliott felt his heart break. Ilena's love and Matt's friendship were the two things that counted most in his life. For ten years, they had been each other's best friend, supported and understood each other . . .

But today, Elliott was in a situation he could only get out of by himself. Incapable of keeping up the act with his friend, he made a painful decision. He had to push him away just as he'd pushed Ilena away.

'You want to do me a favor, Matt?'

'Yes.'

'Get out of my life . . .'

Matt hesitated as though he wasn't sure that he'd heard right. Then his blood froze, and he said in a flat voice: 'If you want.'

He bowed his head and moved toward the door. When he got to the threshold, he turned back toward Elliott, in the vain hope that everything was not lost. But all Elliott said was: 'I'll give you my share in the vineyard, but don't bother coming to see me again. Ever.'

SEVENTEEN

You don't learn anything just by reading books.
You learn only by receiving blows.

Swâmi Prajnânpad

San Francisco 2006
Elliott is 60

When Elliott opened his eyes, he was feverish and shaking, as though he had the flu. It was that filthy cancer together with the side effects of time travel. He stood up with difficulty, dragged himself into the bathroom, and vomited into the sink. He would end up dying from it, but not right now. As was his habit, he checked the number of pills: four left. He had already sworn several times that he wouldn't take any more, but now he was certain: he would never set foot in the past again!

He got into the shower and slowly recovered his spirits. A few minutes earlier he had left his double after a violent argument in the rest room of a Chinese restaurant. The poor kid didn't look so good, and he was sorry he hadn't found the right words to comfort him.

He quickly dressed in front of the bedroom mirror.

I hope you won't do anything stupid, he thought, looking in the mirror, but really talking to his younger self.

He glanced out the window: this Christmas morning a handful of joggers were already running on the beach, and a young girl was playing frisbee with her dog on the grass of Marina Green.

He got into his car, and despite the chill of the morning drove with the windows open, intoxicated with the air and the simple feeling of being alive. Since he had learned that the end was near, he had felt a curious mixture of euphoria and exhaustion. He was facing death, but he was also facing the truth. For the first time he was managing to live fully in the present, making each second count as if it were the final one.

He drove through North Beach at a good clip and headed for Coit Tower. He was supposed to meet Matt for a sailing expedition. It would be a quiet trip around the bay with just the two of them, during which, he had decided, he would reveal the secret he'd kept for too long: the nature of his illness and the imminence of his death.

One hell of a Christmas present . . .

He really didn't know how Matt would react. Their friendship, which had lasted decades, had never failed. It was a strange chemistry made up of attachment, camaraderie and tact that had started forty years before in an event that remained one of the decisive moments in his life.

As he headed north, Elliott remembered the day in 1965 when he had met, at the same time, Matt and Ilena.

New York City 1965
Elliott is 19

It's the middle of winter, early evening, in the city that never sleeps. A sudden unexpected downpour falls on Manhattan . . .

A young man with dripping wet clothes goes down the steps to a subway station. His name is Elliott Cooper. He is nineteen and doesn't really know what to do with his life. Two months earlier he left school to travel around the United States. A way to see the country, make some decisions about his future, and get away from his father in California.

> At the same moment, Ilena Cruz, an eighteen-year-old Brazilian, is coming back from the Bronx Zoo where she's gotten a summer internship allowing her to realize her life's dream: to take care of animals. She floats across the street, avoiding puddles and oncoming cars, and enters the subway station. Her triumphant mood is reflected in her radiant smile.

Elliott stops for a minute in front of a black guitarist playing in the subway, giving a talented performance of Otis Redding's repertoire, and, since it's the era of the Civil Rights Movement, asking for more respect for his community. Elliott is mad about music. It's a way for him to take refuge in his own world, far from everyone else. Why doesn't he trust anyone? Why does he have no real friends?

Why does he feel useless? He doesn't know it yet, but in less than five minutes, he will learn that events often make the man.

> Lille a flame, Ilena lights up the long corridor leading to the platform. The rain has soalled her hair and her strappy T-shirt. Despite themselves, people hurrying by pause for a second, lose themselves when they glimpse the depths of her clear green eyes. She has a gift for that: she attracts people and inspires their trust.

It is 5:11 when the train comes into the station. It's a weekday, at rush hour. The station is mobbed. Elliott edges his way down the platform to get into one of the front cars, when suddenly, this girl . . .
She simply brushes against him. It's almost nothing, just a touch, a look, a presence. And the world blurs around him . . . Why this dizziness, this void in his stomach? Why this feeling that no one has ever looked at him like that?

> At first Ilena is flattered that she's provoked so much interest from such a good-looking boy. Then she feels disturbed, not really knowing why. She is damp; she's perspiring. She adjusts the strap that has slipped down her arm and turns away to escape the boy's visual hold on her. Why does she have the impression that there is something dangerous in the air?

Elliott has walked along the platform to get into the second car. But Ilena picks the third. The young man hesitates, then, as though drawn by a magnet, plows through the crowd and changes cars just before the doors close.

The third car instead of the second . . .

Sometimes a life hinges on things like that: a lingering glance, a flicker of the eyes, the movement of a strap . . .

> The train pulls out. She has sat down on one of the few empty seats and sees him at the other end of the car. She hopes and fears that he will come up and talk to her. She feels her heart beating in her chest almost painfully.

He doesn't take his eyes off her and tries to move to the rear of the car. He wonders how to approach her, tries to find something amusing to say, but nothing comes. No, he won't manage it. He's never been very good at that game. And a girl like that could never be interested in him. *Give up, Elliott, she's too good for you. Stop pretending you're in the movies.*

The train stops at the next station. *Get out of this car, imbecile! You're out of your league.* He hesitates. The train pulls out, passes through another station, then another. This time, Ilena gets up. *Too late. She's geting off at the next stop. Come on, say something, buddy! It's now or never.*

He pushes past a few people to get closer. He can no longer feel his legs. His head is empty. This is it, she's there, a few inches away from him. He sees the perfect curve of her lips. Then he leans a little closer and says—

There was what felt like an explosion in the next car, a few yards from them. A huge blast, a deep sound of incredible force, followed by a powerful shock wave that made the train vibrate on the rails and threw everyone to the floor.

Oddly, a moment went by before people became aware of what was happening. A brief instant of stupefaction before screams filled the car.

A second earlier, it had been an evening like any other, the end of the work day, the quiet routine of everyday life . . .

Then the train had derailed in the middle of a tunnel. The lights had gone out and everything had been blown to bits.

A second earlier, a boy was about to approach a girl.

Then suddenly, noise, fear, and horror.

Elliott and Ilena get up with difficulty. The car is filled with a thick dust cloud that burns the eyes and makes it hard to breathe. The two young people look around: the other passengers are stunned, their bodies spattered with blood, clothing torn, faces twisted in terror. Most of the roof has collapsed into the car, trapping people under the debris.

Cries of panic fill the car. In a terrified voice, a woman screams: 'Help us, Lord!' while people push against each other, looking for a way out. Ilena tries to keep as calm as she can and comforts a little girl who is sobbing next to her.

Elliott's hair is full of shards of glass, and his shirt is spattered with blood. He is injured too, but he doesn't bother to find out where. With the help of those who are unharmed, he tries to rescue the injured people trapped under the collapsed roof. They manage to free a few, but some bodies have been torn apart by the violence of the explosion.

'We have to get out of here!'

His words sound like an ultimatum. And it's true that now everyone is thinking of only one thing: getting out of this suffocating nightmare. But the automatic doors are twisted together. The survivors finally have no choice but to jump out of the windows.

Elliott looks around him. He can barely see a thing. The flames whipping through the train make it hot as an oven. His entire body is dripping with sweat. He's never been so afraid in his life. A nauseating odor is coming from the floor. An odor that he will learn to recognize and fear in the years to come: the odor of death.

He gets ready to leave. But should he? He knows that there are still injured people in the train. In order to breathe more easily, he gets down on his knees and crawls toward the rear of the car. There he sees body parts – an arm, a leg, a foot in a shoe – and he starts to cry. What can he do?

Nothing.

'Come on!'

It's Ilena calling him. She's already halfway through the window and is making sure he'll follow her.

Elliott turns around. He is about to obey when he retraces his steps. Near him, a young man of his own age is stretched out, motionless, under the debris from the roof. Elliott leans over him to see if he's still breathing. He thinks he can detect a heartbeat. He really isn't sure but he decides to believe it's there. He furiously tries to release the man from this tomb of twisted metal, but without success. The young man is immobilized by an iron bar lying across his chest.

'Come on!' Ilena repeats.

She's right: there's too much smoke, it's too hot . . .

But Elliott hesitates, then, with an effort born of despair, he tries again.

'Don't die!' he screams at the wounded man.

For the rest of his life, he will wonder how he managed to twist the metal bar, free the man, and pull him clear. But there it is, he's done it! Now Elliott picks him up, slings him over his shoulder, and leaves this place of darkness.

Following Ilena, he jumps onto the track and they go down the tunnel single file. In front of them, a man with his arm torn off staggers on and almost falls several times. Elliott feels a warm liquid flowing onto his face. It's the wounded man he's carrying over his shoulder who is losing blood. Elliott doesn't know what to do to stop the bleeding. He stops for a few seconds, tears off his shirt, rolls part of it into a ball, and with all his remaining strength, uses it as an improvised tourniquet to stop the blood flow.

Everything is blending together in his head. He has no more strength, as though the guy he is carrying on his shoulder weighs a ton, but he has to forget his own pain. To do that, he decides to focus on something calming.

So he looks at the girl walking in front of him. They've hardly exchanged a single word, but they're already connected by something. He lets himself be guided, convinced that nothing bad can happen to now. If it weren't for her, wouldn't he have gotten into the wrong car, the one where the explosion happened?

After a minute, they see light at the end of the tunnel: it's a station. Only a few more yards, but they are the hardest ones. Elliott can hear nothing, he's about to collapse . . .

Then a firefighter comes up and takes the wounded man and puts him on a stretcher.

Finally released, Elliott turns to Ilena.

And faints.

At the same time, in the stifling depths of the tunnel, the devastated train continues to burn, soon to be nothing more than a smoking ruin.

In one of the cars, on top of a seat buckled by the heat, lies a book that the flames are starting to devour, but these strange words are still legible:

> *You are your own refuge*
> *There is no other*
> *You cannot save another*
> *You can only save yourself.*

When Elliott opens his eyes a few hours later, he is lying in a hospital bed. The sun has come up. His shoulder is bandaged and sharp pain radiates down his spine. Sitting next to his bed, the girl from the subway is watching him.

'How are you?' she asks, leaning toward him.

He nods and tries to sit up, but the tube from the drip in his arm restrains his movements.

'Don't move, I'll fix that.'

Ilena pushes a button, and the upper part of the bed slowly rises.

Up on the wall in a corner of the room, a black and white television set shows pictures of Manhattan in disorder, and then an announcer informs Elliott that:

New York has just experienced the worst blackout in its history. At 5:16 this November ninth, 1965, all the lights went out in Ontario and along the east coast of the United States and only came back on ten hours later. The possibility of sabotage was soon dismissed when a transmission failure in the hydroelectric station at Niagara Falls was found . . .

Then come pictures and a commentary on the subway accident that the reporter attributes to the interruption in current. No question of a bomb or an attack, even if the country is going through troubled times: Kennedy was assassinated two years earlier, and the previous summer race riots in Los Angeles caused dozens of deaths. Most importantly, America is beginning to send large numbers of troops to Vietnam, provoking an anti-war movement on the campuses, where student activism is sometimes assuming very violent forms.

Ilena turns off the set.

'Is he dead?' asks Elliott after a minute.

'Who?'

'The guy I tried to save. Is he dead?'

'I think the doctors are operating right now. You know,' she explains, on the edge of tears, 'he was in bad shape . . .'

Elliott nods his head. For a moment no one speaks. Still stunned, each of them returns to their inner landscape of chaos and confusion.

Then the girl breaks the silence: 'You wanted to say something to me?'

Elliott frowns.

'Just before the explosion,' Ilena explains, 'you leaned in my direction to say something to me . . .'

'Well . . .' Elliott stammers.

The rays of the early morning sun fill the room with a soft light. For a few unreal seconds, it's as though the accident never happened. There's just a boy filled with confusion looking at a girl he thinks is pretty.

'I just wanted to ask you to have a cup of coffee with me.'

'Oh, I see,' she says, timidly.

They are rescued from their embarrassment by the sonorous voice of the doctor who has just come into the room. 'I'm Dr Doyle,' he announces as he approaches the bed.

While the doctor gives him a thorough check-up, Elliott regretfully notices that the young woman has taken advantage of this interruption to disappear; then he has to endure a little speech in which he manages to pick out a few expressions like 'thoracic trauma with depression of the sternum', and 'erosion of the lower cervical area'. The doctor finally concludes his visit by applying an anti-inflammatory cream and putting a surgical collar on Elliott.

Before he leaves the room, Elliott asks him for news of the man he rescued. He learns that the operation has just ended, but that they now have to 'wait for the patient to wake up before making a prognosis'.

Words he will utter himself on numerous occasions in years to come.

Alone in his room, Elliott remains stretched out on his bed until the door opens slightly and a pretty face appears in the gap. 'I accept.'

'What?'

'The coffee, I accept,' she says, brandishing two cardboard cups.

All smiles, he takes a cup from her. 'By the way, I'm Elliott.'

'And I'm Ilena.'

That day, on the sixth floor of a hospital in the middle of a Manhattan winter, two people that destiny has just brought together talk late into the night.

They see each other the next day, and on the days after that; they walk around the city, picnic in Central Park, and scour the museums. They return to the hospital every night for news of the injured man, who is still in a coma.

And then there is the kiss exchanged in the rain on the way out of the Amsterdam Café where they stopped for some hot chocolate and cinnamon cheesecake.

The kiss that will change everything.

For Elliott will never have been happier than with this girl, funny, down to earth and bohemian, who dreamed of remaking the world as she ate her pizza.

And Ilena will never have felt more beautiful than through the gaze of this mysterious and appealing boy that fate had thrown in her path in such a strange way.

In the afternoons, they spend hours talking in the huge park spread out amid the skyscrapers. That's where they get to know each other.

She tells him about her studies in biology and her ambition to become a veterinarian. He, too, is interested in math and science. She wants to know why he left school in spite of his good grades. It's true he's brilliant, but he claims it has nothing to do with him. It's just that things are easy when you have an IQ of 166.

When Ilena asks about his future plans and he doesn't know how to answer, she intuitively understands his lack of self-confidence and the acute sensitivity which often makes him retreat into himself.

Then one day, almost in passing, she asks the question: 'Why don't you become a doctor?' First he pretends he didn't hear, and then when she insists, he shrugs.

But the question sits there, in the back of his mind, until the amazing evening in the hospital when he's told that the young man he saved has come out of his coma and wants to see him.

Elliott walks into the room and approaches the bed.

The man he saved is French. Despite the ten days he's been in a coma, his eyes are bright, he has a friendly face, and a gently ironic smile.

'So, you're my savior!' he jokes, with a slight accent.

'I guess so,' Elliott answers.

They've barely exchanged a sentence and there's already a current of friendship flowing between them.

'Now you'll have me on your back all the time,' the Frenchman informs him.

'Really?'

'Until I do the same for you, and I have the opportunity to save *your* life . . .'

Elliott smiles. The vitality emanating from the other man has immediately charmed him. Sensing in him both his opposite and his perfect complement, he holds out his hand and introduces himself: 'I'm Elliott Cooper.'

'I'm Matt Delluca.'

Later, when he thinks of this period, Elliott will realize how it changed his life forever.

One day, in order to follow a girl in the subway, he got into one car rather than another.

That choice saved his life and allowed him to find . . .

. . . a love,
a friend,
and a vocation.
That year, in the space of a few days, he had become a man.

San Francisco 2006
Elliott is 60

Still bathed in the glow of his memories, Elliott parked at the top of Telegraph Hill and headed down Filbert's Steps, walking past the flower beds to the elegant art deco bachelor pad. He opened the gate into the garden, knocked on the shutter, and shouted through the half-open window: 'Matt, it's me! I'll wait for you out here.'

Matt quickly opened the door and stared at him wide-eyed. 'Elliott?'

'Let's get going, we have to stop at Chez Francis for sandwiches. If we're too late, the gourmet bread will be gone, and you'll complain there's nothing good to eat.'

'What are you doing here?'

'Aren't we supposed to go out in the boat today?'

'What boat?'

'The Pope's boat!'

'What the hell are you talking about?'

'Let's see, you left a message on my answering machine last night to suggest we go . . .'

Matt interrupted him: 'Stop it, Elliott! I didn't leave any message, for the simple reason that we haven't spoken to each other for thirty years!'

This time it was Elliott's turn to stare at his friend open-mouthed.

He looked into Matt's eyes and could see that he wasn't joking.

'Listen,' Matt went on, 'I don't know what you're up to, but I don't have any time to waste today. So, you'll forgive me, but . . .'

'Wait a minute, Matt! You're my friend! We talk on the phone every day, and we see each other several times a week!'

Matt stared into the distance, as though trying to recall an old memory.

'We were friends, that's true, but it was a long time ago . . .'

He was about to close the door, when Elliott pleaded with him: 'What happened? Did we have a fight?'

'Are you going nuts? Don't pretend you've forgotten everything!'

'Remind me what happened.'

Matt hesitated, then said, 'It was thirty years ago. Everything was fine until the day you started to go off the rails.'

'What do you mean?'

'You started to tell strange stories about a guy who had figured out how to travel through time. He was supposed to be you, except older . . .' Anyhow, you weren't in your right mind. I did what I could to help you until the day you went too far.'

'When was that, Matt? When was that exactly?'

'Actually it was on Christmas Day,' Matt suddenly re-called, troubled by the coincidence. 'I remember because it was the same day you broke up with Ilena . . .'

Thirty years to the day . . .

'For a long time, I tried everything to patch things up,

Elliott, but you built a wall between us. And then, after what happened to Ilena, things wouldn't have been the same.'

'What happened to Ilena?'

A veil of sorrow seemed to drop over Matt's face, and he said in a voice that brooked no reply, 'Go away, Elliott!' Then he slammed the door.

Stunned, Elliott slowly made his way back to the car. He was having trouble taking this in. Obviously the Elliott of 1976 had quarreled with Matt, and now he was paying for it.

But how could he explain all his memories of the intervening years? Everything that they'd gone through together wasn't just a figment of his imagination, was it?

Elliott leaned against his car and held his head in his hands.

Suppose there are several streams of time.

He had heard about the hypothesis of 'parallel universes' stirring up controversy in scientific circles. Some physicists said that everything that *can* happen *will* happen in one particular universe. If I toss a coin into the air, there is one universe where it will come down heads and another tails. If I play the lottery, I win millions in one universe and lose in another. So the universe we know is only one among an infinite number of others. There is a universe in which September 11 never happened, where George Bush is not president, one where the Berlin Wall is still standing.

A universe where he fought with Matt thirty years ago and another where they're still friends . . .

The problem was that going back and forth between past

and future, he'd landed in a time stream where events didn't correspond to his memories of them!

So now, unfortunately, he had no choice but to deal with that.

He got into the driver's seat and headed to the hospital.

And there was one thing that was even more important: he had to find out what had happened to Ilena.

EIGHTEEN

*What we call a reason for living is at the
same time an excellent reason for dying.*
Albert Camus

San Francisco
December 25, 1976; 4:48 P.M.
Ilena is 30

High above San Francisco, in the midst of the wind and fog, a
bird with silver wings pierces the clouds and descends toward
the city. Swift as an arrow, it flies over Alcatraz and Treasure
Island and lands on one of the two towers of the Golden Gate
Bridge. Elegant despite its huge size, the famous bridge spans a
mile and a half of the bay to Sausalito. Its enormous towers,
firmly anchored in the Pacific, are unaffected by the icy
currents and the thick fog clinging to their shining metal
surface like ivy.

Perched above the waves, the bird lowers its head to
contemplate the lives of men seething restlessly two hundred
yards below.

On the bridge, six lanes of traffic inch along in an intricate ballet. The noise of horns and vibrating bridge plates is deafening.

Suddenly, on the pedestrian walk, a delicate woman appears, moving like an acrobat on a wire.

Ready to fall.

Ilena couldn't possibly explain why she's there. She had just felt unable to get on the plane back to Florida, so she asked the taxi driver to turn around and take her back to town. Then, since she had to go *somewhere*, she let herself wander, and ended up on the bridge.

She is at the edge of the abyss, trapped in a state of unbearable suffering that she didn't even know was possible. Everyone thinks she is strong, stable, well adjusted, but this image is deceptive. The truth is that she's vulnerable, defenceless, at the mercy of a single sentence – '*I don't love you any more, Ilena*' – which, in less time than it took to say it, had made her lose her bearings, her strength, and her will to live.

She approaches the safety railing to look at the ocean. The view is intoxicating, dizzying. The wind is blowing in gusts, the waves are crashing, giving off spray that makes it look as though the ocean is boiling. Elliott was her entire life. What will become of her without him?

Ilena feels weak, lost. The sorrow in which she is drowning is too powerful, impossible to contain. Suddenly, continuing to live makes her more afraid than dying. She understands now why her steps have led her here. And she leaps into the void.

A fall from the Golden Gate Bridge takes four seconds.

Four seconds for a final journey, four seconds of a no man's land between two worlds.

Four seconds when you are neither entirely alive nor quite yet dead.

Four seconds hanging in the void.

An act of freedom or madness?

Of courage or weakness?

Four seconds at the end of which you hit the water at a speed of one hundred miles an hour.

Four seconds at the end of which you die.

San Francisco
December 25, 1976; 5:31 P.M.
Elliott is 30

Night falls quickly in winter

The afternoon is already nothing but a memory. Lights go on one after the other throughout the city, while a crescent moon makes a timid appearance through a break in the clouds.

With his car windows open, Elliott drives down the Embarcadero, following the shoreline. After what he has been through today, he doesn't have the courage to spend the night alone, cloistered in his glass house. He's afraid he's going mad, afraid of what he might do . . .

So he drives like the wind, allowing himself to be guided by the lights through the business district where the Transamerica Pyramid, the new skyscraper shaped like an arrow, glows with its thousand lights. He distractedly thinks of Ilena, who must be on her plane. How will she react to the breakup? He tries to persuade himself that things won't be so hard for her, that she'll easily find a man who will love her better than he has, but at the same time, he finds this possibility unbearable.

He turns and turns again and finds himself in the hospital

parking lot. He has lost love, he has lost friendship. All he has left is work. Of course, he couldn't possibly operate today or even supervise patient care – he is still suffering from the effects of drugs and alcohol – but he needs to be back in a familiar environment, and this is the only one he knows.

He parks in his usual spot and gets out into the darkness at the very moment that an ambulance tears into the parking lot with its sirens blaring and stops at the emergency entrance. Elliott automatically goes over to help the attendants: Martinez and Pike from Unit 21 whom he's worked with before. He notices the pale faces of the two men, affected by the seriousness of the patient's injuries.

'What do we have, Martinez?'

The attendant thinks Elliott is on call and answers: 'Young woman of thirty, in a coma, multiple traumas. She jumped off the Golden Gate Bridge a half hour ago . . .'

'She survived?'

'Not for long, if you ask me . . .'

The young woman has already been intubated. They've set up venous drips and put on a cervical collar that covers part of her face.

Elliott helps the two men take her off the stretcher.

Then he leans closer to the injured woman.

And he recognizes her.

San Francisco 2006
Elliott is 60

Still troubled by his quarrel with Matt, Elliott was driving without concentrating on the road, not knowing where to go.

What had his friend meant when he'd said, '*after what happened to Ilena*'? Was he simply referring to their breakup or to something more serious? Elliott tried to get his thoughts in order. During his last voyage to the past, on the morning of December 25, 1976, he and his double had managed to avert the accident with the whale which should have cost the young woman her life. Ilena was therefore alive.

Then why had Matt had that *despairing* tone in his voice? He braked suddenly and parked the car next to a fire hydrant outside Washington Park. He walked around North Beach until he found a cybercafé where he ordered a cappuccino so he could sit in front of one of the screens.

With a few mouse clicks he went to an online telephone directory and typed 'Ilena Cruz' in the appropriate box.

The next line started to blink, asking for the city. He typed 'San Francisco' and clicked the search button.

No result.

He broadened the search to all of California, and then to other states.

No result.

The Ilena of 2006 probably had an unlisted number. Or she didn't live on the west coast. Or she'd changed her name . . .

Not giving up, Elliott typed 'Ilena Cruz' into Google. Only one result . . . He clicked on the link. It was a university site devoted to the practice of veterinary medicine for marine mammals. The site recalled that in the 1970s, Ilena had been one of the pioneers in procedures that had now become routine. The article gave as an example the first anesthesia administered to a manatee, carried out by the young woman in 1973. Next to her name, a number referred to a footnote containing her biography. Elliott's hand trembled as he clicked on the link and discovered with horror the dates of Ilena's birth and death: 1947–1976.

There was no further explanation.

His eyes glued to the screen, he tried to understand. If Ilena was still alive on December 25, 1976, and the site nevertheless indicated that she'd died that same year, had her death occurred *in the last six days of 1976?* When? How? Why?

He left the cybercafé and walked quickly back to his car.

I have to consult the newspapers for those days.

That's what he had to do first. He pulled out without signalling and almost got hit by a Lexus coming in the opposite direction. After a dangerous U-turn, he headed for the offices of the *San Francisco Chronicle*, right near City Hall.

For twenty minutes he searched for a parking space, but as he should have known, at this time of day, his chances ranged from slim to none. He gave up and double parked, assuming his car wouldn't be there when he got back. Out of breath, he went into the glass building housing the newspaper offices and explained that he wanted to consult the archives for 1976. The young woman at the reception desk handed him a form to fill out and explained that it would be several days before his request could be fulfilled.

'Several days!' Elliott protested.

She gave the usual excuses: 'national holiday', 'short staff', 'microfilm', 'year not yet digitized . . .'

He took out a hundred-dollar bill; she looked offended; he added two more; she said: 'I'll see what I can do.'

Fifteen minutes later he was sitting in front of a viewer running through the pages of the *San Francisco Chronicle* for the last days of 1976. He found nothing on the front pages, so he went through the news in brief, and in the December 26 edition he came across a little item that he read several times before fully grasping its meaning.

New Suicide Attempt on Golden Gate

Yesterday afternoon a young woman jumped off the Golden Gate Bridge at security point number 69. Her name is Ilena Cruz, a veterinarian from Florida. According to some witnesses, she hit the surface of the water feet first.

Fished out by a police launch and suffering from numerous fractures and internal injuries, she has been taken to Lenox Hospital, where doctors describe her condition as 'critical'.

A knot had formed in Elliott's stomach and he remained motionless in his chair for several minutes, devastated by the dirty trick fate had played on him. Then he consulted the next day's paper, knowing in advance what he would find there.

No Miracle for Golden Gate Suicide

There was no miracle at Lenox Hospital. Ilena Cruz, the young woman who jumped off the Golden Gate Bridge the day before yesterday, died during the night as a result of severe internal lesions (see yesterday's edition).

This new death has revived the debate about the need to install a safety barrier on the bridge, a measure that has consistently been rejected by the Golden Gate Council.

He left the building, feeling utterly destroyed. His car had been double parked for an hour without getting a ticket. Cold comfort. He got behind the wheel and headed for Lenox Hospital.

He had one last thing to verify.

San Francisco
December 25, 1976; 8:23 P.M.
Elliott is 30

Overwhelmed with anxiety, Elliott was waiting for Ilena to come out of the operating room. Since he wasn't on duty, they hadn't wanted him to operate. And since the effects of the heroin were lingering, he hadn't insisted.

The diagnosis was catastrophic: fractures in both legs and both feet, dislocated hip and shoulder, trauma to the thoracic cavity . . . The shock had been so violent that it had also shattered her pelvis, caused damage to the kidneys and spleen, and vaginal bleeding indicated a ruptured intestine or urinary tract.

He couldn't keep still, pacing up and down before returning to the glass doors separating him from the operating room. He had already seen enough to keep him from comforting himself with illusions.

He himself often operated in cases of multiple trauma, and you had to be realistic: at this stage, the likelihood of death was greater than that of survival. Not to mention the fact that an accident like this often caused injuries to the spinal column and the spinal cord. The kind of injuries that frequently leave a patient paraplegic or hemiplegic . . .

For an instant, the image of a paralyzed Ilena pulling herself around in a wheelchair went through his mind, superimposed on a memory of the young woman who only yesterday was swimming and diving with the dolphins.

This was all his fault! He and his double had thought they were saving Ilena, but they'd only succeeded in delaying the outcome for a few hours. Instead of being drowned by a whale, she had committed suicide by jumping off a bridge. What a triumph!

They had tried to defy fate, but fate was stronger.

San Francisco
December 25, 2006; 10:59 P.M.
Elliott is 60

Torrential rain was falling on Lenox Hospital.

In the third sub-basement of the building, in the light from a sputtering neon bulb, Elliott was searching through thirty-year-old records, looking for Ilena's medical file.

The room was lined with metal shelves sagging under the weight of boxes. In the distant past, all of these documents must have been classified in a precise order, but now the whole room was nothing but a colossal shambles. Months, years, departments: everything was mixed up, confused, scattered.

As he frantically opened every box and every file, Elliott tried to make sense of what he'd gone through in the last three months. At first, he had naïvely believed that he could change fate, and fate had reminded him of its power. He had to accept the evidence: free will, the ability to influence your own destiny, that was all an illusion. The truth is that our lives are pre-programmed and it's futile to fight against it. Some

217

events are irrefutable, and the hour of our death is one of them. The future is not created step by step. In essence, the road is already laid out, and there is nothing to be done but to follow it. Everything hangs together – past, present, future – and it all answers to the dread name of destiny.

But if everything is already written, who is holding the pen? A superior power? A god? And leading us where?

Knowing very well that he would never have an answer to that question, Elliott concentrated on his search, and after a full hour he finally laid his hands on what he was looking for.

Ilena's admission file had not disappeared, but the ravages of time had made the contents practically illegible. The handwritten notes were faded, and dampness had stuck some pages together. Elliott feverishly brought the sheets of paper close to the neon tube and managed to decipher the essential information in the document.

Ilena's injuries were even more horrible than he'd imagined, but contrary to what he'd read in the paper, she hadn't died from multiple lesions, but from the effects of an emergency operation to remove a cerebral hematoma.

He looked at the name of the doctor who had operated on her: Dr Mitchell.

He remembered him: Roger Mitchell was a competent surgeon, but . . .

Why didn't I operate myself?

He was also surprised by the absence of an MRI report. Looking through the notes, he managed to reconstruct what must have happened. Around four in the morning, a nurse had reported irregularity in Ilena's pupils, indicating the presence of a hematoma. There had been an emergency operation, but it had not succeeded.

The hematoma was deep and located in a difficult position, complicated by a wound in the sinus canal that could not have been predicted without an MRI. A very delicate operation on a patient with respiratory distress and low blood pressure.

Even the best surgeon wouldn't have saved her. Except perhaps by anticipating what needed to be done . . .

A final bit of information drew his attention: the time of death.

4:26 A.M.

He couldn't help looking at his watch.

It was not yet midnight.

San Francisco
December 26, 1976; 12:23 A.M.
Elliott is 30

'I've removed the spleen and restitched part of the intestine,' Dr Roger Mitchell explained to his young colleague.

For the first time, Elliott, filled with anguish, found himself on the other side: with the patients and their families.

'How are the kidneys?' he asked.

'They may be all right. But I'm worried about the respiratory system: several connected ribs are fractured in at least two places.'

Elliott knew what that meant. One segment of the thoracic cavity was detached from the thorax, increasing the risks of pneumothorax, hemothorax, and respiratory distress.

'Lesions of the spinal column?'

'Too soon to tell. Maybe at the dorsal vertebra . . . As you know, at that level it's all or nothing: it may be benign . . .'

'. . . and it may lead to permanent paraplegia,' concluded Elliott.

Mitchell pursed his lips.

'We have to wait. For now, we can't do much.'

'You're not giving her an MRI?'

'Not tonight, there's a problem with the software: the program has been constantly crashing ever since this morning.'

'God damn it to hell!' Elliott yelled, banging his fist against the door.

'Calm down. We have her under close supervision. A nurse will look in every fifteen minutes. And in any case . . .'

He was about to say something, but thought better of it.

'In any case?' asked Elliott, forcing him to finish his sentence.

'The only thing we can do at this stage is to pray. Pray we don't have to open her up too soon, because in the condition she's in she won't hold up.'

San Francisco
December 26, 2006; 1:33 A.M.
Elliott is 60

Elliott went upstairs, clutching Ilena's old medical file to his chest. Even if he'd stopped operating two months ago, he was still on the hospital staff and had the right to keep his office. The lights came on automatically as soon as he opened the door. He stood motionless in front of the window, contemplating the torrents of rain still falling on the city.

Then he paced up and down the room, his mind tormented, wondering if he could still do something. He went through

Ilena's medical file again, and put it on his work table next to a stylized marble chess set with a very spare design. Pensively, he picked up two pieces: a bishop in a conical shape and a cylindrical rook.

Cone and cylinder . . .

That reminded him of a fable he'd read in school.

He laid the cone on its side on the table and flicked it with his finger: the solid form rotated around itself. He did the same thing to the cylinder: it rolled over the table and broke on the floor.

The two pieces had received the same force, but had followed different trajectories. The moral of the story: people react differently to the same blow of fate. *Even if I can't escape my destiny, I'm still master of the way I face it.*

Encouraged by this idea, Elliott put his hand in his pocket and grasped the bottle of pills.

He had lived through a trying day and it was far from over. But now he felt surprisingly calm.

Because a man is never as strong as when he is fighting his last battle.

NINETEEN

Seventh and Eighth Encounters

If youth knew . . .
If old age could . . .

San Francisco
December 26, 1976; 2:01 a.m.
Elliott is 30

The hospital was dozing, lulled by the sound of the rain.

Ilena was lying with her eyes closed in a small darkened room. She was surrounded by a tangle of drips and she had a breathing tube in her mouth.

Elliott was sitting next to her. He cautiously pulled the sheet higher as though he was afraid she would get cold. Overcome, he moved his trembling hand toward the young woman's face. As their skin touched, he felt razor blades slashing through his heart.

Beneath the bruised features and the blue lips, he felt a life struggling to keep its flame alive.

A life hanging by a single thread that was ready to break at any moment.

*   *   *

The door to the room opened quietly. Elliott turned around, expecting to see the floor nurse.

But it wasn't her.

'She has to be operated on!' said his double in a tone that would not allow contradiction.

Elliott jumped to his feet.

'Operated on for what?'

'A subdural hematoma in the brain.'

Panic-stricken, the young doctor lifted Ilena's eyelids, but he saw no anomaly in the pupils indicating a hematoma.

'Where'd you get that from?'

'From an autopsy report. If you'd done a scan you would know it too.'

'Easy,' Elliott defended himself, 'it's only 1976. Machines break down, software crashes half the time, don't you remember?'

His double didn't bother answering; all his attention was on deciphering the EKG.

'Tell them to get an operating room ready, quickly!' he said, pointing to the phone on the wall.

'Wait – she's got several chest lesions: if we open her up right away, she might die.'

'Yes, and if we don't open her up, what's now a risk will become a certainty.'

Elliott considered this before making another objection: 'Mitchell will never operate on Ilena on a hunch.'

The old man shrugged his shoulders. 'If you think I'm going to let Mitchell operate . . .'

'Who, then?'

'Me.'

Elliott agreed, including himself in the 'me', but there was a further problem: 'The two of us alone can't do the operation. We need at least an anesthetist and a nurse.'

'Who's the anesthetist on call?'

'Samantha Ryan, I think.'

The old doctor nodded and looked at the clock on the wall.

'I'll see you in the operating room in ten minutes!' he said, as he left the room. 'Prepare Ilena for the operation and I'll take care of Ryan.'

The sixty-year-old Elliott rushed into the almost empty lobby, which smelled strongly of ether. To make himself inconspicuous, he'd replaced his jacket with a white coat. He knew the hospital like the back of his hand and had no trouble finding the rec room where Samantha Ryan was resting.

'Hi, Sam,' he said as he turned on the light.

Being used to having her sleep interrupted when she was on call at night, the young woman quickly got up and covered her eyes with her hand to protect them from the glare. Although the face in front of her looked familiar, she couldn't seem to remember his name.

Elliott handed her a cup of coffee, which she took as she brushed the hair out of her eyes.

She was an unusual woman: thirty, of Irish descent, gay, and a practicing Catholic. She had been working at the hospital for two years after severing ties with her family in New York, where her father and brothers were pillars of the NYPD.

In the years to come she and Elliott would become good friends, but at this point in time Samantha was solitary, introverted, and ill at ease with herself. She seemed to have no friends in the hospital, and her colleagues kept their distance.

'I need you for an operation, Sam.'

'Right away?'

'Right away. A subdural hematoma to be drained in a patient suffering from respiratory distress.'

'The suicide victim?' she said, and took a gulp of coffee.

'Exactly.'

'She's not gonna make it,' she said calmly.

'Only the future can tell,' Elliott replied.

She unwrapped a few Oreo cookies from some tin foil.

'Who's operating?' she asked, and dipped a cookie in her coffee.

'I am.'

'And who are you, by the way?'

'Someone who knows you.'

She exchanged glances with the doctor, and for a minute felt unsettled – she had the fleeting impression that this man could read her like a book.

'We have to move quickly,' said Elliott.

Samantha shook her head. 'Mitchell's the chief resident. I can't work on an unauthorized operation, I'll get fired.'

'There are risks,' Elliott agreed. 'But you will help me . . .'

'I don't owe you anything,' she said with a shrug.

'Not me, but you owe Sarah Leeves something . . .'

He let the sentence hang, and she looked at him in panic. Sarah Leeves was a two-bit hooker who'd come into the hospital two years earlier having been beaten and stabbed. She'd been given emergency treatment, but she hadn't survived.

'You were starting out here and you were on call,' said

Elliott. 'You're a good anesthetist, Sam, one of the best, but that night you really screwed up . . .'

Samantha closed her eyes and for the thousandth time relived the events in her mind: a wrong move, one drug confused with another, an elementary mistake, and the poor woman never woke up.

'You were clever enough to cover your tracks,' said Elliott, 'and I have to admit that nobody was especially interested in the death of a hooker.'

Samantha's eyes were still closed. She'd made the mistake because she hadn't been on her toes. That night, her mind kept wandering, back to New York and a father who called her 'slut, tramp, little whore,' and her mother repeating the word 'shame' over and over, and her brothers telling her to leave town.

When she opened her eyes, she looked at Elliott in terror.

'How do you know all that?'

'Because you told me about it.'

Samantha shook her head. She'd never told anyone about the incident, not even in confession. On the other hand, she'd grown more deeply religious in the last two years and prayed constantly as if to expiate her sin. More than anything, she wished she could turn the clock back, make it so that horrible day had never happened. She had constantly prayed that heaven would send her the possibility of redemption.

'Save a life to make up for a death . . .' said Elliott, figuring out what she was thinking.

After a few seconds' hesitation, Samantha buttoned her coat and said simply: 'I'm on my way.'

Elliott was about to come after her when he felt his hands start to tremble.

Already?

He took refuge in the bathroom, which was fortunately deserted at that time of night. He was panic-stricken as he felt himself disappearing. He bent over the sink to throw water on his face. Unlike Samantha, he didn't believe in God, but this didn't stop him from praying.

Let me operate on her! Let me stay a little longer!

But the God in whom he didn't believe didn't give a damn about his pleas, and Elliott had no choice but to let himself be sucked into the labyrinth of time.

He woke up in 2006, drained, on his office chair. In panic he looked at the digital clock on the shelf. 2:23.

He still had a little time, provided he returned immediately to the past. He hurriedly swallowed another pill, but nothing happened. This was to be expected: the substance only worked when he was asleep. But he was too anxious to fall asleep on command. So he hurried into the corridor and called for the elevator to go down to the hospital pharmacy. He dug up a vial of a narcotic used to prepare patients for anesthesia; rushed back up to his office to get a disposable syringe out of his bag. He prepared a small dose of the medicine and injected it into a vein. The hypnotic didn't take long to kick in, and Elliott was soon in the land of dreams and fantasies.

At the same moment, in 1976, thirty-year-old Elliott was finishing the preparations for Ilena's operation. He'd shaved her head and had just disconnected the breathing tube. He set up an inflatable balloon so she could breathe on the way there, and wheeled her to the operating room as discreetly as possible.

Samantha Ryan and a nurse were waiting for him. There was, on the other hand, no sign of his double, then he heard someone rapping on the window. The old doctor signaled that he should come into scrub up and Elliott complied without a word. Finally together, the two surgeons rolled up their sleeves above their elbows and prepared in silence, methodically scrubbing their hands with antiseptic, then each putting on a gown, mask, rubber gloves, and a surgical cap.

Then they both enter the operating room.

Elliott stands back, letting his double manage the affair. The older man is at ease, very calm, coordinating every gesture involved in placing Ilena on the operating table. He keeps her head steady, avoiding any flexion or rotation. He knows that she has vertebral lesions and does not want to aggravate them by any sudden movement.

Finally, the operation begins. The older doctor has a strange feeling: he hasn't operated for two months and he thought he'd never hold a scalpel again. His actions are precise. Over time he has learned to handle the pressure of these critical moments. He knows exactly where he has to cut, his hands don't shake, everything is going well until . . .

'Who gave you permission to operate?'

Mitchell has just come into the room and he is livid with anger. He looks one after the other at Samantha, Elliott, and his double.

'Who is he?' he asks, indicating the old surgeon, who calmly points out, 'You're not sterile, Doctor Mitchell, and you just failed to diagnose a hematoma.'

Angered, Mitchell puts a mask to his face and promises: 'You won't get away with this!'

'Please disinfect yourself,' Elliott repeats, forcing the furious doctor to leave.

The operation continues surprisingly calmly. Outside, the storm is raging, and rain can be heard lashing at the windows and flowing through the drains. Elliott at thirty looks at his senior with a mixture of admiration and mistrust. Elliott at sixty remains focused on his task. Even though everything is going well, it is obvious that the depth of the hematoma, its size, and Ilena's respiratory problems make the prognosis very uncertain. He knows that even in the best case, her comatose state will cause lack of blood to the brain with severe after effects.

What are the chances of her coming through this?

Medically, one in twenty that she'll survive.

And maybe one in a thousand that she won't suffer serious consequences.

But in the course of his career he's learned to consider these figures with skepticism. He's known patients to whom doctors had given three months who'd lived for ten years. Just as he's seen routine operations end in tragedy.

This is what he's thinking when a stream of blood splashes his face. This is what he's been fearing: a wound in the sinus compressed by the hematoma. It's bleeding profusely, but he's warned the others, and the blood is carefully drained. He makes an effort to freeze his feelings, focusing entirely on the area of the operation, not even thinking that it's Ilena he's operating on. Because if he starts to visualize her face he knows that his hand will start shaking and his vision might become blurred.

The operation continues calmly until Mitchell re-enters the room with a duty manager. They take note of the infraction of the rules, but do not attempt to interrupt the operation, which is in any event coming to an end. As he anticipates the start of his trembling, Elliott at sixty turns to his younger self and suggests: 'I'll let you close up.'

He takes off his gown and his cap, removes his blood-stained gloves, and looks at his hands: they have withstood the shock without shaking for longer than he'd hoped.

'Thank you,' he whispers, not really knowing to whom he's offering his gratitude.

This was his last operation. The most important one of his entire life.

At the very moment that he disappears before the stunned gaze of the others, he tells himself that he has done enough.

Now, he is no longer afraid to die.

TWENTY

Last Encounter

At twenty, you dance in the center of the world.
At thirty, you wander inside the circle.
At fifty, you walk on the circumference, and you avoid
looking both outside and inside.
Later on, it makes no difference, it's the privilege of
children and the old to be invisible.

Christian Bobin

San Francisco 2006
Elliott is 60

When Elliott opened his eyes he was lying on the cold tile of his office floor, his face in a little puddle of blood. He struggled to his feet and brought his hand to his nose, which was flowing like a fountain. His blood vessels had once more paid the price of his journey in time and it took several cotton swabs to stop the bleeding.

As day broke, one question still tormented him: had he managed to save Ilena?

He sat in front of his computer to consult the online phone

directory. The day before he had gotten no results when looking for Ilena Cruz. Elliott tried again, extending his search throughout the state of California. This time it came up with something: an address in Weaverville, a little town in the northern part of the state.

A wild goose chase? Too soon to rejoice?

There was only one way to find out.

He left his office, went down to the lobby, made a brief stop at the coffee machine, and went out into the parking lot to find his car. If he drove fast he could get to Weaverville in less than six hours. Like him, his old VW was worn out, but he hoped it would come through. Just for a little while longer . . .

It was still early morning when he got on the road. The sun had not yet risen, but the previous day's heavy rain seemed to have painted the sky a metallic blue.

He left San Francisco on Route 101 and quickly covered the first two hundred miles.

A little past Leggett, he left the highway to follow the scenic route that wound its way as far as Ferndale, following the coast around Cape Mendocino. The road clung to the edge of the land, the sea, overlooking steep cliffs that plunged into the swells of the Pacific. Elliott followed it to Arcata, then picked up Route 299, the only passable road over the mountains. The area looked as wild as ever, with huge sequoia trunks and vast forest preserves of silver firs.

He had been driving for more than five hours when he got to Weaverville, a tiny town lost in the mountains. He parked the VW on the main street and went into the town drugstore to ask for the address of Ilena Cruz. He was directed to a forest road on the way out of town, and decided to go on foot. Twenty minutes later he came to a little wooden house built on a spot just down from the road. The sound of a waterfall could be heard nearby. Elliott stopped in his tracks and hid behind a sequoia that had survived the clearcutting a hundred years earlier. Using both hands to protect his eyes from the glare, he squinted and stared.

A woman was sitting under the cottage's awning, facing the snow-capped mountains.

That afternoon, Elliott saw her only from behind, but he didn't doubt for a second that it was her.

They had been separated for thirty years. Now there were only thirty yards between them.

For an instant he made himself believe that he would cross that space, that he would tell her everything, that he would hold her in his arms, and would once again be able to smell the aroma of her hair.

But it was too late. His last journey in time had considerably weakened him. Now more than ever he knew that his life was behind him and that he had lost his battle against the disease sapping his strength.

So he sat against the trunk of the thousand-year-old tree and was content just to look at her.

The air was warm, and in this solitary and peaceful place he finally felt free of the weight of time and sorrow.

For the first time in his life, he was at peace.

San Francisco 1976
9 A.M.
Elliott is 30

Two days had passed since Ilena's operation.

The young woman had come out of her coma a short time ago, but her prognosis was still very uncertain.

The circumstances surrounding the operation were the talk of the hospital; people were either skeptical or incredulous. For a few hours hospital management had debated what course of conduct to follow. Should they report the incident to the police and risk compromising the prestige of Lenox Hospital? The hospital director and the chief of surgery were too attached to their reputations to sign a report about a 'man from nowhere' who 'disappeared in the middle of the operating room'. They merely imposed a penalty of two months' suspension for Elliott and Samantha.

The young doctor had just learned of his suspension and was about to leave the hospital when a nurse called to him. 'It's for you, doctor!' She held out the wall phone receiver.

'Hello.'

'I'm across the street,' his double informed him. 'Come and join me.'

'Across the street?'

'At Harry's place. Should I order something for you?'

Not bothering to answer, Elliott hung up and crossed the road.

You could hardly see your hand in front of your face. Patches of fog were blowing in the wind, enveloping lampposts and cars in their shifting shapes. Harry's Diner was a real old-fashioned steel dining-car across the street from the emergency room entrance. Entering it was like going back into the fifties. Elliott went in and saw a number of his medical colleagues having a quick breakfast before going on duty.

At one end of the smoke-filled room, he saw his double sitting at a table with a mug of coffee.

'Well?' asked Elliott, sitting down in the booth.

'She made it!'

'Ilena is alive, in the future?'

The old doctor nodded.

Elliott couldn't believe it for a moment. Then he asked: 'After effects?'

But his double evaded the question. 'Listen, she's alive. We saved her . . .'

Elliott decided to hang on to this assertion and for a few minutes the two men sat facing each other in silence, united in contemplation.

Both had drawn features and circles under their eyes. Both were exhausted from lack of sleep and the accumulated nervous tension of the last few days. They had thrown all their strength into a strange battle against fate and they'd apparently emerged victorious.

Elliott was the first to break: tears of exhaustion streamed down his face, and he didn't know himself whether they were making him feel better or worse!

He rubbed his eyes and looked out the window. Outside, the fog was spreading its white-gray waves, obliterating the sidewalks and the fire hydrants.

'It'll be all right . . .'

'No, it will not be all right! I've lost everybody I loved: Matt! Ilena! And all because of you!'

'Maybe, but that's the way it is: you have to keep your promises, the way I've kept mine . . .'

'Easy for you to say!'

'We've already talked about that! Listen, I don't know by what miracle we were able to save Ilena, so don't go spoiling everything. Lead your life the way you promised to, because if there's one thing I'm sure of, it's that miracles never happen twice.'

'It will be too hard to bear . . .'

'The next few years will be difficult,' the old doctor admitted. 'Afterward, everything will be better. You are able to bear it, but you'll have to do it alone.'

Elliott looked at him and frowned. His double explained, 'This is the last time we'll see each other.'

Elliott shrugged. 'You say that every time.'

'This time it's true. I won't be able to come back, even if I want to.'

In a few words, he told the story of the pills: the circumstances in which he'd received them, the unexpected effect they'd had on him, the way they'd allowed him to travel through time . . .

Before he had finished his story, his double had stood up to leave the restaurant. Elliott was dying to ask him hundreds of questions, but he understood that he would learn nothing further, that this was indeed the last time they would meet.

While the old man gathered himself together, the young surgeon felt overcome by an emotion he had not foreseen. Two nights earlier, during the operation on Ilena, his older self had astonished him with his skill and his ability to make the right decisions. Elliott now regretted not having had more time to get to know him.

The old doctor took the time to button his coat. He felt himself leaving, but from experience he knew that he still had one or two minutes.

'I'd just as soon not disappear in the middle of the diner.'

'You're right, it might make trouble for me.'

236

At the moment of his departure, the sixty-year-old Elliott simply put his hand on the thirty-year-old Elliott's shoulder before walking away.

He'd almost reached the door when he turned around one last time to nod to his double. They looked at each other, and in the eyes of his younger self, he saw what he had already seen in some of his patients: the sorrow of those who had never gotten over the pain of their childhood.

Instead of leaving the restaurant, he retraced his steps. He still had one more thing to say to his double: a sentence that he himself had waited to hear for years, but that no one had ever taken the trouble to say to him.

A very simple sentence, but one that he'd taken a lifetime to understand. 'It wasn't your fault . . .'

At first the young surgeon didn't understand what his double was talking about. The old man repeated: 'It wasn't your fault . . .'

'What?'

'Mom's suicide, the beatings Dad gave you . . .'

The Elliott of sixty left his sentence hanging when he realized that his voice was choked up. He needed to take a deep breath before he could repeat, like a litany: 'It wasn't your fault.'

'I know,' Elliott lied, troubled by this unexpected conversation.

'No, you don't know yet,' his older self calmly asserted. 'You don't know yet . . .'

A kind of communion followed between the two men, a moment of understanding that lasted just the blink of an eye, and then the old man was shaken by the trembling that announced his return to the future.

'Goodbye!' he said as he walked quickly away. 'It's up to you now!'

Elliott had sat down again. Through the window he watched his double disappear into the fog.

He would never see him again.

TWENTY-ONE

Living Without You

> *Life will have gone by like a*
> *great sad castle buggered by the winds.*
>
> Louis Aragon

1977
Elliott is 31

A summer night in San Francisco.

Staring into space, Elliott is smoking a cigarette on the hospital roof. The city is spread out at his feet, but he pays no attention to it. He hasn't seen Ilena since she was transferred to Miami, and it's killing him.

A gust of wind stirs up a little dust.

The young surgeon looks at his watch and stubs out his cigarette. He has an operation in five minutes, the sixth of the day.

Living like a ghost, getting drunk on work, taking on any number of shifts . . .

To keep from letting himself die.

*   *   *

Ilena opens her eyes as the sun is rising over Miami.

She's been lying in a hospital bed for six months, her body devastated, her legs shattered. She's already gone through four operations and it's not over yet.

Mentally, it's even worse. There's nothing but chaos, screaming animals, and slamming doors.

She speaks little, she has refused all visitors: Matt, her colleagues from work . . .

She feels vulnerable, helpless.

How can she pull herself out of this sorrow and shame?

Matt is on the highway to Seattle, driving fast with the roof down. His brutal split with Elliott has ripped his life apart. He, too, has lost his bearings and everything he believed in. He feels lonely and miserable, so he thinks of Tiffany, the amazing girl he was stupid enough to let slip through his fingers. Now he's ready to try anything to find her. Every weekend for months, he's been scouring different parts of the country. All he has to go on is a first name and a telephone number that's long been out of service.

Why her? He doesn't even ask himself the question. On the other hand, he's certain of one thing: he has to find this woman, because he senses that she could be the fixed point in his life.

The one to come home to.

1978
Ilena is 32

January, a rehab center in Florida. Chopin's Nocturnes are playing in the background.

For the first time this century, snow is falling on Miami. A young woman in a wheelchair looks through the window at the delicate white flakes swirling in the air.

If only I'd been able to die . . . Ilena thinks regretfully.

Late August, a godforsaken town somewhere in Texas.

The barmaid looks at her reflection in the mirror.

Three days earlier she celebrated her thirty-fifth birthday. *Some party! More like a funeral . . .* thinks Tiffany as she straightens her uniform.

She's been back home for a few weeks and spends her days serving beers to hicks who stare at her breasts. She's back to square one; back to the life she'd left at seventeen to take her chances in California. At the time, everyone thought she was as pretty as a picture. She could sing, dance, act, but it hadn't been enough to separate her from the herd; not in San Francisco, and not in Hollywood.

'Let me have another, sweetie!' says a customer, waving his mug.

Tiffany sighs. Her dreams of glory are definitely over.

The heat is stifling. The windows are wide open and suddenly there's a squeal of tires in front of the bar, then a few seconds later a new customer comes in.

At first she can't believe her eyes, but she's forced to recognize that it's really him.

She hasn't forgotten him and has often regretted having left before things even started between them. He glances around the room and his eyes light up.

Then she understands that he's come for her and that life sometimes gives us gifts when we least expect them.

Matt approaches, almost timidly. 'I've looked for you everywhere.'

And Tiffany answers: 'Take me with you.'

1979
Elliott is 33

It's fall. While Elliott is spending a few days' vacation in Sicily, a series of earthquakes hits southern Italy. Almost without thinking, he volunteers to help and is sent to join a Red Cross team in Santa Sienna, a little village built on a mountainside. This episode marks the beginning of a long collaboration with the well known NGO, but he doesn't know that yet. In the old village, the earthquake has destroyed everything in its wake: houses, cars . . .

In torrential rain, the rescue workers are struggling to dig through the ruins. They find twenty or so bodies, but also a few survivors trapped beneath the wreckage.

Night has almost fallen when they hear the groans of a six-year-old boy trapped at the bottom of a well. They lower a torch at the end of a rope. The hole is deep and the well, which has half collapsed, is in danger of caving in completely. The kid is in mud up to his chest, and the level of the water is rising constantly. They try to pull him up with the rope, but the kid is unable to hang on.

At the risk of looking like a hothead, Elliott ties a rope around himself and goes down into the well.

He doesn't deserve any admiration. He knows that today is not the day he will die. He's learned enough about his future to know that he'll live to be *at least* sixty.

For twenty-seven more years, he will be 'immortal'.

1980
Ilena is 34

Winter. A deserted windswept beach.

Supported by a cane, Ilena walks a few yards and then lets herself fall onto the wet sand.

The doctors tell her she's still young, that she has an iron will, and that she'll walk almost normally again some day. In the meantime, no matter how many painkillers she takes, nothing works: the pain is still everywhere, in her body, in her head, in her soul.

December 8, Lenox Hospital, in the room for medical personnel.

Collapsed on a couch with his eyes closed, Elliott is resting between two operations. His colleagues' conversations are murmuring in his ears: for or against Reagan? Who shot J. R.? Anybody heard the latest Stevie Wonder?

Someone turns on the television and suddenly they hear:

'John Lennon has just been assassinated in New York outside the Dakota by a disturbed individual named Mark Chapman. Even though emergency medical services came immediately, the doctors at Roosevelt Hospital were unable to save the former Beatle.'

1981

It's a sunny day in Napa Valley.

Matt and Tiffany are walking hand in hand between the rows of vines. For three years they have lived in perfect unity, in complete harmony, experiencing the kind of happiness everyone dreams about . . .

Are there many people on earth this happy? Can love last for an entire lifetime?

1982

Two in the morning in the bedroom of a small apartment in Lower Haight.

Elliott slips out of bed, trying not to wake the woman lying beside him, whom he met a few hours before in a downtown bar. He picks up his underwear, his jeans and his shirt and gets dressed in silence. As he's about to slip away, a voice calls to him: 'You're leaving?'

'Yes, but stay in bed. I'll lock the door behind me.'

'By the way, my name is Lisa!' the woman grumbles and buries herself under the covers.

'I know.'

'Then why did you call me Ilena?'

1983

Matt and Tiffany are in each other's arms, lying in bed after making love.

A tear is running down her cheek. They've been trying to have a child for five years.

She's just turned forty.

1984

Days, weeks, years go by . . .

For Ilena, life once more has meaning.

She's walking again; stumbling, limping, dragging her foot. But at least she's walking again.

It's impossible to return to her old profession, but she's made her peace with that. Overflowing with energy, she is teaching courses in marine biology at Stanford and has become one of the leading members of Greenpeace, playing an active role in new campaigns against burying radioactive waste at sea and helping set up the first European offices in Paris and London.

It's summer in San Francisco.

A ray of sun illuminates the hospital lobby. Elliott gets a Coke from the machine, sits in one of the chairs, and looks around.

The television is tuned to a new cable channel called MTV. On the screen is 'Like a Virgin', featuring a young singer writhing lasciviously on the floor, making a series of suggestive movements and leaving nothing of her lingerie to the imagination: this is the beginning of the Madonna phenomenon.

The hospital is amazingly calm. Someone has left a Rubik's Cube on one of the tables. Elliott picks it up and in a few moves restores uniform colors to all six sides.

Like everyone, he has his good days and his bad days. Today he feels pretty good. He doesn't really know why, but he feels serene. At other times it's harder: solitude combines with weariness to drag him toward a precipice of sadness and depression. And then an ambulance brings in another patient. Quickly, he's needed, they have to operate! And for a moment, life makes sense again.

That's the blessing of this job.

1985

Verona, early spring.

Elliott has been in Italy for two days for a surgical conference. If he remembers correctly what his double told him, today is the day he will meet the mother of his daughter.

Sitting on the terrace of a trattoria, he is watching the sun set on the Piazza Bra. Orange-tinted rays gild the top of the Arena, the magnificent Roman amphitheater overlooking the square.

'For you, sir . . .' says the waiter, bowing and setting a dry martini with two olives before him.

Elliott sips his drink, but he can't manage to calm down. Just what is he supposed to do? He knows that he has an appointment with fate, but he's afraid he'll pass it by. He goes over and over his double's words in his head. They're a good ten years old, but he has never forgotten them: 'On April 6, 1985, during a surgical conference in Verona, you'll meet a woman who will show interest in you. You'll respond to her advances, and you'll spend a weekend together, during which our daughter will be conceived.'

It all seems simple, except that today is April 6, it's almost seven in the evening, and he's still waiting for some curvaceous Italian woman to come and whisper sweet nothings in his ear.

'Anyone sitting here?'

He looks up, surprised to hear these words in English, spoken with a New York accent. Standing in front of him is a young woman in a light pink suit. Maybe she noticed the *International Herald Tribune* on his table . . . In any event, she seems delighted to have come across a fellow American.

Elliott nods and invites her to sit down. Her name is Pamela, she works for a large hotel chain, and she's in Verona on business.

Is she the one? he wonders, suddenly anxious. *It must be her. Everything fits.* After all, his double never specified that she'd be Italian . . . He scrutinizes her as she orders a glass of Valpolicella. She's an eighties-style beauty: tall, statuesque, bouffant blonde hair, shoulder pads.

By the time the entrées are served, they've gone past introductions and are talking about the 'heroes' of the new America: Reagan, Michael Jackson, Spielberg, Carl Lewis . . . Elliott is on automatic pilot. He is keeping up his end of the conversation, but his mind is somewhere else.

Strange – I never imagined it would be like this . . .

He can't bring himself to believe that this woman will be the mother of his daughter. It's hard to explain why. There doesn't seem to be anything the matter with her. Except that her conversation is vapid, her remarks are predictable, she's a Republican, she thinks more about having than being, and she doesn't have that certain something in her gaze, that extra spark called charm.

And yet here it is: if he hadn't met his double, he'd have no way of knowing this flirtation would end up creating a new life!

Still, it's weird that I'll let myself be taken in by this woman's chatter . . .

Sure, after a few hours of gabbing, there's the prospect of a night of sex, but even so, despite Pamela's obvious attractions, Elliott tells himself it won't necessarily be an unalloyed pleasure.

The meal continues with the local specialties: *pasta e fasoi,*

247

risotto all'Amarone, tournedos con taleggio, all of it washed down with several glasses of Bardolino.

The lights in the square are now illuminating the Palazzo Barbieri, the town hall, and the wide sidewalk where, despite the late hour, a crowd of Veronese are strolling.

He asks for the check, but when it seems to be taking a long time, he decides to get up and pay directly at the bar. While the owner is adding up the bill, Elliott takes out a Marlboro and puts it to his lips. As he's about to flick his lighter, a flame touches the end of his cigarette.

'Not bad, your presentation this morning, doctor.'

He looks up at the speaker: a woman of about thirty sitting on a stool with a glass of white wine in front of her.

'You were at the conference?'

'Giulia Batistini,' she introduces herself and holds out her hand. 'I'm a surgeon in Milan, a cardiologist.'

She has green eyes, and red hair that doesn't look at all Italian.

Their eyes meet and he notices in hers the little glimmer that he'd missed in Pamela's: charm.

With relief, he understands that *she's the one*, not Pamela, who will be the mother of his daughter!

'I would have liked to talk more with you,' Giulia begins, 'but . . .'

'But what?'

She glances at the terrace. 'I think your friend is waiting for you . . .'

'I think she's not my friend.'

She smiles slightly, the modest triumph of someone who had been ready to fight harder. 'In that case . . .'

1986
Elliott is 40

San Francisco, five in the morning. A call from Europe, ignoring the time difference. A woman with an Italian accent telling him what he already knows.

Elliott takes a plane to Milan, jumps into a taxi to the hospital, goes up four floors on foot, and knocks at the door of room 466; hello Giulia, hello Giulia's new partner, hello doctor, hello nurse.

Finally he approaches the cradle. He sees babies every day in the hospital, but this time it's different. This one is his. At first he's afraid he'll feel nothing, then she opens her eyes, looks at him, blinks, and he's hers for life.

It's February outside; snow, cold, traffic, car horns, angry drivers, pollution. But inside this room there is nothing but warmth and humanity.

'Welcome, Angie . . .'

1987

And there is life again.

All at once, he's at the end of the tunnel, he's turned the page, light has come back when he no longer expected it.

A little baby in the house and everything is turned upside down: there are bottles everywhere, packages of diapers, baby formula.

After five months, her first tooth. And five months later, her first steps on her own.

Everything that is not her seems pathetic. October 19,

market crash – Black Monday, the Dow Jones down 20 percent.

So?

1988

Angie's hungry! Angie wants a cookie! Angie's thirsty! Angie wants a colacoca!

It's already Christmas. The house is decorated and a vigorous fire is crackling in the fireplace.

Elliott has picked up the guitar again and is picking out his own personal version of 'With or Without You', the hit of the moment.

Lying on the rug, Tramp is watching over the family, and Angie is dancing in front of the flames.

1989

Angie is three. She can write her name in block letters with a large felt pen.

On March 24, the tanker *Exxon Valdez* runs aground off the coast of Alaska, spilling 300,000 tons of crude oil and unleashing a black tide. CNN broadcasts an impassioned attack on Exxon by Greenpeace delivered by its new spokesperson, Ilena Cruz.

In October, Rostropovich plays his cello in front of the Berlin Wall as it's demolished.

On television, they explain it's the end of the cold war and from now on people will live happily in a world full of democracy and the free market economy . . .

1990

The lines stretch out in front of the movie theater.

In the first line are lots of families and noisy children. Elliott and Angie are waiting for *The Little Mermaid*, Walt Disney's latest, while people in the other line are waiting to see Meg Ryan in *When Harry Met Sally*.

Angie is a little tired and yanks on her father's sleeve so he'll pick her up.

'Get ready for takeoff!' he yells as he grabs hold of her.

As he picks up his daughter, he turns his head and catches sight of Matt and Tiffany waiting in the other line.

An exchange of glances lasting half a second, that seems to take place in slow motion. Elliott feels his heart go cold. The two men haven't spoken in almost fifteen years. Tiffany looks at Angie with a sad smile and then turns away. Then the two pairs each go into a different theater.

The time for explanations has not yet come.

But one day, maybe . . .

1991

Elliott and Angie have gotten involved in a complicated recipe for pancakes. A brilliant smile lights up the little girl's face. Her mouth is smeared with maple syrup. It's early evening, the air is warm, a beautiful orange light filters through the kitchen windows.

The television next to the microwave is on, but the sound is off. A few blurry pictures of Kuwait: Operation Desert Storm, the first Allied military intervention against Iraq.

On the radio, U2 is singing 'Mysterious Ways', and Angie keeps time with Bono, banging on the table with a wooden spoon.

Elliott immortalizes the moment with his video camera. He always manages to spend the maximum amount of time with her, even at the expense of his career. He still loves his profession just as much, but he has rejected the compromises that would have allowed him to rise up the ranks more quickly. Others have overtaken him and he's done nothing to catch up with them. Being a good surgeon in the eyes of his patients is enough to satisfy him.

And besides, his daughter comes before everything else. He now understands his double and all the efforts he made to save Ilena without sacrificing Angie. But the serenity he feels when he looks at his daughter is sometimes tinged with vague unease. Life has already taught him that moments of happiness can extract a heavy price, and he's learned the lesson well. Life has been sweet again for the last six years, but he knows that that could end at any moment.

The problem with happiness is that you get used to it so quickly . . .

1992

At six, you lose your baby teeth . . .

So Angie does her homework with a pretty, toothless smile, sitting at the glass table in the living room.

Visibly angry, Elliott comes into the room and looks at his daughter severely. 'I've told you before to turn off the television when you do your homework!'

'Why?'

'Because to do good work, you have to concentrate.'

'But I am concentrating!'

'Don't get smart with me!'

He picks up the remote from under a cushion and is about to turn off the set when his finger freezes on the button.

On the screen, a reporter is speaking from Rio where the second Earth Summit is being held. For a few days, the great powers will talk about the state of the world's environment. The reporter is interviewing a representative of an NGO. For several minutes, this woman speaks knowledgeably and with conviction about climate change and the destruction of bio-diversity. She has enormous melancholy eyes. As she speaks, her name appears on a banner at the right of the screen: Ilena Cruz.

'Daddy, why are you crying?'

1993

It's almost 6:30. Elliott slips out of bed before the alarm clock goes off. All that can be seen outside the covers is a head of long brown hair belonging to a flight attendant he met at the airport the night before, when he sent Angie to visit her mother in Italy for a few days.

He leaves the bedroom without making a sound, takes a shower, and gets dressed quickly.

He picks up a pad in the kitchen and is about to scribble a note when he realizes he's forgotten the girl's name. So he writes only the bare minimum:

When you leave, could you put the keys in the mailbox?
Thanks for last night.
Maybe I'll see you again one of these days.

He knows it's pathetic, but that's the way it is. His affairs seldom last more than a week. It's by choice: he refuses to stay in a relationship if he's not in love. That would be hypocritical and cowardly. And in a sense, that's the way he's found of being faithful to Ilena.

You make the best arrangements you can . . .

He gulps down a cup of coffee, picks up a stale doughnut, and leaves for work. On the way out he picks up the paper that's just been delivered. A huge photograph is spread over the front page: the handshake between Rabin and Arafat under the attentive gaze of Bill Clinton.

1994

An early evening in late summer. The sky is mauve, with streaks of red. Elliott parks his faithful VW in front of Marina Green. He's arranged not to get home too late, but he knows that Teresa, the nanny he's hired to take care of his daughter, has already been gone for almost an hour.

'Angie!' he shouts when he opens the door. 'I'm home!'

She's eight now, but every time he leaves her alone, he can't help worrying.

'Angie, are you all right?'

He hears her light step coming down the stairs, but when he looks up he sees her beautiful face bathed in tears.

'What's going on, honey?' he asks, and rushes toward her.

She falls into his arms, crushed by the greatest sorrow in the world.

'It's Tramp!' she says finally between sobs.

'What did he do?'

'He's . . . he's dead.'

He picks her up and carries her up to the bedroom. The old dog is indeed lying there on the rug as though he were asleep.

'Will you take care of him?' the little girl asks.

As Elliott feels for a pulse, Angie's sobs are accompanied by pleas: 'Please, cure him, Daddy! Cure him!'

'He's dead, honey, he can't be cured.'

'Please, Daddy!' she screams and falls to her knees.

He picks her up and takes her into her room.

'He was very old, you know. It's already a miracle he lived so long.'

But she's not yet prepared to hear this. For now the pain is too strong and nothing can ease it.

She lies down on her bed and buries her head in the pillow. Elliott sits by her side, doing his best to console her.

Things will be better tomorrow.

The next day, they drive for more than an hour to the little forest in Inglewood, north of San Francisco. They pick an isolated spot, not too far from a large tree, and Elliott digs a deep hole with a shovel he's brought along. Finally he puts the body of the Labrador into the hole and covers it with earth.

'Do you think there's a heaven for dogs?' the little girl asks.

'I don't know,' says Elliott as he covers the grave with leaves and branches. 'But if there is, Tramp will certainly be there.'

She silently nods and then her tears start to flow again. Tramp has always been part of her world.

'I can't believe I'll never see him again.'

'I know, honey, it's hard to lose someone you love. There's nothing harder in life.'

Elliott makes sure everything's done right, then he suggests to his daughter: 'You can say goodbye to him if you want.'

Angie steps toward the grave and says in a solemn voice: 'Goodbye, Tramp, you were a great dog . . .'

'Yeah,' Elliott agrees, 'you were the best.'

Then they get into the car and head back to the city. They're both quiet on the way back. Since they deserve some comfort, Elliott suggests they stop at Starbucks.

'Would you like a hot chocolate?'

'Okay. With whipped cream!'

They sit down at a table and, with her face covered in whipped cream, Angie asks: 'How did you get Tramp?'

'I never told you?'

'No.'

'Well, you see, at first we didn't like each other very much . . .'

1995

'Daddy, can we see *Toy Story*?'

'What's that?'

1996

'Daddy, can we see *Romeo + Juliet*? I adore Leonardo!'

'Did you finish your homework?'

'Yes, I promise!'

1997

A Saturday afternoon in December. For the first time, Angie has decided to go to the movies with her friends instead of with him.

Like millions of adolescent girls, she couldn't wait to see DiCaprio kiss Kate Winslet on the deck of the *Titanic*.

Feeling peaceful, Elliott makes some coffee in the kitchen. Everything is fine. So why does he have this deep feeling of solitude?

He goes upstairs and opens the door to Angie's room. She's left the music on. The Spice Girls are belting out their hit 'Wannabe' on the stereo. On the wall next to the ever-present Simpsons hang posters from television shows he's never heard of: *Friends, Beverly Hills 90210, South Park* . . .

He feels an abrupt emptiness, realizing suddenly that his daughter is no longer really a child.

That's normal. Kids grow up. That's life.

But why so fast?

1998
Elliott is 52

The television is on in the hospital break room. On the screen, some guy is saying that men are from Mars and women are from Venus. All the nurses in the room seem to agree. Elliott frowns. More and more often, he has the impression that he's out of synch with the world around him. He finishes his can of Coke and leaves the room. For the first time, he feels the burden of being over fifty. It's not that he feels old, but he no longer feels young. And he knows his youth will never return.

The hit show on television is *ER*. Some patients in the hospital ask to be treated by Doctor Green or Doctor Ross . . .

One Thursday in January, the gloomy face of Bill Clinton, forced to defend himself, appears on television: 'I did not have sexual relations with that woman, Miss Lewinsky.'

At the same time, north of the Arctic Circle, the ice keeps on melting because of global warming.

But who really cares?

1999

It's the end of April.

Elliott pokes his head into the break room. Empty.

He opens the little refrigerator to take out a piece of fruit. A nurse has stuck a Post-it with her name on a green apple. Elliott raises his eyebrows, takes off the note, and bites into the apple.

He sits on the windowsill and distractedly watches some of his colleagues playing basketball outside. The scent of spring is floating through San Francisco. Today is a perfect day: a day worth living, when all operations are successful and no patient is inconsiderate enough to slip through his fingers.

He hesitates to turn on the television. Why take the risk of ruining this good mood by inflicting on himself his daily dose of bad news? He's about to leave it off, when he tells himself that maybe today things will be different. He starts to daydream for a minute: the announcement of a vaccine against AIDS, permanent peace in the Middle East, a real global plan to fight pollution, doubling of the federal education budget . . .

Bad guess. A special correspondent on CNN, speaking from Columbine High School in Littleton, is explaining that two students have just shot twelve of their fellows before turning the weapons on themselves.

He should have left it off . . .

2000

'Daddy, can I get a piercing?'

'Daddy, can I have a cell phone?'

'Daddy, can I get a tattoo?'
But also:
A gerbil, an iMac, an iPod, a DKNY T-shirt, Diesel jeans, a fur bag, New Balance sneakers, a clown fish, a Burberry raincoat, Marc Jacobs perfume, D&G glasses, a chinchilla, a Hello Kitty bag, turtles, a Tommy Hilfiger polo shirt, an IKKS T-shirt, a seahorse, a Ralph Lauren sweater, a . . .

2001

Elliott parks his VW in the lot and glances at his watch. It's still early. Theoretically, he doesn't start work for two hours, but he's decided to come in early.

He knows today will be a special day.

When he comes into the hospital lobby he sees dozens of

patients, doctors, and nurses crowded around the television set. They all look pale, and many of them have their cell phones out.

Of all the things his double told him in their various encounters in 1976, there's one he's never forgotten: 'Something happened on September 11, 2001, at the World Trade Center in New York.'

Elliott has been wondering for a long time what that *something* could be.

He gets closer to the television and pushes his way through a few people to get a glimpse of the screen.

Now he knows.

2002, 2003, 2004, 2005 . . .
Elliott is 56, 57, 58, 59 . . .

'It's not that we have little time, but more that we waste a good deal of it.'
Seneca

2006
Elliott is 60

Manhattan, the second week in January.

Elliott has taken a few days' vacation to help Angie get settled in New York where she's about to begin medical school.

His daughter is all excited by her new life, and Elliott has left her for a few hours to make a rather special trip. The taxi drops him off in front of a glass and metal tower at the corner of Park Avenue and 52nd Street. He goes into the building and takes the elevator to the thirty-third floor, the offices of a prominent medical practice. The day before, he went through a whole battery of tests and scans, and now he's come for the results. Elliott decided to have all these tests done in New York instead of San Francisco where half the doctors in town know him. In theory, of course, there is such a thing as medical confidentiality, but in this world as in others, rumors spread fast.

'Please come in, Elliott,' says John Goldwyn, one of the doctors in the practice. The two men went to medical school together in California and they've kept in touch. Elliott sits in a chair as Goldwyn opens a file and takes out several X-rays that he spreads out on his desk.

'I won't lie to you, Elliott,' he says, and hands him one of the pictures.

'I have cancer, don't I?'

'Yes.'

'Is it serious?'

'I'm afraid so.'

He takes a few seconds to digest the information, then says, 'How much time?'

'A few months . . .'

Fifteen minutes later, Elliott is on the street again, amid the skyscrapers, the car horns, and the traffic. The sky is blue, but it's icy cold.

Still stunned from learning of his disease, he wanders through Manhattan, lost, feverish, shaking.

As he walks through a shopping mall he comes face to face with his mirror image in the window of a luxury shop. Suddenly he sees that he has the same age and the same appearance as his double who appeared to him thirty years before.

That's it: I've finally become him . . .

Looking at his reflection in the window, he waves the X-ray of his cancerous lungs. As though he could still speak to his double across time, he says in a choked voice: 'That's something you made sure not to tell me, you bastard!'

TWENTY-TWO

And leaving me to my fate,
he went out into the light-filled morning.
Edith Piaf

February 2007
Elliott is 61
Three Minutes Before Death . . .

Wrapped in blankets and stretched out on the couch on the veranda, Elliott is watching the sun set on San Francisco for the last time.

He is shivering, and even with the oxygen mask he can no longer breathe.

He feels as though his entire body is on the point of dissolving.

Two Minutes Before Death . . .

The dreaded moment has finally come, the moment when he embarks on the great journey.

It is often said that the value of a life comes not from how long it lasts but from the way it is lived.

Easy to say when you're the picture of health!

Elliott believes he's tried his best, but in the end has he done well?

Only time will tell.

Only death will tell.

Last Minute . . .

He would have liked to die with the serenity of a Zen master.

But it's not that easy.

In fact, he's helpless, like a kid.

He's afraid.

He didn't want to tell Angie.

He has no one by his side.

So that he won't leave this life entirely alone, he thinks very hard about Ilena. And at the moment he breathes his last breath he manages to convince himself that she is by his side.

TWENTY-THREE

It's human to have a secret,
but it's just as human to reveal it sooner or later.

Philip Roth

February 2007
Three days later

Bright winter sunlight was shining on the verdant walks of Greenwood Cemetery, making it look like a park.

The burial had just taken place, and people who wanted to say a last goodbye to Elliott walked past his grave and tossed a handful of dirt or a flower onto the coffin.

Angie came forward first, along with her mother, who had come from Milan. Then came his colleagues and many of the patients he had operated on in the last thirty years. If he hadn't been six feet under, Elliott would have been surprised and touched by the crowd. The presence of one person in particular would have warmed his heart: the retired detective Malden, who was over ninety, and who came valiantly forward, supported by his old colleague, Captain Douglas, now in charge of the city police.

The ceremony ended a half hour later, just before nightfall. Everyone quickly scattered to the parking lot and the familiar comfort of their cars. When they arrived home, many of them thought: *My day will come too*, and immediately afterward: *I hope it's as late as possible.*

The windswept little cemetery was now deserted.

When he was sure he was alone, a man who had stood apart during the ceremony finally ventured to approach the grave.

Matt.

Tiffany had tried to dissuade him from coming. She saw no need to honor the memory of a man who hadn't spoken to him for thirty years.

But Matt had come all the same.

With Elliott's death, a whole period of his youth had disappeared, along with the hope of reconciliation that he'd always secretly nourished.

For Matt couldn't help thinking that he'd missed something essential thirty years ago. What was the explanation for Elliott's sudden change in behavior toward him? How could he possibly have left Ilena when they were so much in love?

These were all questions he would never be able to answer now.

'You decided to take your secrets with you, old pal,' he said helplessly.

As he stood before the newly erected gravestone, memories rushed through his mind. And they were painful. They had once been so close. Even though the end of their friendship was forty years ago, to him it seemed like yesterday.

Matt crouched in front of the gravestone and remained motionless for a good while as his silent tears fell on the ground. As he grew older, tears would sometimes come from nowhere, and he could do nothing to stop them.

As he got up he said with a kind of ironic anger: 'Since you went first, you'd better keep that damned spot in heaven for me . . .'

He was about to walk off when he felt a presence behind him.

'You must be Matt . . .'

He turned around, surprised by a voice he had never heard before.

A young woman in a long black coat was standing before him.

'I'm Angie, Elliott's daughter,' she said and held out her hand.

'Matt Delluca,' he introduced himself.

'My father told me that at his funeral, you would be the one who stayed the longest at his grave.'

'We were friends,' Matt explained, almost embarrassed. 'Very close friends . . .'

He let his words hang in the air for a few seconds, and then explained, 'But it was a long time ago, well before you were born.'

As he looked hard at the young woman, Matt couldn't help being troubled by her resemblance to Elliott. Angie had inherited her father's regular features, but not his anxious expression. She was a radiantly beautiful young woman who, despite her sadness, seemed at ease with herself.

'My father left this for you,' she said, handing him a brown paper bag.

'Oh?' he said in surprise as he took it.

Angie hesitated, and then went on, 'A few weeks before he

died, he told me that if something serious ever happened to me . . .'

'Yes?' said Matt, to encourage her to continue.

'If I had a problem, I shouldn't hesitate to come to you.'

Touched and comforted by this mark of trust, Matt took a moment before saying: 'Of course, I'll do whatever I can to help you.'

'Maybe we'll meet again soon,' she said, and moved off like a shadow.

Matt waited until he'd lost sight of her and turned back to Elliott's grave.

'You can count on me,' he promised. 'I'll look after her.'

Then he left the cemetery, his heart a little less heavy than when he'd arrived.

His eyes glistening, Matt was on Route 29 headed for Calistoga, the little Napa Valley town where his vineyard was located. Tiffany was in Europe promoting their wine, and he didn't want to go back to a cold and empty house in San Francisco.

He drove through Oakville and St Helena on the way to the property that was his pride and joy. Matt was a rich man. For thirty years he had spared no efforts to make his vineyard one of the most highly rated in the region.

He pressed a button on the remote and the gates of the winery opened. He drove past gardens with ornamental fountains and parked his car at the end of a gravel driveway. The old wooden house had been torn down long ago and replaced by a handsome building that was both classic and contemporary.

He greeted the watchman and went directly down to the

tasting cellar. It was a huge room decorated with paintings and sculptures by renowned artists: Fernand Léger, Dubuffet, César, and a priceless Basquiat he'd given Tiffany for her last birthday.

The lighting was soft, lending the floor a rich bronze color. Matt sat down on an oak bench and eagerly opened up the paper bag, curious to see what his friend might have bequeathed to him. Inside was a wooden box containing two bottles of wine that he examined carefully: Château Latour 1959, Château Mouton Rothschild 1982. Splendid vintages for two of the finest wines in the Médoc, a kind of perfection in this fallen world . . .

Matt smiled ruefully as he picked up a bottle and was surprised to find a large leather notebook stuck at the bottom of the box.

In an instant, his mood shifted from amusement to surprise and then to excitement, and his hands shook as he opened the notebook. It had about a hundred pages covered with neat handwriting that he recognized as Elliott's.

As he glanced over the first page, Matt felt his skin prickle.

My Dear Matt,

If you're reading these lines, that means that the damn' cancer finally got the best of me. I fought to the bitter end, but there are enemies you can't beat.

You probably saw my obituary in yesterday's paper, and since you're good-hearted, you figured out a way to get to my funeral. I even bet you hid behind a tree until you could have a quiet conversation with my gravestone . . .

I know you're still mad at me. I know you never understood my behavior and you suffered the way I suffered. I would have liked to explain things sooner, but that was impossible. You'll understand why . . .

So, here's the incredible adventure that I fell into and that affected all of us: you, Ilena, and me. I tried every time to make the right decision, but as you'll see, my room for maneuver was limited.

Once you've read these pages, please above all, don't blame yourself for anything. You were always there for me and I was tremendously lucky to have you for a friend. Don't be sad. Before starting to read, open one of the bottles of wine – you see how highly I thought of you – pour a glass and drink a toast to me.

As I write these lines, I know I'm living my final days. The bay window of my bedroom is open: the sky is glowing with that intense blue that you see only in California, a few puffy clouds are scudding by, and the wind carries the sound of the waves.

All the little things we never take the time to appreciate . . . It sounds stupid to say it, but it's so hard to leave them.

Take care of yourself, Matt, and take advantage of the time you have left.

If you only knew how much I've missed you.

Your friend in life and death,

Elliott.

It was past two in the morning.

Matt's eyes were red when he'd finished reading the astonishing tale his friend had left for him. Elliott's encounter with his double, the time travel, the strange pact to save Ilena . . . The story that he hadn't wanted to believe thirty years ago came back to him today in a different light.

270

Matt closed the notebook and stood up with difficulty. His head was spinning, and he'd made a good dent in the bottle of Latour, but that had not been enough to obliterate the enormous pain of his remorse and regrets.

What should he do now? Kill the bottle to drown his sorrows? He considered the idea for a minute, but quickly dismissed it. He went behind the tasting counter and splashed his face with cold water. Then he put on his coat and went out into the dark. A few gusts of the icy wind were enough to sober him up. Elliott was dead and he couldn't do anything to change that. But there was still one thing he could do.

But did he have the right?

Instead of his sports car, he got into the four-wheel drive belonging to the business. As he left the property he turned on the GPS system and entered an address in northern California.

Then he headed for the mountains.

He drove through the night, heading west through snow-covered country. It was still winter and the roads were slippery and obscured by thick fog.

He almost ran out of gas a little past Willow Creek and was saved only by a drugstore owner who agreed to sell him a containerful for a king's ransom. When he got to Weaverville, the fog had finally lifted and he could see the sun peeking over the snowy caps of the Trinity Alps.

He took the forest road and soon came to the little wooden house that he'd already visited with Tiffany.

Hearing the noise of the car, Ilena had come out onto the porch.

'Matt!' she cried, in a worried voice.

He waved and joined her on the porch, giving her a big hug.

Every time he looked at her he felt distinctive emotion, a mixture of compassion and respect. Ilena had fought all her life, first to overcome her handicap and then to defend the causes dear to her.

'You're looking good,' he said.

'You, on the other hand, look like hell! What happened, Matt?'

'I'll explain, but first make me some coffee.'

He followed her into the house. The cottage was tastefully decorated with a mixture of traditional wood and designer furniture. Bay windows, a fireplace, the latest computer equipment: nothing was lacking to make the place cozy and comfortable.

'Well?' Ilena asked and turned on the espresso machine. 'Your wife kick you out?'

'Not yet,' answered Matt with a hint of a smile.

He looked at her tenderly. Despite the ordeals she'd gone through, Ilena still exuded an amazing charm. At Stanford, where she taught a few courses, she was considered one of the stars of the campus. In that nursery of intellectuals and Nobel Prize-winners, more than a few brilliant men had been given a gentle brush-off when they tried some strategy of seduction on her. Matt knew that Ilena had given up any love life after her accident. In the hospital she'd fought to survive repeated surgical procedures. In Greenpeace, she'd worked tirelessly against lobbies and governments. But she'd never tried to find love again . . .

'Here's your coffee,' she said, and set down a tray with two steaming cups and an assortment of cookies.

A cat with long silky hair entered the room to ask for his first meal of the day, too.

Ilena picked him up and petted him for a little while. She was about to go back to the kitchen when Matt suddenly confessed the reason for his visit: 'Elliott is dead.'

Deep silence filled the house. Ilena dropped the Persian cat, who landed with a complaining meow.

'Cigarettes?' she asked, turning back toward Matt.

'Yes, lung cancer.'

She nodded pensively. Her face was impassive, but Matt noticed that her eyes were glistening.

Then she headed for the kitchen with the cat at her heels.

Left alone, Matt sighed. His eyes wandered to the glaciers coming down the mountains like frozen lava flows.

Suddenly the whole house was shaken by the noise of breaking dishes. He ran into the kitchen and found Ilena collapsed on a chair. With her head in her hands she was giving free rein to her sorrow. Matt kneeled down next to his friend and hugged her with all the affection that was in him.

'I loved him so much . . .' she confessed, her face on his shoulder.

'Me too . . .'

She looked up at him, her eyes full of tears. 'In spite of everything he did to us, I kept on loving him.'

'There's something you need to know . . .' Matt whispered.

He stood up and took the large notebook out of his coat pocket.

'Elliott left me this before he died,' he explained, and handed it to Ilena.

She took the notebook with shaking hands. 'What is it?'

'The truth,' he said simply.

Then he left the house and got back into his car.

*   *   *

273

Puzzled, Ilena went out onto the porch to try to stop him leaving.

But Matt had already gone.

The morning air was chilly in spite of the sun. Ilena picked up a shawl and covered her shoulders before settling into the rocking-chair.

She opened the leather notebook, immediately recognized Elliott's handwriting, and felt as though an ice pick was plunging into her heart and lacerating her soul.

After reading the first lines, she understood she was finally going to get the answer to the question that had made her suffer for thirty years.

Why did you abandon me?

Matt drove like an automaton toward San Francisco, sad and downcast.

Elliott's confession had at first given him some comfort, but that soon gave way to melancholy, and then depression.

In fact, this posthumous reconciliation gave him a feeling of things left. Matt had an Epicurean side. What he believed in was *life*. A 'good death', the ideas of leaving in peace, of drawing up a positive balance sheet for his life, all left him cold.

What he would have liked to do was relive their glory days. Get in the boat and sail round the bay, have a drink in a café in the old port, eat a trout Chez Francis, go for a hike in the Sierra Nevada forest . . .

Live.

But he shouldn't give way to dreams. Elliott was dead, and his own turn might come soon.

Naïvely, he had always imagined that everything between them would work out. But life had decided differently, and the years of estrangement had passed by.

It was now three in the afternoon. As he drew closer to the city, traffic got heavier. He stopped at a gas station to fill up and to get something to eat.

In the rest room, he threw water on his face several times, as though he expected that would wash away his weariness and his age. The mirror reflected a dismal picture. His stomach was rumbling and his mind was clouded by exhaustion and depression.

Why did he have the troubling feeling that he was missing something essential? Something that had been tormenting him since the night before. The circle didn't seem quite complete, but he couldn't figure out why.

He ordered a sandwich and sat down at a table by the window, looking out distractedly at the heavy traffic on Route 101.

He felt guilty biting into his BLT. Since his latest tests had shown an alarming cholesterol level, his wife had forbidden him to eat bacon.

But today Tiffany wasn't there to take care of him.

Unbidden, between bites he took the bottle of anti-cholesterol medicine out of the jacket pocket where he always kept it. The bottle was almost empty. He took the last capsule and washed it down with a swig of coffee.

This mechanical procedure made something click in his head.

He left his sandwich behind and hurried back to his car.

Because he had just understood what had been bothering him for the last few hours: he had read and reread Elliott's story. It explained clearly that the old Cambodian had given him *ten* pills. But Elliott had made only *nine* journeys through time!

Ten pills, nine journeys.

What had happened to the remaining pill?

TWENTY-FOUR

Last Pill

*When several roads are offered to you and you don't
know which one to choose, don't take one at random,
but sit and wait. Keep on waiting. Don't move, keep
silent, and listen to your heart. Then, when it speaks to
you, get up and follow where it leads.*

Susanna Tamaro

2007
Matt is 61

Matt got back to town in less than half an hour.

Something was running though his head. The idea was a
little crazy, but it eased his heartache.

He roared onto Marina Boulevard and, as in the good old
days, parked his car in front of Elliott's house. He'd hoped to
find Angie there, but apparently the house was empty. After
ringing the bell and pounding on the door, he went around the
house and climbed over the fence into the garden. The place
was virtually unchanged. The old Alaska cedar still stood
there; its branches had spread by now to meet the glass wall.

Matt was almost certain that, unlike the other houses in the neighborhood, this one didn't have an alarm system. He took off his coat, rolled it up around his arm, and, with all his strength, jabbed one elbow into the bay window in the kitchen. The glass was thick, but Matt still had impressive physical strength. When the window gave, he slipped his hand between the shards and opened the door from the inside.

He crept into the house and for three long hours went through the place from top to bottom, methodically searching every room, opening all the drawers, inspecting every closet, even lifting up a few loose floorboards, hoping to get his hands on the last pill.

But he couldn't find it.

Night had already fallen. Matt was about to go back home when he stopped in front of a frame containing a photograph of Elliott surrounded by several pictures of Angie.

Then he gave vent to his anger and disappointment. 'You really had us going, didn't you?' he shouted at Elliott's picture.

He was yelling as if his friend were in front of him: 'It's all a load of crap, isn't it? Tall tales you made up to justify your behavior . . .'

He stepped closer to the photograph and stared into the doctor's face. 'There never was an old Cambodian! There never were any pills! There never was any time travel! You were crazy thirty years ago and you stayed crazy until the day you died!'

In an outburst of fury he picked up the picture frame and hurled it against the wall.

'Bastard!'

Then, at the end of his rope, he collapsed in a chair.

It took him a long time to calm down.

The room was now completely dark.

Matt got up to turn on the lamp that stood on a painted wooden chest. He picked Elliott's picture out of the fragments of glass and set it on one of the bookshelves.

'No hard feelings.'

Bookshelves . . .

He went over to them. He remembered the day when he had come here to put the telegram between the pages of an atlas. Standing in front of the shelves, he cast his eye over the titles until he found the book he was looking for. He picked up the old atlas, blew on the edge to remove the fine layer of dust, and shook it hard.

Nothing. Then, suddenly, a last flash of inspiration.

He grabbed a paper cutter from the desk and inserted it in the narrow space between the binding and the spine of the atlas. He felt some resistance and then a tiny square of plastic fell to the floor.

Matt picked it up, his heart racing. It was a minuscule sealed pouch which he immediately opened, sliding the contents into his palm.

Sitting there now was a little golden pill . . .

He tried to keep from getting carried away, but he was overwhelmed by a flood of adrenaline.

One last pill.

One final journey . . .

Now what should he do?

What had Elliott intended when he'd left himself one last chance to go back to the past? And why had he chosen to hide the pill *in that spot*, exactly the one hiding place that *only Matt* could know about?

He was pacing the living room, going over the same questions, when his cell phone rang.

He looked at the screen and recognized the number.

'Ilena?'

'Yes, it's me, I've just read the notebook . . .'

She was speaking in a flat voice, trying to hold back waves of fear and emotion.

'It's a crazy story, Matt, you have to tell me more.'

Matt didn't know what to say. He closed his eyes and rubbed his eyelids.

Of course Ilena had trouble believing Elliott's story! How could it be otherwise? How could he ask her to accept this improbable tale, when she had never had the least suspicion of the extraordinary drama that had blighted the life of the man she loved?

'I can't explain right now,' Matt answered.

'Oh, yes, you will explain!' Ilena retorted. 'You come barging in on me, force me to stir up memories I spent thirty years burying, and then you run off like a thief!'

'I'm going to bring him back to you, Ilena.'

'Who?'

'Elliott.'

'You're crazy, too. Elliott is dead, Matt. DEAD!'

'I'm going to bring him back to you,' Matt repeated. 'You have my word.'

'Stop torturing me!' Ilena screamed and hung up.

Matt put his phone back in his pocket and stood by the window. A fine rain lashed the glass but at last everything seemed clear to him.

This last pill was for him . . .

*   *   *

He found a bottle of Perrier in the refrigerator and took a big gulp to wash down the pill.

It was done.

Too late to turn back.

He went back to the living room, sat in a chair, and put his feet up on the desk.

Now he only had to wait.

But wait for what?

Indigestion?

Stomach cramps?

Or to go back in time thirty years in his turn?

He waited and waited.

In vain.

Frustrated, he went upstairs, rummaged in the bathroom and found a bottle of sleeping pills. He took two, went back down to the living room, and stretched out on the couch.

He closed his eyes, counted sheep, opened his eyes, changed position, turned off the light, turned it back on . . .

'Shit!' he said and jumped to his feet.

Too excited to fall asleep, he put on his coat and went out of the house into a freezing downpour. He ran to his car to get out of the rain and roared off. He headed up Fillmore to Lombard Street. It was after midnight in the middle of winter, and the streets were deserted.

He'd reached the highest part of Russian Hill – the place where the street plunges down to North Beach in a series of hairpin turns – when sleep hit him like a fist. Pain suddenly radiated through his neck, his mind clouded, and he felt blood pounding at his temples. He lost consciousness and collapsed at the wheel of his car, without even having time to park.

The car scraped against the curb, crushed two hydrangea bushes, and came to rest against a metal barrier.

1977

When Matt opened his eyes, he was lying face down on one of the curves of Lombard Street. It was deepest night, shrouded in rain and fog.

Soaked and shivering, he stood up with difficulty. How long had he been there? He looked at his watch, but it had stopped. He looked around for his car: the four-wheel drive had disappeared.

Higher up, on Hyde Street, a drugstore's neon sign was hissing in the rain. He hurried into the store. The place was empty except for an Asian employee arranging soda cans on a shelf. Matt went up to the magazine rack. Feverishly, he picked up a copy of *Newsweek*: on the cover, Jimmy Carter was smiling awkwardly. The date at the top was February 6, 1977.

He rushed out of the store.

The pill had finally worked! This time, *he'd* gone back to the past – thirty years back!

But he knew that these trips in time were brief. He only had a few minutes to find Elliott. He had at first intended to go to the marina, but according to the notebook, during this period Elliott often worked at night.

He took a few seconds to make up his mind.

Lenox Hospital was a little less than a mile away as the crow flies. A short distance by car, but a hefty distance on foot. He stood in the middle of the street to try to stop a cab, but all he got were drivers beeping at him angrily and several splashes that soaked him even more.

He finally summoned up his courage and started to jog through the night toward the hospital. He ran up and down the hills of San Francisco, pausing, out of breath, on California Street. With his hands on his knees, gasping, he bitterly regretted not having followed Tiffany's advice to jog daily and lose the extra twenty pounds he was carrying. His coat was now nothing but a gigantic sponge. He left it on the sidewalk. His load lightened, he took off again in the driving rain. He'd rather die of a heart attack than give up so close to his goal.

He'd been waiting for this day for forty years. The day when it was his turn to save Elliott.

Finally he saw the blinking lights of the emergency entrance. He covered the last hundred yards as quickly as he could and pushed open the door as though his life depended on it.

'I'mlookingfordoctorelliottcooper!' he said in one great rush.

'I beg your pardon?' said the receptionist.

'I'm looking for Doctor Elliott Cooper!' he repeated, more clearly.

The young woman graciously handed him a towel so he could dry off while she looked at the schedule. She was about to answer, when a nurse spoke first: 'Elliott is in the cafeteria,' he explained as he bit into a chocolate bar. 'But that—'

Matt raced across the lobby as the nurse finished his sentence: '—is reserved for the staff.'

Matt pushed open the double doors to the cafeteria. The place was deserted and dark. The wall clock indicated 2 a.m., and the voice of Nina Simone could be heard faintly from the radio behind the counter.

Matt walked to the middle of the row of tables. Leaning against the wall at one end of the room, with his legs stretched out on a bench, Elliott was smoking a cigarette and making notes on medical files.

'I see you're still working.'

Elliott jumped and turned toward the man who had just come in. At first he didn't recognize him. Then he disregarded the wrinkles, the excess weight, and the thinning hair.

'Thirty years have changed the way I look, haven't they?' said Matt.

'Is that you?' Elliott stammered, slowly standing up.

'In the flesh.'

There was a brief hesitation and then the two men embraced.

'Where the hell did you come from?'

'From the year of our lord 2007.'

'How could you . . .?'

'There was one pill left,' Matt explained.

'So you know everything?'

'Yes.'

'I'm sorry about what happened,' Elliott said apologetically.

'Don't worry about it.'

The two men stood looking at each other, simultaneously moved and shy.

'How are you in 2007?' Elliott asked, still eager for information about the future.

'I'm getting old,' Matt answered, with a hint of a smile, 'but I'm doing all right.'

'We still on bad terms?'

Matt paused, then looked his friend in the eyes, and confessed, 'You're dead.'

Silence fell, the storm raged, and the bittersweet voice of Nina Simone was drowned out by the rain.

Unable to utter a word, Elliott blinked and nodded.

Matt was going to say something more when a spurt of blood landed on his shirt and the trembling began to hit his body.

'I'm leaving!' he shouted, hanging on to Elliott.

Shaking uncontrollably, he convulsed as though his body had suddenly been hit by an electric charge.

'I came to save you,' he said, straining to get the words out.

He was shaking so hard that Elliott helped him sit on the floor.

'How do you propose to do that?' he asked, kneeling next to him.

'Like this,' said Matt. He took the cigarette out of Elliott's mouth and ground it out on the cafeteria floor.

Elliott gave his friend a worried look. Matt's neck was rigid and his limbs were flailing.

'You're not the only one who can save lives,' he whispered, trying to smile.

'If I'm still alive, I'll see you in 2007,' Elliott promised.

'You better be, old man.'

'Thirty years is a long time,' said Elliott and took him by the hand.

'Don't worry, it'll go fast.'

In a few seconds, Matt's breathing grew loud and hoarse. His eyes glazed over and a spasm distorted his face. He had just enough time to add: 'It always goes too fast,' and then he disappeared with a cry of pain.

Elliott stood up, full of anxiety. Matt's return to the future had been more painful than that of his double. Had he gotten back to the right place? And if so, what kind of shape was he in?

As he always did when he was anxious, he reached for his pack of cigarettes and quickly lit one. Despite the downpour, he opened the window and stared in fascination at the torrents of water coming down from the sky.

Elliott took all the time in the world to smoke this cigarette. He'd understood Matt's message perfectly.

Distracted, hypnotized by the curtain of rain, he thought about the risks his friend had just taken to save his life.

'You really impressed me there,' he muttered to himself, hoping that merely by willing it Matt would somehow hear him.

He put out his cigarette on the windowsill, threw the pack he'd just opened into the wastebasket, and left the cafeteria.

That was the last cigarette he ever smoked.

2007

It was after 2 a.m., but the lights were still on in Ilena's little house.

On the desk, between the laptop computer and a mug of cold tea, the notebook with Elliott's story was open at the last page.

Sitting at the desk, her eyes sore from crying, Ilena was starting to doze off when the Persian cat sleeping on the couch suddenly arched its back, gave an unearthly growl, and ran to hide under a chest of drawers.

In an instant, the house started to shake, the walls vibrated, a light-bulb exploded, and a vase shattered on the floor.

Ilena sat up, terrified.

There was a low rumble and a hissing sound, then the notebook disappeared right before her eyes.

The vibrations gradually subsided and the cat slowly crept out of its hiding place and emitted a plaintive meow.

Ilena was petrified, overwhelmed with emotion. In her mind was a crazy hope:

If the notebook no longer existed, then Elliott hadn't written it.

If Elliott hadn't written it, then he was . . . alive.

Epilogue

February 2007

'Sir! Are you all right, sir?'

When Matt opened his eyes, he found himself collapsed against the steering-wheel of his car. Two cops, one on each side, were banging on the windows, worried about his condition.

Matt sat up with difficulty and unlocked the doors.

'I'm calling an ambulance!' one of the officers said when he saw the blood on Matt's shirt.

He was in bad shape. His head was buzzing and his eardrums felt as though they'd burst. He got out of the car, covering his eyes with his hand to protect them from the light. His legs were stiff, as though he'd been asleep for months.

The cops were already asking him questions. After crashing through the metal barrier, the car had ended up on the steps running down the steepest street in the city. Matt gave them his license, accepted complete responsibility for the accident, and submitted to an alcohol test, which turned out negative.

Having fulfilled his obligations to the police, he left Lombard Street without waiting for the ambulance.

Last night's storm had given way to a beautiful morning of wind and sun.

Feeling groggy, Matt limped back to the marina, limping. His head was swimming. Right now, he wasn't sure about anything. Had he dreamed his trip back in time? Had he succeeded in saving Elliott?

When Matt got to the marina, he pounded on his friend's door like a madman.

'Open up, Elliott! Open the goddamned door!'

But the house was empty.

Time hadn't erased their friendship. But their friendship, it seemed, couldn't erase time.

Exhausted and depressed, Matt sark down on the sidewalk in tears. He sat there until a taxi turned the corner of Fillmore and stopped in front of him.

Ilena got out of the car, her face full of hope, but Matt shook his head, indicating that he'd failed.

He hadn't kept his word, he hadn't been able to bring Elliott back.

Ilena crossed the street and took a few steps toward the beach. The Golden Gate Bridge was very close by and for the first time she had the courage to look at the accursed place from which she'd jumped thirty years before.

It still had the same fatal allure that made it so fascinating.

As though hypnotized by the morning light, Ilena walked toward the ocean.

A man was strolling along the shore at the edge of the surf.

When he turned around, Ilena could see his face, and her heart stopped.

He was there.

Note

The 'grandfather paradox' mentioned in Chapter 7 (page 88) is taken from *Le voyageur imprudent* by René Barjavel.

Translator's Note

The translator would like to express his appreciation for the remarkable skill and care that Lynn Curtis brought to the editing of his work.